His
Governess

By

ALYSIA S. KNIGHT

Heart Dreams
PRESS

His Governess
By Alysia S. Knight
Published by Heart Dreams Press
Copyright © 2015 Alysia S. Knight
Cover design: by Kelli Ann Morgan @
www.inspirecreativeservices.com

The views expressed within this work are the sole responsibility of the author and do not represent Heart Dreams Press or any of its affiliates.

This is a work of fiction. Names, characters, place and events are product of the author's imagination. Any similarities to actual persons, living or dead, business establishments or events are purely coincidental.

ISBN:1942000073
ISBN-13:978-1-94000-07-5

Also available from Alysia S. Knight

Letting Love Win

ରୟ

Past To Die For

ରୟ

Temperature Rising

ରୟ

Kare for Me

ରୟ

Blind Witness

ରୟ

Beauty and the Chief

ରୟ

Trail to Her Heart

Love, best wishes and happy reading.

Alysia S. Knight

Chapter One

Jake McCarron brought the lasso around in another circle before letting it go. As the loop floated neatly over the calf's head, Shasta began to pull back. The horse was so well trained that if she didn't need him to throw the rope, she could have done the job without him.

"Good girl," he patted the horse's neck. He maneuvered the calf to where he wanted it before swinging down to catch the calf and tip it onto its side.

Jess, his hired hand ran up with the branding iron, tag and antibiotic. While Jake pinned the calf, Jess placed the brand. Jake took the needle, giving the shot, before adding the tag to the ear, reading off the number to be double checked by Ben, his foreman.

"That's the last one," Jake yelled letting up the calf to go find its mama.

A cheer went out from all the men milling around.

"Hey, Todd." He got the attention of the man off by himself. "Wrap it up." Jake waved his arm over his head in a circle.

"Fine looking little heifer," Ben ambled up beside him. His gait wasn't as smooth as it had been in his younger days.

"That's why we're keeping her." Jake turned to his foreman. "Hopefully, we'll get some good future generations from her."

"I don't doubt it. She's got a good bloodline. We have

3

a real fine looking batch."

Jake nodded. "It's been a good year for the cattle." Before he could say more his cell phone rang.

Ben shook his head as Jake pulled it out. "They don't give you rest anywhere."

"It's Chance." Jake hit accept. "Hey."

"Hi, Jake." His little brother's voice sounded sad over the phone.

"What's wrong?" Losing their father eight months ago was a lot for a seven year old to handle but Chance had been excited when he'd left for a vacation with their grandmother.

"Mrs. Harwell's sister got sick. I guess it's bad. She's catching a plane back to Massachusetts to be with her. Gran'ma said we're still going to Yellowstone, but there won't be anyone to walk me around to see anything."

"I'm sorry." His heart went out to his brother. "Tell you what, I'll try to take you back sometime later this summer and we'll go see everything."

"Okay." He sounded a little happier. "What you doing?"

"Finishing up branding the stragglers."

"Aww."

"Before you complain, you helped me do most of them this year." In his mind, Jake could see Chance digging his toe through the dirt. Chance was his shadow when he could be. Jake didn't mind it though. He needed Chance as much as Chance needed him.

Sometimes, he felt more like Chance's dad then his brother. At eighteen years older, he could have been Chance's father. He had custody of him, which was good because their stepmother was no mother. Gran did what she could, but they needed each other. "So what are you doing?"

"We're in Wyoming getting gas. Gran'ma said I could call you while I was stretching my legs. She just found us a place to stay about two hours from here. We're not going to make it to Yellowstone Park tonight. We were late leaving. Clarissa has a headache and wants to stop at the first acceptable place."

Jake almost laughed. He knew Chance was repeating what he'd heard.

"I've got to go. Knowlton is finishing up."

"Okay. Try to have fun." He wished he could be there with his brother. It was just a bad time for him to get away.

"Love you. Bye."

"Love you." Jake didn't hesitate saying the words. It was one of those things he wished he could have said just one last time to his father. He hoped his brother would have a good time.

ભ૪ৢ

"What's wrong?" Amy asked the small boy staring up at the wall of the information booth.

The forlorn look on the boy's face pulled at her. His large hazel eyes took in all the pictures of the mountain scenes. His shoulders went up and down in a huge sigh of hopelessness. Compelled, Amy slid from her stool to her knees beside the boy.

His head tilted thoughtfully to the side. "Does the water really stop and start?"

"Yes, that's why it's called a Periodic Spring or around here we say 'the Intermittent Spring'. There's only four in the world and this one's the largest. The water in the drinking fountain out there is piped from up there."

Another sigh escaped his young body. He stared with longing at the pictures on the wall.

She grinned as his head tilted to the side in a thoughtful way. "Pretty isn't it?" She glanced at the picture. The Intermittent Spring was one of Afton, Wyoming's claims to fame. "It's just settling down into its regular cycle, stopping and starting about every eighteen minutes."

"Chance, we're about ready to go to the hotel."

Amy turned to face the older woman who spoke, shocked to see the wheel chair.

"Gran'ma." The boy took a couple steps forward. "Isn't there some way I can go see it?"

"I'm sorry, dear. I can't take you, and you know your stepmother has a headache and she hates walking." The woman caught the boy's small hand.

"What about Knowlton?" He pleaded his case.

"I'm afraid not. He already let us know hiking is not his job."

"I know, he's a driver not a walker." The little face looked forlorn.

A wrinkled hand patted his arm. "Maybe we can take a drive up the canyon." The old woman tried to placate the boy.

Amy bit her lip as he nodded, twisting his foot into the ground. Brushing a lock of long brown hair behind her ear, she stepped forward. "Excuse me. Is there something I can do to help?" She wasn't sure exactly what she was volunteering.

The old woman's gaze turned to her, scrutinizing her with none of the softness as when she talked to her grandson.

Amy straightened under the woman's stare. Though aged and in a wheelchair, there was nothing frail in her gaze.

"I could hike him up if you'd like. I'm to be replaced here in about ten minutes," Amy put forth, breaking the silence.

A smile crossed the little face and Amy couldn't help but return it before she shifted her attention back to the woman.

"How long will it take to get to the springs and back?" the older woman questioned.

"Around two hours to give us time to watch the water stop and start again."

The woman seemed to think a moment than asked. "Will forty dollars be enough?"

"I wasn't meaning that you had to pay me. I was just …." Amy shifted uncomfortably.

"Nonsense. I am willing to pay you for watching my grandson. We will be waiting outside," the woman continued in a curt fashion.

Amy could do nothing but nod. "I should be only a few minutes more. By the way, my name's Amy Mathews." She extended her hand.

The older woman took it in a surprisingly firm shake. "Maggie McCarron."

"May I stay in here with her?" the boy spoke up with a big grin.

"Of course, dear." Maggie patted his hand before maneuvering out the door.

The little face beamed as he looked up at her. "My name's Chance. Will you really hike me up to it?" He pointed to the picture on the wall.

"Nice to meet you, Chance. You can call me Amy, and as long as it's okay with your grandmother, I'd love take you to the Intermittent Springs. It's a beautiful hike, and I haven't been up yet this year."

"Why not?"

"I just got back from college."

"I'm going to school."

"That's great. So how old are you?"

"Seven. I'll turn eight in a month."

"I see and where do you live?"

"Nevada."

"So you're on vacation."

"Uh-huh, we were visiting an old friend of my Gran'ma's in Colorado, and she had some business. We're going to Yellowstone Park. I hope to see buffalo and bears."

"It's getting pretty hard to see bears anymore. They try

to keep them away from people. Here, would you like this card of the spring?" She handed him a postcard.

"Thank you. May I send it to my brother?"

"Of course, whatever you like. It's yours." Amy was surprised at how grown up the little boy seemed.

"Jake had to stay home and work. He's older than me," Chance continued matter-of-factly.

"I see." Amy smiled, turning to straighten the things on the counter.

"Have you ever seen a bear before?" he asked with what Amy guessed was the ever inquisitiveness of youth.

"Yes, a couple of times, but they were always quite a ways away. We might be able to see a moose on the way up to the springs. There has been one up the canyon lately."

"Good afternoon, Amy. Boy, that's somethin' you don't see often." The deep voice of a man in his late sixties greeted her from the doorway.

"Afternoon, Fred. What is?" she greeted.

"That big old limo. Didn't you see it?"

Amy stepped to the doorway to see the long, white, luxury vehicle parked off to the side. Looking back at Chance, she assessed the smartly dressed young man. *No wonder his grandmother had offered so much just to take him on a hike.* She shrugged. "Come on Chance, let's go." She extended her hand to the boy who didn't hesitate to accept it.

Amy wasn't at all surprised when they stepped out into the sun that the man leaning against the limo opened the door.

"Ready?" Maggie McCarron greeted from within. Chance was already scrambling in but Amy hesitated.

"Maybe it would be better if I borrowed my aunt's truck." She shifted uncertainly.

"The road's passable isn't it?"

"Yes, but—"

"Then let's go. I would love the drive up your canyon,

and we will be quite comfortable waiting for you in here." The woman motioned her in.

Amy had never been in a limousine before. As she settled into the seat, her faded jeans made quite a contrast. Instantly, her eyes were drawn to a woman leaning back against the opposite side. From high heeled sandals to her cream, linen pants, her silk shirt, to prefect make-up and styled ash blonde hair, the woman looked as if she fit in the limo. Her accessing gaze was cold and daunting.

"This is Chance's stepmother, Clarissa," Maggie McCarron said.

"Mrs. McCarron." The woman voice was honey sweet and unmistakably condescending.

Amy picked up the stone cold tone that hadn't been in Maggie's authoritative voice before and realized the way Maggie McCarron said Chance's stepmother, not her stepdaughter, that she didn't like her stepdaughter.

After giving directions to the driver, Amy settled back, answering all the questions Chance came up with.

"Have you lived here all your life then?" Maggie broke in.

"Mostly, except for three years away at college."

"You're still a student?" Maggie questioned.

"I will be when I earn enough money to finish up. I'm taking about a year off," she said with a little shrug.

"Your parents aren't helping you?" Maggie's eyebrow arched.

"My parents are both gone," she said, looking over to see what Chance was playing with.

"You can't be making much at the information center." Maggie McCarron drew her attention back.

"Oh, I'm not doing that as a job. I was just helping out today. I have some applications out but so far nothing yet."

"And what are you studying?" the younger Mrs. McCarron asked.

Amy was surprised when the question came from her.

"Art and business. I hope to have my own studio someday," Amy said brightly.

"You're an artist?" Clarissa McCarron looked disbelievingly at her.

"Yes. I mainly do wildlife and scenery."

"With where you live, I would say that is understandable." The older woman nodded as if giving her approval.

The younger Mrs. McCarron made what almost sounded like a snort. "I suppose you like to be outside all the time."

"I enjoy the outdoors very much; hiking, fishing, horseback riding," Amy said in defense.

"So you ride?" Maggie jumped on the word.

"Yes, all my life. My parents always had horses. My mother was an excellent horsewoman."

The older woman gave another nod and fell silent. Amy wondered if she might have fallen asleep but her eyes remained wide open as if lost in thought. There was no doubt Clarissa's attention was focused elsewhere.

 C380

Amy smiled down at the boy beside her. Chance McCarron was the basic seven-year old, full of excitement and questions. She'd learned more about his family than she figured they'd want her to know.

His mother had died a year after his birth. His father had died eight months ago, just a month after marrying Chance's stepmother. He had a brother that was eighteen years older than him, and who was the greatest. His name was Jake, and he had to stay home and run the ranch and 'stuff'. His brother could ride and do about anything better than anyone.

Though Chance didn't say much about his stepmother, certainly nothing out right negative, it wasn't hard to see he didn't like her much. She took very little time with him and had no desire to be the mother the small lonely child needed.

The maternal influence was his grandmother. There was no doubt she loved him but she wasn't able to handle an active little boy.

ॐ

The first thing Maggie McCarron noticed when her grandson came around the bend was his hand clasped and swinging in the young woman's hand. There was a natural ease between them. Their faces where turned to each other. Chance chattered vividly. His free hand waving to whatever he was telling her, and her attention seemed intent on him.

Maggie placed a hand to her heart. It had been so long since her grandson had looked so bright and happy. It was just what she'd hoped this trip would bring about, but until now, it had been failing miserably.

Maggie focused her attention on the young woman. She seemed open and friendly, once she'd gotten past her initial intimidation of the limousine. Her offer to help said a lot about her character. She liked her, Maggie thought, her mind already forming an idea. First, she would have to have Amy Mathews checked out.

Chance looked up. "Gran'ma!" He broke into a run. "It was cool. The water stops. Just stops. The whole waterfall stops, and then it goes again. You can hike right up to where it comes out of the mountain. There's a big cliff up behind it. We saw a moose with a calf. It was at a small lake that Amy says was formed by a slide." He finished as he reached the car.

"Wow. That is something. So I take it you had a good time."

"The greatest," he exclaimed, full of excitement.

"Why don't you get in and get a drink? I want to talk to Amy." She waited for Chance to comply before turning to the young woman. "I want to thank you."

"It was my pleasure. He's a lot of fun." Her smile said

she meant what she was saying.

"Yes, well, I appreciate it. And I'm glad you think that. I was wondering if you could come by our hotel tonight, at nine o'clock? There is something I would like to discuss with you."

ᏣᏤᏮ

Pinpricks of excitement rushed through Amy as she moved toward the room where she had been told the McCarrons were staying. All evening she felt as if she was on the edge of a new point in her life, though she didn't know what to expect.

Passing the open window just before the door, a loud voice carried out, reaching her, and giving her a hint of what lay ahead.

"The girl is obviously less than satisfactory. How could you even consider it?"

Amy froze in mid-motion of knocking on the hotel suite door.

The shrill, feminine voice continued to float through the open window. "There is nothing satisfactory in this little hick town. National parks. Wyoming. You could find this kind of terrain not far from the ranch. I can't believe you are thinking of taking someone from this place to be a guardian and companion for your grandson. It's unforgivable that Mrs. Harwell left us in such a predicament. She certainly will not get a recommendation from me when she starts her next job."

"Her sister had a stroke, for goodness sakes. There was no one else to take care of her. Can't you find a little compassion in your heart?" The older woman's tone was unyielding to the ranting going on in the room.

"As for the girl, Chance likes her. You saw his face as he came down the trail with his hand locked in hers. Since you don't seem to be willing to care for him, and most of the women that you have hired for him have been stuffy bores that I couldn't even stand to be stabled with, I think it is my place to choose what's best for him. I think the girl is quite satisfactory."

Amy could hardly believe it. She was going to offer her a job taking care of Chance.

Maggie McCarron's voice continued. "The police officer that I talked to knows her family well. They are honest, hard-working people. She has never been arrested or even had a ticket. She has even passed the Red Cross First Aid Course and lifesaving. She rides horses and likes the outdoors. She has finished three years of college and is working for her last."

Amy wasn't sure how they found out so much about her, not that she had any big secrets in her life. She felt guilty for eavesdropping but couldn't force herself to move away.

"More importantly though," Maggie McCarron's voice came clearly, "is Chance likes her, which is more than you can say about any of the governesses that you have hired. You are drawn more to the title some of those crones have had than what is good for my grandson. He needs someone young and active. Someone who will care for him, spend time with him."

Amy felt her heart jump. It only took a second for her to realize she would like taking care of Chance. He was a great little boy, and she desperately needed a job and there really wasn't anything for her here now with her parents gone. This visit had proved it.

She wondered what a nanny made. If this afternoon was any hint, she thought they might pay well. As long as it was a decent amount with room and board, in just one year she could put away enough to cover her year of school, housing, books, tuition, everything, and maybe even have a little to carry her until she got settled.

But what do I know about being a governess? She knew several girls that had become nanny's, most said it had been a good experience, but it still made her feel uneasy putting her life in the hands of people she didn't know anything about, except that they traveled in a limo and stayed in the nicest room in town.

She liked the older Mrs. McCarron with her blatant forth-rightness. It testified the woman had made her way in life with backbone and fight. Pioneer stock was a term that fit her well.

The younger Mrs. McCarron, Amy guessed, was in her mid-thirties. It was hard to say with all the make-up she used to perfection. Everything about the woman screamed of perfection, from her bleached blonde hair, down her lush body decorated with glittering diamonds, to her bright-red toenails. Clarissa McCarron made her feel more than a little intimated. She seemed to be looking down on her full red lips pressed with distaste.

Amy looked down at her clothes. She was wearing a pair of twill pants and a plain, lightweight sweater. Her accents were a small fire agate ring her father had made for her with matching necklace and earrings. She loved them, but like her, they were simple not showy. At a slender five-eight with brown hair, she was all right, but next to a woman like Mrs. McCarron, she'd never be noticed.

I don't care about being noticed. I would like to be Chance's governess.

Steeling herself, she knocked on the door. A resounding grunt echoed inside.

The door opened. "You're late," the younger Mrs. McCarron said coarsely. Amy knew it couldn't be more the two minutes after nine.

"Come in, dear." The aged voice sounded more welcoming as Amy entered.

Chapter Two

Jake McCarron sighed as he dropped his hat on the hook and stopped to pull off his boots. He left them in the mud room, and walked silently down the hall on stocking feet. The excited, youthful chatter coming down the hall would have let him know Chance and his grandmother were home even if he hadn't seen the limo in the garage as he pulled in.

By the noise, traveling through the National Parks in Wyoming had done his little brother a world of good. Chance sounded more like the happy boy he'd been before their father's death.

Jake stopped just inside the kitchen and watched. Chance sat at the counter eating apple slices dipped in caramel. George, their portly chef, paid close attention as Chance described bubbling mud pots.

"We hiked all the way around–Jake!" Chance jumped off the stool and was across the floor almost before Jake was ready to catch him. Chance leapt from two feet away.

"Whoa," Jake let out with the impact. "What a tackle." He lifted his brother over his head like he had been doing since he was a baby.

Chance laughed happily. "We're home!"

"I see. Did you have a good trip?"

"Uh-huh." The small head bobbed up and down, as Chance settled against his chest. "I wish you could've come."

"I wish I could've, too."

"Guess what, I got a new governess."

"You did?" Jake felt a jab of shock then displeasure. He hadn't been happy with any of Chance's 'governesses'. He didn't see why Chance needed one. There were plenty of people on the ranch to keep an eye on him. Though, he guessed it was better than Clarissa having anything to do with him. He looked at his brother, and realized he'd never sounded excited about any of the governesses before.

"So where did you find a governess?"

"In Wyoming. She took me hiking and knew all about Yellowstone Park."

That was a surprise. He couldn't image anyone Clarissa hired being willing to take Chance hiking.

"I tried to call you to tell you.

"Sorry. I was out on the range for your last couple of calls and in a meeting for your other."

Chance's head bobbed again.

Jake wondered how Clarissa had ever managed to find a nanny, correction, 'governess' on the road. Then again with the internet, he shouldn't be surprised. He was just surprised the woman knew how to use it. Jake had to jerk his attention back to Chance.

"Amy had to boost me up, and I had to hold onto her hand the whole time. But when we got to the top, we could see forever."

"Really?"

"Yeah, I got to take a lot of pictures. Amy showed me how to position them so they will have a good composition."

"Composition?" Jake repeated the word in surprise that Chance knew it, but Chance was already explaining it.

"That's so it will look nice when you look at it. You don't want to cut things in half with the sky or put some things right in the middle. You balance it. I still didn't get it right sometimes, but Amy said that was okay, that we can fix it with the computer before we print them or set them to a slide show."

"I take it Amy is your new governess?"

"Yes."

"Is it all right if you call her Amy?"

"Uh-huh. She likes it better, but around Clarissa I have to call her Miss Mathews, so she calls me Master Chance." He laughed like it was a great joke.

"So you like your new governess?" Jake could hardly believe it was true. So far they had been some of the most dreadful, boring women he'd ever seen.

Chance's head was bobbing up and down again. "We went for hikes and swam. She reads books with different voices and is teaching me to draw. She can also ride horses, though we haven't gotten to do that yet. She said we could in the morning if we can get it cleared. Can we?"

"Of course. So she can really do all that?"

"Yep, and she's beautiful."

"Really?" Jake figured she sure must've really won Chance over for him to think she was beautiful, because one thing he could guarantee was, Clarissa would not let a beautiful woman stay. The woman would have to be old enough to be Clarissa's mother. Well, he didn't care what she looked like just as long as Chance liked her. And it sounded like she was active enough to do things with Chance instead of just making him sit all day and do lessons.

"Tell you what, let me grab a quick shower, and you can tell me all about your trip over dinner. That is, if you haven't filled up on apple slices."

His brother shook his head. "George only let me have four slices for my appetizer. I was starving."

"That sounds normal." He flipped Chance over as he put him down. "I'll be right back." He headed down the hall to his room, his hands already opening the buttons on his shirt. He was just passing the hall bathroom when the door opened and someone stepped in front of him.

There was no stopping the impact. All he had time to do was put his arms out to catch the woman to keep her from being knocked over, then he felt like he was knocked over as a set of sky blue eyes, wide from being startled, came up to meet him.

For a minute, he forgot to breathe as he took in her womanly curves shrouded in a fluffy, soft, blue robe. He had no idea what color her hair was or its length because it was wrapped in a towel piled on her head, but her face was perfect, high cheekbones, long lashes, totally free and clean of makeup. Her lips were slightly full and parted in a small O as she stared up at him. The thought of lowering his lips to hers came out of nowhere, shocking him. He'd never had such an instantaneous reaction to a woman.

One fine-boned hand rested against his bared chest right over his heart as if that was where she was settling. He could feel her heart pound, and his seemed to match the rhythm. He had no idea how long they stood there before the woman blinked and lowered her eyes.

"I'm sorry. I didn't know anyone was down here. Chance is in the kitchen, and Maggie's in her room resting. Clarissa is in the other wing. I–" The words ended as abruptly as they spilled out.

Something in her flustered reaction made him smile. "It's all right. I was just going to take a shower."

"I was just...." Her head came up and the O reappeared. "You're Jake."

His name helped bring him back to reality, and he started shaking his head. It couldn't be. "You can't be, Amy?" Jake drew the name out slowly, testing it. It fit well.

"Yes, I, I need to ... I thought you'd be younger."

A smile tugged at his lips at her flustered remark. "And I thought you'd be older."

"I ... I excuse me." She broke from his arms and disappeared through the door across from Chance's room so fast Jake almost thought she was a dream. He still tingled from holding her, and he could still feel the impression of her hand over his heart.

Jake stood there for a full minute more before moving to his room. By the time he'd finished his shower, he'd decided she had been his imagination. There was absolutely no way Clarissa would allow a younger, beautiful woman in the house.

He pushed his hands through his damp hair. It had to be Chance's talking about her. That, and the fact that, it had been nearly a year since he'd had a date and even longer since a woman had affected him like this. What had happened to him?

He lowered his hands to press his fingers over his eyes. Jake knew what had happened. He couldn't escape it. He'd been the one who had encouraged his father that he needed a break. He'd insisted he could handle everything while his father took a month long world cruise, he just hadn't ever consider his father would come back married, especially to someone like Clarissa.

If his father had been happy it might have been okay, but there were signs he wasn't. Then, in just a month, his father was dead of a heart attack, and he really did have to handle everything on his own.

It wasn't just his part of the ranch and holdings he had to worry about, but he was responsible for Chance's share, his inheritance. It didn't bother him stepping into a role of father figure to Chance. With the difference in their ages their relationship was already sort of like that, though they were surprisingly close.

No, his challenge was Clarissa, his stepmother. What a joke. The woman's obvious plays for him started before they'd hardly had his father buried. He wished he could kick the woman out. His father had protected the ranch and business in his will. Unfortunately, along with the large allowance the woman received, she also retained the right to stay at the house until she remarried or moved out on her own accord. Jake didn't see that happening. Clarissa liked living in the house too much.

He still couldn't figure out how his father ended up with her. Clarissa didn't fit his father's no-nonsense manner. His father never had patience with fluff and high maintenance women. It just didn't fit, just like the woman that he dreamed up earlier didn't fit Clarissa's idea of a governess. With the last button of his shirt done up, he decided it was time to go down and meet the real woman.

Jake reached the dining room just in time to hear Chance say. "But where's Amy?"

"She's a servant," Clarissa answered, her condescension ringing loud and clear. "She'll eat in the kitchen with the rest of the staff."

"You used to let my other governesses eat with us."

Jake felt like applauding Chance's argument. He was right. All the other governesses had eaten with them, sending scowls at both Chance and him when they got into subjects they didn't deem fitting, and jumped down Chance's throat for any deficiency in his manners.

"Yes, well it's best she learn her place until she has earned her right."

"But it is Amy's right, and I want her here."

"She needs to know what's proper for her to teach you. You don't want to act like some small town bumpkin. You are above that."

Jake grimaced. Clarissa sounded in a fine snit. He wished there was some way he could get out of dinner or eat in the kitchen. There was no doubt it would be more pleasant. He sighed and was about to step in and face a slice of purgatory when another voice stopped him.

"What's going on here? What this about?" There was a demanding tone to his grandmother's voice that made him smile. She definitely sounded like she'd handled the trip well.

"I want Amy to eat with us." Chance took his case to a higher court and won.

"Well, of course she will eat with us. Where else would she eat?" There was no missing the directive from his grandmother.

Before it could be argued, Jake decided to make his entrance. "Hello everyone. Welcome back." Jake caught the seething look on Clarissa's face before she pasted an over-sweet smile in its place.

"Oh, Jake." Clarissa stood and came toward him with her arms open. He back up, stepping out of the hug before she could lock it down, giving her barely a perfunctory kiss on the cheek before heading to his grandmother. Leaning over, he wrapped his arms around her giving her a tight hug, being careful of his strength. "You look wonderful." He sent her a conspiratorial wink he'd learned from his father that always made her smile.

"Oh you, it's good to be home." His grandmother squeezed his hand.

"Did you have a good trip?"

"Yes. It was quite wonderful. We had a fine time. We have a new nanny."

"Governess," Clarissa snapped out.

Jake knew it was no slip of the tongue especially when his grandmother answered, "Oh, yes, governess. Chance, why don't you go get Amy so we can all sit down to eat."

There was no holding back a smile when Chance let out a whoop and ran from the room.

"I take it he had a good time."

"Grand. At least, the last half when Amy joined us."

"That was fast. So how did you get a governess to join you in Wyoming?" He figured now was a good time to curb his curiosity with Chance out of the room.

"Chance found her," his grandmother said taking him by surprise. "We stopped at a visitor information booth in Star Valley, Wyoming, and she was at the booth. When

Chance said he wanted to hike to the Periodic Spring there, she volunteered to take him."

"And from that your grandmother hired her," Clarissa broke in, her disapproval blatant.

"Chance likes her. She is good with him, and I like her," Maggie said plainly.

"She has no qualifications." Clarissa turned her nose up in offense.

"That is not true. Just because you didn't pick her from one of those listings of old battle axes doesn't mean she won't be good. If anything, it speaks higher of her. We've had four of your 'governesses' in the last eight months and none of them have stayed, though I won't hold Mrs. Harwell's leaving against her. The others though, have not lasted, and I wasn't sad to see any of them go. Even if the girl only makes it through the summer, we are ahead. The girl is staying," Maggie McCarron said forcefully, leaving Clarissa no room to debate.

Fury burned off of Clarissa that she couldn't mask. She glanced at him then turned striding off to the dining room.

"Ruffled her feathers, didn't I?" There was a lilt in his grandmother's voice when she spoke again.

Jake let out the laugh he'd been holding back. "That you did." He leaned down and kissed her cheek. "I'm glad you're home. Things have been dull without you."

"Posh." She swatted at him but her face glowed with pleasure.

"Shall we go into dinner?" He stepped behind her to push the chair.

"Yes. We better get in there before Chance gets there with Amy so Clarissa won't start ripping into them. Clarissa doesn't like that Chance likes Amy but I think what really gets her is Amy's younger and prettier than she is without all that goop on her face. It burns her."

"So she is young?" Jake said.

"And pretty." Maggie looked at him.

Jake picked up an odd tone in her voice and stopped. "You aren't planning on playing matchmaker are you?" he asked suspiciously.

She just laughed. "I know better than that. You'll get around to finding someone one of these days, and though I wouldn't mind seeing a great-grandbaby, I won't press you. I like her, but this girl, I got for Chance. In just an hour with her, I saw him happier than he's been in months, except when he's with you. I was not going to give Clarissa another opportunity to find another one of those harpies she favors."

"I agree with you there. Where does she find them? They make me shudder."

Chapter Three

Amy opened the door and peeked out into the hallway. The coast was clear. She'd spent the last half hour trying to calm her heart and still wasn't feeling too steady, and the main problem was she wasn't sure what was wrong with her.

She'd seen good looking guys before. In some of her art classes, she'd had to sketch some very nice male specimens, and some so-so ones, but never had she been bowled over by a man before. She could still feel the warmth of his skin on her palm. His eyes were hazel, a lot like Chance's, but with flecks of vibrant gold and green in them. She wanted to study the color.

Amy shook her head. She was being foolish. If she tried to open her mouth to talk to him, she'd end up tongue-tied. She might have gotten over most of her shyness since high school, but one look at him made her feel all funny inside. There was no way she was going to say it was love at first sight. A man like him would never give her a second look. Add to the fact, she was way out of her league in this house.

Amy looked down the hall again and stepped out. Spotless, thick, beige carpet muffled her footsteps as she walked forward. Wide moldings accented the walls. Just ahead it opened to a large family room with a beautiful hardwood floor and an opulent beamed ceiling.

Amy stopped and looked around. This area acted as a

junction to other parts of the house, but it was still a comfortable room with a grouping of two couches and chairs angled to take in one wall and the massive stone fireplace with French doors on either side. A huge TV was set in one of the recesses on the wall. The French doors stood open allowing her to see out to the patio, swimming pool and the amazing view all the way up to the hills beyond.

It was a place she could easily sit and paint for hours and never run out of something to inspire her.

From her initial tour of the house she knew Chance's room, and every room on the back of the house, had a similar set of doors giving easy access to the pool, back of the house, and the view. Her room looked out front with its landscaped yard and wide circular driveway.

Amy walked to a large inlaid table that stood in the exact center of the house, like a hub, directly behind the couches and in front of the main entry. She couldn't resist leaning over to smell a lily from the gorgeous floral arrangement which sat there. She wondered if there were always fresh arrangements. It made a great focal point, visible from every direction of the house.

Looking to the main entry, she could just glimpse into the formal living room that sat off to the side of it. She was tempted to go take a peek but decided that could wait. She knew on the other side it opened up to the formal dining room, where the family would be gathering.

She hadn't seen the dining room yet, but Chance said it could seat thirty people. When he'd told her that, she thought he was probably exaggerating, now she wasn't sure. He'd given her a pretty fair description of the place from what she'd seen so far.

Taking a stepped into the family room, she let her gaze follow the set of stairs that curved along the wall up to the library loft and felt another wave of temptation to go up and check it out. Besides her curiosity about the books up there, it would be a great view of the family room. Instead, she forced herself to cross the family room to the kitchen.

She wasn't sure what she was to do now. She was nervous to go in. She didn't want to just barge in. She'd been introduced to Mr. Davidson, the chef, and Mrs. Jeffers, the maid, and they'd been very polite. Still, she wondered how they felt about her being given a room down by Chance's instead of in the staff quarters, which were down the other hall past Clarissa's suite and the garage.

If Clarissa had gotten her way that was where she'd have been–actually she wouldn't have been there at all. But, Maggie insisted she needed to be close to Chance if he ever needed her. So she was across the hall from Chance, and just past their rooms, at the end of the hall, in the other master suite, was Jake McCarron. She tried to think of the man she'd bumped into in the hall. He was Chance's brother. Her boss.

She focused her attention back on the house. Maggie's room was closest to Chance's, next to the family room, giving her easier access. Across from Maggie was Jake's office. Amy glanced back across the family room toward it. The glass panel doors stood open letting her see the mahogany desk and bookcase. It made her think of the man she ran into, and her hands trembled.

She was not going to think of him or let herself be nervous. She pushed through the door into the kitchen. The chef was the only one there. He looked up when she entered.

"Hello, again. Come in, you don't have to be shy here." He seemed to read her easily. "This is your home now." The smile on his face made her relax.

"I wasn't sure if I'd be disturbing you with getting dinner ready." She got the words out.

"Never, I can cook in my sleep, but I'm definitely better when I have someone, especially a beautiful someone, to talk to."

Amy relaxed at the flattery. "Is there something I can do to help?"

"Everything is done. Just sit." He reached up and turned off a burner. "You have certainly made an impression on Chance. You made his trip wonderful."

"I didn't do anything but walk with him. He's a wonderful boy." She stepped farther into the room.

"That he is." The man nodded. "Still, Ms. Mathews, it is nice to see him so happy. It's been a hard year for our boy."

"Please, just Amy." She slid onto the stool at the marble counter. "How long have you been here, Mr. Davidson?"

"You just call me George. Four years now. I ran a restaurant with my wife but after she passed away, my heart wasn't in it. So I sold the place, but it didn't take me long to get bored with my own company. About that time I saw a notice John, Mr. McCarron, had about looking for a cook. It ended up being a good fit." There was a fondness in his smile. "Mrs. Jeffers, the housekeeper, has been here twenty-one years. Constance, her helper, is married to one of the hands. She's worked here three years."

"And Mr. Knowlton?"

"The younger Mrs. McCarron hired him right after John passed away." There was a slight frown that flickered on the edge of his lips.

"Do–"

"Amy!" Chance's voice preceded the boy into the kitchen, cutting off her next question.

"Hey, slow down there." She turned to him. "What is it?"

"You get to eat with us in the dining room." He ran up and caught her arm, tugging her off the stool.

"Oh, Sweetie, your stepmother said that I'm to eat in here," she said gently.

He was already shaking his head when she finished

speaking. "Gran'ma said you were to eat with us like my other governesses."

Amy glanced at George. He nodded his head. "They did."

Amy looked back at the hopeful face. She wasn't sure she wanted to eat in the formal dining room, but there was no way she could disappoint him. "You're certain?"

His head bobbed up and down as he drew her forward. Helplessly, Amy followed trying not to gape as she entered the large dining room. It could easily fit twenty people at the cherry-wood table. The ceiling was recessed in the center with thick crown molding around the fabulous crystal chandelier.

Clarissa already sat, back stiff, at the table when they entered. Maggie and Jake McCarron were just coming in from the living room. Amy almost froze when she saw him. His eyes came right to her. He looked her over from head to toe before coming back to her face. His eyes seemed to intensify, and she was tempted to bolt, but Chance had her hand, continuing to pull her forward.

"Jake, this is Amy. She's my new nanny." Chance announced with enthusiasm.

"Governess," Clarissa hissed out at the table. "And it's Ms. Mathews."

Amy glanced her way then back to Jake McCarron.

"Amy, this is my brother, Jake."

"Actually, we bumped into each other in the hall." There was a glint in his eyes. "But, I didn't get to say welcome. I hope you enjoy your stay here."

Amy wondered if he was a womanizer. That was all she needed, to be living with a man who thought he was a gift to all women and they couldn't resist him. Well, no matter how he made her heart jump that was one thing she found easy to avoid.

Funny, from how Chance talked, she didn't think he would be that way. Then again, Chance thought he was the greatest. But the things Maggie had said about him seemed to agree with Chance, and then again, she was his grandmother.

"Thank you," she managed to get out and felt color heat her face.

He moved Maggie into place before he took the spot at the head of the table. Clarissa was seated at his right. Chance led Amy around the table. He took his place next to his grandmother. There was no other place setting. Amy wasn't quite sure what to do.

"Have a seat dear. Ruth will bring a setting in for you. Just give her a moment," Maggie said.

"I am really fine to eat in the kitchen." Amy fidgeted.

"Nonsense, how are you to get to know the family from in there," Maggie insisted.

Amy caught the scowl Clarissa sent her way before the woman masked as she turned to look at Jake. Amy couldn't get an objection out as a woman in her late fifties came in carrying a tray with a place setting and a dish of appetizers. Ruth Jeffers placed the food on the table before coming around and arranging the dishes next to Chance's. Not knowing what else to do, Amy slid into the chair.

"We try to eat together for evening meals. Otherwise, we wouldn't get to spend any time together. Breakfast and lunch are usually eaten in the kitchen or out on the patio, quite often individually," Maggie turned to her.

"You will be expected to take all your meals with Chance," Clarissa interjected.

"No problem." Amy looked down at Chance and gave him a wink when he smiled up at her.

Clarissa made a slight huff.

"Amy, I'm afraid I didn't get your last name." Jake spoke up.

"Mathews. But Amy is fine."

"So Amy, I was wondering what your plans were. How long are you planning to stay?" There seemed to be a tightness in his voice, and she wasn't quite sure what was behind it. Did he think she would quit or just take off?

"I'd like to be here for at least a year. I think it will take me that long to save enough to be able to finish school. I have one year left."

"So no student loans?" He raised an eyebrow.

"No. I was afraid I could never get out from under them and be in a position to start my own gallery."

"Gallery ... photo?"

That confused her. "Art–all mediums."

"Chance said something about you showing him how to take pictures with composition," he said in way of clarifying.

"Oh, he has a very good eye." She smiled again at the boy.

"I can't wait to see the pictures he took." Jake looked at his brother and sent a wink similar to how she had earlier.

It was easy to see the love there. Amy decided maybe Jake was okay.

Just then Mrs. Jeffers came out with their dinner, juicy looking prime rib, small red potatoes with rosemary, and long, butter glazed green beans. It looked amazing.

"I hope you like beef," Jake spoke up. "We're a cattle ranch, among other things."

"This looks amazing, and I'm always up for a good steak," she said truthfully.

"You'll have some of the best here. It's one of the perks of the job." He smiled.

"Really Jake, let me guess," Clarissa spoke up, her voice the softest, sweetest Amy had ever heard it. The woman almost purred. "All the time we were gone, you spent all day out with those beasts. You have people to take care of that for you. Your time is so valuable."

"They're my responsibility." His voice seemed to tighten.

Clarissa leaned toward him and rested a hand on his arm. "But you could've come with us and taken care of the business in Colorado yourself." The purr turned into a pout but it didn't seem to have any effect on him.

He pulled back his arm. "Gran handled it just fine. I've already gone over the reports faxed to me." He looked at his grandmother, and his eyes softened. "You got a better deal than I could have."

Maggie shrugged. "They were putty in my hands."

Jake laughed. "They're probably still trying to figure out what hit them."

Amy was trying to take it all in. She never doubted Maggie's love for her grandsons, but the byplay between her and Jake was interesting to see, but what was going on with him and Clarissa? She was his stepmother but only about twelve years older than him, and she was a very beautiful, sexy woman. Still, Amy shuddered at the thought. Deciding it wasn't her place to worry about it, she focused on eating.

Chance chattered with his brother about the things they saw in Yellowstone until Clarissa interrupted him. "Ms. Mathews, please take Chance to get ready for bed now. I want him to read at least thirty minutes before he goes to sleep."

"But we just got home. I wanted to spend more time with Jake, and we haven't had dessert yet," Chance objected.

"Don't whine or you won't get dessert," Clarissa said coolly.

Amy reached under the table and squeezed Chance's knee before he could snap back. "I'll take care of it. Come on. If you'll excuse us."

"I'll come in and see you before you go to bed and I settle down in the den. If you're up early enough, we can have breakfast together," Jake said as they stood.

"Why don't you grab your bath?" Amy suggested as

they made their way down the hall, "I'll unpack your bag then go down to get us some dessert."

"Okay." He smiled. "Can we play a game, too?"

"Sure." Amy turned on the water while Chance got his pajamas. Once he was in the bath, she gathered his clothes and put them in the laundry.

"I'm going to get dessert," she said as soon as he was out of the tub and getting dressed. "Pick your books and game, and I'll be right back."

George looked up as she entered. "Thought you might show up. It's right there." He nodded toward a tray with two bowls full of dark chocolate pudding cake with whipped cream peaked on it.

"Oh man, do you know what you're going to do to me?" Amy let out a groan. "I'm going to have to take up running five miles a day."

"You probably will get that just chasing after Chance, or you could look like me." He padded his ample tummy. "I got this fair and square."

She laughed, picking up the tray. "He'll be on such a chocolate-high he'll never go to sleep."

"It's not as bad as it looks."

"That's what I'm afraid of."

That brought a laugh from the man.

"Goodnight," she said going out the door. She was humming when she crossed the family room. Just outside Chance's bedroom, she heard a gurgled outcry then a rattling sound she'd never heard before in real life but knew exactly what it was. The next step let her see into Chance's room.

Her heart lurched. Chance stood in the doorway to his bathroom. Curled in the middle of the floor, not three feet away from him was a large snake, its head up facing Chance, tail high in the air, shaking with its terror-provoking sound.

Chapter Four

"Chance, don't move," Amy whispered the words, barely managing not to drop the tray. Afraid that any sudden movement or sound would make the snake strike, she eased into the room, sliding the tray onto the dresser.

"Amy," Chance whispered.

"It's okay, sweetheart. Don't move." In slow motion she made her way to his bed, easing down to pick up the corner of the spread she'd pulled back earlier. At the motion of the spread unfolding, the head of the snake swiveled her direction. Amy threw the thick quilt a split second before the snake struck. The force of the snake hitting the spread pushed it back toward her as the material closed around the snake.

Amy's scream was echoed by Chance's cry. She stumbled back, almost going down, before she leapt to Chance, pulling him up in her arms. There was a sound of heavy footsteps running their way then Jake appeared into the doorway.

"What the …"

"Don't come in. Rattlesnake—under the spread." Amy gasped out, her heart still pounding too hard to move.

He stared at them a second before looking at the quilt on the floor. He moved into the room.

"Don't," she cautioned.

"It's okay." He pressed the quilt down with his booted foot. When it shifted, he trapped the snake under his foot then gathered the edge of the quilt around it until he could pick it up.

Amy couldn't keep back the gasp.

"It's okay. It can't get to me to strike. I'm just going to get it out of here. Don't worry. It will never bother you again." He looked at his brother then her, waiting until they both nodded. "I'll be back in a few minutes." Instead of going out into the hall, he left through the French doors right out onto the patio.

Amy could do nothing but continue to hug Chance to her. His head cuddled down on her shoulder, legs wrapped around her waist. She ran her hand up and down his back. "It's okay, it's over now," she said the words for both of them. Cupping his chin, she tipped his head back so she could look into his face. "You okay?"

He nodded. "You saved me. That was great."

"I would say it was scary." She hugged him tight.

"What is all the commotion going on down here?" Clarissa snapped as she stepped into the doorway. "If you cannot keep a civilized tone, you are fired."

"Amy saved me." Chance went from terrified to her defender in an instant.

"Pppah," Clarissa made a face of complete doubt.

"What is it, love?" Maggie appeared behind her with George.

"There was a rattlesnake in my room." He burst out, now excited to tell the tale.

"What?" Maggie gasped and moved her chair forward making Clarissa step aside.

Clarissa scowled. "Just how would a snake get in here?"

Amy let Chance down, and he ran to his grandmother climbing up onto her lap. "There was a giant rattlesnake when I came out of the bath. Amy threw the quilt on it and it struck at her."

Maggie's head shifted toward her. "Are you all right?"

"Yes," Amy said along with a nod. "Just scared me a little. I've never seen a rattlesnake outside a case in the zoo."

"Then it probably wasn't even a rattlesnake," Clarissa scoffed.

"It was." Chance beat her to the comeback.

"It was." Jake stepped back into the room echoing Chance. "Big sucker, about four feet long."

"We've never had a snake get in the house before." Maggie sounded stressed.

Jake nodded, looking serious.

"Well, we'll just have to be more careful about keeping the doors closed," Clarissa snapped and walked away.

"But I didn't have my door open." Chance looked at his grandmother.

"It's okay, love." She ran her hand over his cheek, brushing her fingers through his hair. "I don't think you have to worry about that happening again."

"That's right." Jake crossed the room to lift his brother into his arms. "Somehow the old guy just managed to get in but it won't happen again. I'll get someone out to do an inspection just to be sure. Okay?"

Chance laid his head on his brother's shoulder.

"You about ready for bed?" Jake asked.

"We were going to eat our dessert then play a game first." Chance pointed to the tray on the dresser.

"How about I go get my dessert and come join you?"

"That sounds like fun. I think I'll join you, too," Maggie spoke up.

"I'll get it for you," George volunteered and left.

They gathered around the table set on one side of his room while Chance got out the game. As they played the tension faded. Amy found herself laughing, especially when Jake, who was leading and about to win, hit a slide that took him almost back to the beginning and Chance snuck in for the win.

"I admit defeat." Jake put his hand over his heart. "Maybe I better go over record books the rest of the night." He stood and ruffled his brother hair. "Goodnight."

"Night." Chance hugged him around the waist.

"I'm for doing a little reading before I turn in for the night." Maggie gave Chance a kiss when he leaned into her. "Sleep well, love."

When they were left alone, Amy handed him the game. "Why don't you go put this away and pick out a book for us to read?"

She just laughed when Chance came back with three books. He climbed into bed, and she tucked the blankets around him like she'd been doing since the first night with him. She sat beside him on the bed, and they began. First, she read a page then he read the next. They were on the third book when he finally fell asleep.

Amy stood and placed the book on the nightstand, straightened the blankets around him and kissed his forehead. When she turned to leave, she found Jake McCarron watching her from the hall. For a minute, she thought he was going to say something, but he just turned and walked away instead.

Amy shrugged it off and went to her room to finish unpacking but found herself too restless. Giving up, she left the room. Reaching the family room, she continued across, going out the doors onto the patio.

Lights within the pool made it glow. Overhead, the stars shone brightly with only a crescent moon lighting the sky. Amy tipped her head back, listening to the night sounds, and sighed as the remaining tension left her body.

After a second, she moved over to sit in one of the lounges. It was beautiful. She was tempted to go for a swim but decided just to take in the calm of the evening. A warm, gentle breeze caressed her, drawing a sigh from her.

If you excluded the snake, she shivered at the thought

and pushed it out of her mind, it was like a dream. Living in a place like this and having the job of watching Chance couldn't get any better.

Well, when her paints arrived it would be perfect. There was so much she wanted to paint. Maggie had assured her she would have free time, and Amy thought it would be fun to teach Chance. He was eager to learn.

She looked around her. Across the pool, on the other side of the white slat, shade awning, she could see the lights, in what she knew was the other master suite where Clarissa lived.

She thought it was funny having two master suites, one in each wing, but she guessed it made sense with two generations living there. Well, actually three with Maggie. There was something kind of wonderful about the idea of the family staying together. She wondered if it would stay the same when Chance grew up and started his family. Would he take over the other wing and would they remain there together?

Funny, she didn't see Clarissa in the picture. Just getting to know Clarissa over the last few days, it was plain the ranch wasn't for her. No matter how beautiful and fancy the house and even though it was close to town, she just didn't fit. In fact, Amy was surprised she was still here. She wondered why Clarissa hadn't taken her part of her husband's inheritance and left. Her thoughts really weren't very nice, but she couldn't help it. She figured Clarissa would have been hunting another husband.

The idea made her pause. Maybe Clarissa had found the next one. Maybe it was Jake, and they were just waiting for it to be decent. She didn't know if that idea fit either. Clarissa obviously played up to him, but Jake didn't really seem to reciprocate. In fact, she'd say Clarissa annoyed him.

"You're not worried?" The voice of the person she was just thinking about made her jump. A squeak escaped her, but she managed not to scream. A different kind of squeak slipped free as she turned. Jake McCarron stood there in a pair of swim trunks. The light from the pool made the ridges of his chest stand out.

She just stared at him. He was a great looking man. His sandy-colored hair was tousled from running his fingers through it. His lips twitched and one corner kicked up giving him a dimple on that side.

"It beautiful here," she finally managed to get out.

"I like it, but I'm surprised you can say that after the snake."

She shook her head. "That was one of those one in a million things. As you said earlier, it's never happened before. What are the odds it would happen again?"

"Don't ask me, I'm not a gambling man. Odd, I know, for living in Nevada. But I risk enough with everyday life on the ranch and with other things to possibly throw money away on a game I have no control over."

"That's an interesting way to look at it."

"Are you a gambler?" he asked as he dropped his towel next to the pool.

"Can't say it's ever had an appeal to me."

He nodded and just stayed where he was staring at her.

Amy felt her heart pick up. "I better turn in and let you get to your swim."

"You're welcome to stay." He stepped toward her.

"It's been a long day." As she stood, he moved closer.

"Do you always kiss the children you look after goodnight like that?" He was so close it was hard to breathe.

"I don't know. I guess so. I've never been a nanny before."

"Governess," he corrected with a smile.

"Yes, of course. I didn't even know people still had governesses." She wrinkled her nose.

"Clarissa thinks it sounds more dignified." He rolled

his eyes then looked serious. "She'd send him away to a boarding school if she could."

Amy couldn't help shudder at the thought of the little boy who had already lost so much alone in a boarding school. "No." She didn't realize she said it aloud.

"My thoughts exactly." He shifted a little, cutting off her retreat. "I wanted to thank you."

"Thank me?"

"For saving Chance. That took a lot of courage."

Embarrassment ran over her, amplified under his intense scrutiny. "I did what anyone else would do."

He shook his head. "I'd say that was over and above the job description of a governess. Most would run for help or shriek with panic. Either of which could have gotten him bitten. That is if they didn't faint dead away. The governess, two governess ago, I'm sure would have done the shriek and faint."

"I would think a governess should be ... more composed then that. I mean, you can't go freaking out over everything kids will do, especially active little boys."

"I don't think they believe in 'active little boys'. They expected him to be well behaved, seen but not heard."

"Were you that kind of a boy?" She couldn't believe she'd actually asked the question.

"No." He gave a laugh. "I was always on the go, all over the ranch. My dad's shadow. I think my first memory was of sitting on a horse."

"That sounds normal. There's a picture of me sitting on my mom's horse and I was probably only two or three. I used to follow my dad around moving sprinkler pipes and everything until I got big enough to do it myself." Amy smiled at wonderful memories.

"So you were a country girl?"

"Kind of. More a tomboy. I felt more comfortable doing sports and being outdoors. I was very shy."

"I don't see that." He eyed her up and down again.

"I was and can still be," she said, then was amazed to realize she felt so comfortable around him.

"So where did the art come from?" he probed, rocking back on his feet a little, drawing her attention down his legs. He had well-formed calves, lightly dusted with hair that picked up the light from the pool. It took her a second to get her focus back on what he'd said.

"My father. He was what you would call a Jack-of-all-trades. He could do about anything. He was very talented. On a whim, he took up painting so I decided to give it a try also. I loved it. It just fit for me. Though, he liked acrylics and I prefer oils. I like to shift mediums also. Clay's fun and I took a class on doing bronze and loved it. I'm hoping to continue with that in the future."

"Why do you say hoping?" He moved closer.

"It's kind of expensive. When I'm out on my own, it may be a while before I can afford to do it."

"Which is why you took the job watching my brother?" It really wasn't much of a question but there was a tightness in his words.

"Yes," she said honestly. "I'm hoping to save enough to pay for my last year of school."

He stared at her, quiet, brooding. She wasn't sure what his thoughts were until a scowl creased his brow. "My brother's had it hard, but still he's handling it pretty well. He needs love. I'm going to ask you not to hurt him."

"I would never hurt him." She stiffened.

"I don't mean physically. Chance has lost a lot of people. He's becoming attached to you. He never cared for any of his other governesses so he didn't care when they left. Though you've only been with him a few days, I can tell he already cares for you. If you leave, it will hurt him."

"I have no plans to leave him. I committed to Maggie to stay for at least six months. I always keep my promises."

He stared at her. "Six months," he said softly as if adjusting things in his head. After a second, he nodded.

"Goodnight, Amy." He turned and walked to the edge of the pool.

Amy took the opportunity to make a break for her room.

CR80

Jake watched the woman walk away—the governess, Amy. She was a surprise to him. He wasn't quite sure what to think about her. He still couldn't believe she had taken on a rattlesnake to save Chance. It might have been without conscious thought, but she had done it, put herself between him and a rattlesnake.

True, if the snake had bitten her, odds were likely she would've survived. Still, it wouldn't have been pleasant, and it was natural instinct to pull back from them. He'd bet none of Clarissa's other hand-picked governesses would've done anything. If they didn't go into hysterics, they'd have probably reacted like he'd said, screamed and ran. Chance would have gotten bit. But Amy had protected him as if he were her own.

Her image came clearly to his mind, her rich brown hair that seemed to shimmer with hidden light. Her eyes were a surprising blue that reminded him of the sky on a crisp fall day. Her body was naturally slender, toned from athletics, but not lacking any of the feminine curves. She had very nice curves, in fact.

Her head would come to just above his shoulder. It would rest perfectly there so he could breathe in her soft clean scent. He wasn't sure what it was, it was so subtle, but it called to him.

Jake froze, realizing he was still staring after where the woman had disappeared. Forcing her from his mind, he turned and dove into the pool. As he glided back to the surface and started to pull long strokes through the water, he hoped it would wash her away from his thoughts.

CR80

Amy stopped in the hall and looked in on the young,

sleeping boy. She felt a tug at her heart. She didn't know how Chance captured a part of her heart so easily, but she loved him already. He was easy to love with those large, soulful, hazel eyes and sweet smile.

She glanced to the middle of the floor where the snake had been curled and shuddered again at the memory of it. Shuddering a second time as the question hit her of how the snake had gotten there. It was extremely odd. Chance's door hadn't been open. She didn't remember it being open at all since they had arrived. He hadn't been in there long, wanting to go find his brother to tell him all he'd seen on the trip.

The image of his brother came to her mind. She tried to push it back but it came in detail, those hazel eyes, almost identical to his brother's. Lips that cocked slightly to one side when he saw something of mirth.

His broad chest was lightly covered with the same pale hair that dusted his legs. She wondered how it would feel. She had a weakness for texture. His skin would be warm but that hair—Amy pulled back her thoughts.

She took one last glance to make sure Chance was all right. Smiling at the sleeping boy, she left the door partially open so she would hear him if he woke with a nightmare, and crossed to her own room to prepare for bed.

She peeked out into the hall to make sure the coast was clear before hurrying to the bathroom. It was still clear when she came out. She wondered a second if that meant Jake was still out swimming then remembered the doors leading out to the pool from all the rooms on the back side of the house.

Amy lay in bed staring at the ceiling, letting her mind drift with the peace of the night. What an amazing place, but it, like all the emotions running rampant through her threatened to overwhelm her.

It was just all too incredible. Just five days ago, she'd been doing a favor and helping out at the information booth. With no job, and low on funds, she'd been feeling frustrated. Now here she was. She had already figured the McCarron's were wealthy but the ranch was immense. Chance said the ranch stretched up on the mountain which was several miles away.

Chance had also said they had over three thousand head of cattle. It seemed unbelievable until she'd seen the place. Chance had also said something about mining, but that didn't really interest him. Still, in this area of the state, it definitely was possible.

One thing for sure, she was not going to complain about the amount Maggie offered her for watching Chance. It was over twice what she'd hoped to make. Maggie had also assured her everything would be covered for her. Even personal stuff could be put on the house account.

It hadn't only been just money that had made her say yes. In fact, foolishly, she had already agreed before Maggie told her the amount. It was the pull Chance had on her from the first moment she'd seen him. He needed her.

Now that sounded foolish. What do I know about raising little boys? Sure, I babysat a lot, but that hardly qualifies. The thought of the little boy tugged her from her bed.

The house was dark, completely quiet. Not even the creak of settling could be heard. Amy tiptoed across the hall and peeked in. The glow from the nightlight on the dresser gave off plenty of light to see Chance by. He still slept peacefully, not a sign of a nightmare in sight.

Smiling, she turned away and found herself looking straight at the older McCarron male. Barely visible in the darkness, his eyes seemed to burn with a light of their own. He turned and disappeared back inside his room, closing his door softly behind him.

Amy fled to her bed, her heart once more pounding so hard she knew sleep would be a long time coming.

Chapter Five

Jake lay back in his bed but the tension didn't leave his body. The woman was actually checking on Chance in the middle of the night. Even in the faint light, he'd seen her face clearly. The softness on her face turned the pretty to downright beautiful, but the tug he felt within him was for more than for a beautiful woman.

He'd had a lot of immensely beautiful women chase him. He frowned staring up. He was one of the area's most eligible bachelors but had no delusions it was him or even his looks that made him so.

Maybe that was why Chance's governess affected him so. You didn't buy the look that was on her face when she was looking at Chance. It came from inside—pure beauty, real and deep.

He pictured her out by the pool when she'd looked at him. He'd seen something in her eyes then, too, and it wasn't the same tenderness that she'd had when she looked at Chance. He wouldn't say it was plain desire either, more like awareness, that she wasn't sure what to do about.

He wondered if she knew how easy she was to read, or maybe he was reading things that weren't there. Was it wishful thinking, or was it a spark of interest in her eyes, interest in him as a man and not a bank account?

He knew not every woman thought of him that way, but way too many of them did, and that made dating uncomfortable for him. He wanted a relationship, something like his father had with his mother, not like what his father had with Clarissa. There was no love there or even companionship. It had been pure entrapment from Clarissa.

A feeling of sadness swept over him. His father hadn't deserved to have his last days made miserable because of that woman. And, why couldn't Clarissa understand how he felt about her and leave him alone? How could she think he would ever turn to someone like her?

She made him want to shudder. He pushed the thought of her away and concentrated on the more appealing image of Chance's sweet little governess. Funny how the description went together.

撀

Amy found George in the kitchen when she walked in. "Good morning," she greeted the man.

"Good morning, Miss Amy." He glanced away from what he was whipping in a bowl, over his shoulder. "How are you after your dull first night here? I hope it wasn't too calm." The mirth that twinkled in his eyes turned into a chuckle.

Amy joined in. "Oh, yes, very calm." She arched a brow.

"I hope it doesn't put you off us." He looked more serious.

"Oh, no. It's just one of those things."

"Good, good. Now what would you like for breakfast?" he asked as he returned to whipping whatever it was in the bowl in front of him.

"Oh, a bowl of cereal is fine."

"Heaven forbid. That will not do. This is your first morning here. Now what would you like?"

Amy wasn't sure what to say, so she just shrugged. "Anything is fine." It made her feel uncomfortable having someone wait on her. "What are you making?" She moved forward to peek into the bowl at the batter he continued to whip.

"Crepes. Chance's favorite thing. I'm making them as a welcome back."

"Oh, I'd love a crepe. Can I help? I make them quite often myself."

That caught his interest. "You cook?"

She shrugged again, feeling embarrassed. "Well, nothing like you, I'm sure, but I enjoy baking– cookies, desserts and rolls."

"Excellent, excellent." George clapped his hands together. "Chance will enjoy that."

"We all will." The deep masculine voice from behind startled her.

Amy turned to the man standing in the open doors that led out to the patio. The morning sun gleamed around Jake McCarron, highlighting the streaks in his hair. A navy blue T-shirt stretched over his chest, accentuating the width of it. The jeans he wore were well worn. They hugged his hips and made his already long legs look incredible. The cowboy boots he wore were as worn as his jeans, and definitely looked natural on him.

Jake McCarron was a really good-looking man. He wasn't much older than her but he exuded strength and authority. Amy's breath caught. *I'm not going to fall for him. I want this job. I'm not going to foul it up by falling in love.* Amy froze. *What's wrong with me?* This was so unlike her. She was a practical person.

"Mr. McCarron, good morning." She forced the words out with a smile she hoped would hide all the flip-flopping emotions going on inside her. She'd just have to stay away from him.

A slight scowl appeared over his features. "I thought we'd settled this, Jake will do. Would you please join me for breakfast on the patio?"

"Oh, I was going to wait for Chance." Amy grabbed for the first thing she could think of.

"I'm sure he'll be out as soon as he wakes up. I'd like to go over your schedule for today."

So much for staying away from him. Amy wished there was a way she could decline but maybe it was better to get used to him right now and get these silly emotions in check. He was her employer. "Yes, sir."

The scowl lines deepened as he turned out onto the patio, leaving her to follow.

Amy started forward.

"Here." George caught her attention. "Will you take this out?" He motioned to a tray with fruit and whipped cream on it.

"Sure." She picked up the tray.

Stepping onto the patio, she was again taken back at how beautiful it was there. The sun gleamed off the huge pool, but it was the blue sky and meadow that stretched out that stunned her. She turned from it to see Jake standing by the table, holding a chair out for her.

"Oh, thank you." Amy set the tray on the table and slipped into the chair. It was a relief to her when he took the chair across from her.

When he looked at her, she had to keep herself from fidgeting. "Chance seemed to sleep well last night."

"Yes. Thanks to you I'd say." He studied her openly.

Amy wondered what he saw. "It helped that you and Maggie came in with him. He needed to have his family."

"Yes, family is important. While you are here, I hope you will feel part of the family so you can help strengthen and support Chance."

"I will try to do my best." She shifted in her chair, feeling like he was trying to say something more. Before she could figure out what it was, Chance came running across the patio.

"Jake, Amy. Have you had breakfast already?"

Jake turned and smiled at his brother. "We were waiting for you, sleepy head."

"I'm here." Chance practically dove into the chair. "What's for breakfast?"

"I think George said something about pickled-pig's feet and sauerkraut." The older McCarron looked at his brother with a semblance of seriousness.

"Augh." Chance made a face.

Amy couldn't keep from laughing.

George picked that moment to walk out with several crepes stacked on a plate.

"Oh-boy." Chance's expression changed to one of pure joy.

"I didn't know you were here. These are for Miss Amy."

Amy knew he had heard Jakes comment. "It's a good thing that I'm good at sharing." She looked at the chef as he put the plate by her. "Thank you."

"Anytime. I'll have more out in a minute." The man turned and hurried back inside.

"Does that mean you will share with me?" Jake asked.

"Of course she will. Amy's nice," Chance spoke up for her.

"That's nice to know." His eyebrow arched slightly.

"Chance, what would you like on yours?" Amy asked as she placed a crepe on a plate.

The boy looked at the toppings. "Powdered sugar, strawberries, raspberries and whipped cream." Amy loaded the things on the crepe rolled it up, and handed it to Chance along with a fork.

"That sounds good to me, if you're serving." Jake held his plate out to her. He had a grin, as mischievous as any she'd seen on Chance's face in the last week. *They were two of a kind.*

Amy took the plate and focused on loading another crepe and handing it to him before making one for herself.

"Now what are your plans for today?"

"I'm going to show Amy around. She hasn't got to see

anything yet. Not even the whole house." Chance spoke with a touch of whip cream on his lip.

"Really?" Jake looked at her again.

"We didn't get here until just before dinner."

"I have a little time this morning, maybe I'll join you." Jake's comment brought a whoop of excitement from his brother. "I believe you also mentioned something about wanting to go riding."

"Yes," Chance's enthusiasm continued.

"I'm going to be out by the old homestead. Why don't you show that to Amy? If you bring a lunch, I'll join you for a picnic."

"All right!"

"Good." Jake grinned at his brother then turned his attention back to her. "It was mentioned that you ride."

"I'm decent but I haven't done much in the last couple years." She tried not to shift uneasily.

"It'll come back to you quickly enough, I'm sure. What do you think, Chance? Shall we put her on Shasta? I think they'd look pretty good together."

Chance literally bounced up and down in his seat, his eyes full of excitement. "She was born the same day I was. She's beautiful."

Amy looked from Chance to Jake.

"She has a real sweet personality. I think you'll like her," Jake added. There was unmistakable pride in his voice.

His eyes were so intense, Amy felt herself flush. "It sounds like I will." There was a breathless quality in her voice. She swallowed, then reached for a glass of juice and took a drink trying to reel in her runaway reaction. *Practical, I'm practical. I am not going to fall for the man. Oh, but he has beautiful eyes.* She tried not to look at them and was saved by George coming out with more crepes. Amy set herself to filling them while the brothers ate and talked of Chance's trip and the ranch.

Time seemed to pass quickly as she tried to keep out of the conversation, giving them time together. After the last several days, she knew how much Chance craved time with his brother, though he understood Jake was extremely busy.

"Well, how about we take your governess for a tour before I have to get to work?" Jake said suddenly, pushing back his chair to stand.

"Oh, it's not necessary." Amy made her way to her feet as he pulled out the chair for her.

"I know, but I want to. Where to first?" He let Chance make the decision.

"Around the yard." Chance took Amy's hand as he liked to do when they walked. Amy found herself sandwiched between the two.

"Okay, so out here we have the patio. We cook out a lot, especially when its George's evening off." Jake started but Chance cut him off.

"That's because Jake can't cook but on the grill. Otherwise, he burns everything, and George has forbidden him to use his pans."

"Hey," Jake protested.

Chance laughed.

When Amy looked up at him, Jake just shrugged. "I really can't cook."

She found herself smiling and relaxing.

"Make yourself at home here. You can use the pool and hot tub any time you want. The sports court is down this way." He led the way down the path, just over a small knoll.

Amy didn't think the name sports court did it justice. There was an enclosed tennis court and basketball court that could be set for volleyball. There were several tables with umbrellas, a playground with a climbing wall and slide combo like usually found at city parks and a baseball diamond on the far side.

"It's like your own city park." The words came out,

and Amy hoped they hadn't sounded rude.

Jake didn't seem to take offense. "The ranch families bring their kids here to play quite often. In the evenings, the hands will come down and shoot hoops, and they have parties here. The only time it's not available to everyone is from ten to twelve."

Amy picked up a tightness in Jakes voice.

"That's when Clarissa likes to have her tennis lesson and doesn't want to be disturbed." He shifted. "The sports equipment is in the building. There's grill that is for everyone to use."

Amy noticed the little bowery on the side of the building with picnic tables under it. An access road with a parking lot was just on the other side of it. "This is a nice set up."

"It works. Everyone seems to enjoy it."

"Do you play tennis, Amy?" Chance got back into the conversation.

"A little. My dad taught me some when I was young then I took a couple classes in college for fun. I'm better at volleyball and softball."

"So you like sports?" Jake asked.

"Yes. I like to be outdoors."

"Will you teach me to play tennis?" Chance tugged on her arm.

"I think I could get you started."

"Cool, I want to be able to beat Jake. He's good but not great."

"Hey," Jake said in protest and dodged around her reaching for his brother. Chance squealed and ducked around Amy.

The game erupted with Amy in the middle of the two McCarron's as Jake tried to catch Chance and the boy dodging away, laughing happily. Jake faked one direction coming around the other way catching Chance, throwing him up in the air easily, before catching and tickling him.

Chance roared in laughter.

Amy smiled at their antics.

"Give up," Jake demanded until Chance finally gave in. Jake set him on his feet. "Come on, we'd better show Amy the house. We wouldn't want her getting lost. She might end up in Clarissa's room then there would be trouble."

Chance giggled.

The first part of the tour was a quick go over what she'd learned the day before, which was most of the wing where hers, Jake's, Chance's and Maggie's rooms were. They circled through the family room, entry, living, dining room, with a stop in the music room. She found out Jake played the piano and guitar and Chance was taking piano lessons, which were on Wednesday's and he was to practice every day for at least thirty minutes. It wasn't negotiable.

They ducked into the kitchen to say hi to George on their way to the game room. Amy liked the room with the pool and foosball tables. She found out that downstairs there was another game room with table tennis, air hockey, exercise mats and equipment.

"The wintertime outlet is what our father used to call it." Jake winked at Chance as they stepped out into the hall that was actually split into two halls that ran parallel to each down the other wing.

"The first hall is shorter, with only another guest room, and Clarissa's rooms at the end. This hall," Jake directed them down it, "leads to the garage and the elevator at the end will take you to the exercise room, but first through here, there's a bathroom, and another guestroom," he said as they walked down the hall. "Here's the laundry and mud room that goes to the garage. You probable came in that way yesterday." He glanced at her.

"Yes."

"This hall goes past the garage to the staff quarters."

They walked down a hall that was sided with storage cabinets. At the first door they came to, he paused. "Ruth's family usually stays here when they come to visit. This hall leads out to the backyard. Ruth's apartment is here on the left. George's is on the right. This door is to the garage."

He held it open for her. The garage was massive and immaculate. There was a truck and five cars besides the limo and still room for a couple other vehicles. The car in the corner was covered with a dust cover. Jake must have noticed her attention on it because he said, "I'll show you that some other day when I have more time to take you for a ride."

"It's so sick," Chance said then grinned.

"I still haven't gotten used to that term." Jake made a face.

Amy laughed.

"I take it you know what it means?" Jake asked.

"Yes. Your age is showing through, though I prefer awesome or sweet."

"Our country upbringing."

Amy didn't think Jake was that country though he lived on a ranch. There was a well-educated quality about him. Before she could decide if she dared pry, Chance spoke up again.

"It's his favorite toy." Chance rolled his eyes.

"You like it, and you know it."

Chance wrinkled his nose then grinned. "I like your other car." He caught Amy's hand and drew her to a silver convertible that gleamed under the overhead lights.

Amy didn't know much about fancy, high-performance, sport cars, but recognized the logo on it and had to admit it really was pretty with its sleek lines. She looked at Jake to see him shrug. "It's not that outlandish, just good and reliable."

"And stylish," she added holding back a smile.

"Well, yes." He grinned openly. "I got my thing for

cars from my father. He believed in having good automobiles and looking after them. We restored several over the years. We have a couple that are in museums as show pieces." There was pride in his voice. He looked thoughtful. "You didn't get to bring a car with you, did you?"

"No. I rode in the limo."

"We'll have to see about getting you a vehicle to use. The last governess was from back east and didn't drive so we didn't keep a car for her. Do you know how to drive a stick?" The question took her by surprise.

"Yes."

"Then you can take my car until I can arrange for another one."

Amy looked at the beautiful sports car and started shaking her head. "Oh, no. I've never driven anything like that before. When I said stick, I meant an old ranch truck."

"Well, the trucks around here are all in use. And don't worry about the car. It's just a car and it's insured."

She continued to shake her head.

"I'll tell you what. I'll give you a driving lesson on it, and we'll see how you do. It will have to be tomorrow, though, because I better get to work now."

"That's not necessary."

"Yes, it is. I want to see how you drive before you start taking Chance around with you."

Amy was torn with wanting to argue but understood his reasoning. Still, she couldn't imagine driving a car like the convertible.

"It will be all right, Amy," Jake said as if reading the direction her thoughts were going. His gaze seemed to promise more, then he turned his attention on Chance. "You'll have to finish her tour. See you at lunch." With that, he strode over and climbed into a four-wheel drive truck. One of the sets of garage doors opened and he backed out, waving before he drove way.

"Come on, I'll show you the basement." Chance headed out the door Jake just drove through.

"Where you going?" Amy asked, confused.

"I want to show you the outside entrances." He took the path that went toward the front entry. About half way there was a smaller path of stepping stones that curved off behind the landscaping. Chance led her behind the trees to stairs going down. The door at the bottom blended in with the house. What was a surprise was the keypad set in heavy metal.

"Come on. You have to know the code or you can't get in." Chance waited until she was right beside him before he reached out to touch the numbers.

"Are you sure it's okay that I know it?" She shifted uneasily.

"Sure. You can get here from upstairs, and you'll have a key to the house."

Amy knew that made sense, especially since she'd be living there for a year. Jake had told him to show her the rest, she just hoped it was okay. Making up her mind, she decided not to watch. If she was to have the combination, she'd wait until one of the adults gave it to her. Chance opened the door, and the lights came on automatically.

"It's all storage down this way. The vaults are at the end. You'll have to have Jake show you that. There's some real cool things in there."

They reached what was the main hall in about twelve feet. Amy was surprised at the double width of it and the polished concrete floor. Chance took her down toward what he said was the storage area.

"There are holiday decorations in that room, and that one's camping gear." He opened the door displaying shelves that had an array of sleeping bags, pads and tents. Another shelf held an assortment of Dutch ovens, another had lanterns, stoves and water filters. Hanging on the wall were several sizes of backpacks. There was other gear like climbing ropes and helmets; and fishing poles, tackle boxes and bags.

"Wow, where's the canoe?" The comment wasn't meant to be serious but Chance took it so.

"Out in the equipment shed. It won't fit in the elevator."

Amy looked down at the boy and laughed, ruffling his hair. "Looks like you're set for anything."

He nodded. "I have my own bag and tent. Jake promised to take me camping at least once a month all summer."

"That sounds like fun."

"I caught five fish when we went last month," he said proudly.

"Wow, I guess I'll have to get a fishing license so we can go."

"You can fish?" He looked in awe as if she just said something amazing.

"Yes."

"Maybe you can come with us next time."

"I think your campouts sound like they're something just for the guys."

Chance seemed to think on it for a minute then nodded.

"Do you want to show me the workout room?"

"Yeah, it's down this way, back toward the garage." He stopped where another hall ran off. "That goes out to the back patio. That's food storage, and there's a dumbwaiter to the kitchen."

"Sick."

Chance started laughing.

"Hey, what's so funny?"

Chance laughed harder, holding his stomach and doubled over.

"Okay, you little hyena, come on."

He was still laughing when they made it to the exercise room. Sun came in through the windows high on the walls of three sides of the room. Amy was no longer surprised at the amount of equipment. It was a great workout room or place to relax.

She lost to Chance in a game of foosball but won table tennis. Instead of letting him talk her into a rematch, she insisted they head upstairs. "It sounds like you need to get your piano practicing done so we can go riding, and I need to see about getting us lunch."

Chance let out one groan but didn't argue. "Tomorrow can we play tennis?" he asked as they walked up the stairs.

"I think we can arrange that. I need to find out what other duties or lessons you need to do." She rested a hand on his shoulder.

"Will you ask gran'ma or Jake?" He looked up with a hopeful expression she could fully understand.

She smiled. "I'll go see if your grandmother is busy right now." She stayed at the entrance of the music room and watched as he got settled. As soon as he started to play, she went in search of the older woman.

Maggie McCarron was reading on the patio outside her room. "Hello dear. Won't you have a seat?" she greeted as Amy approached. "All settled?"

"Close. Chance just finished giving me a tour of the house and is practicing his piano." Amy settled in a chair.

"Excellent. I figured you might like a list of all his activities." Maggie handed her a paper. "Please, don't try to press all the things on him that I'm sure Clarissa will give you. She does it more for punishment. For what, I don't know, but she wants to make his life miserable."

It was Amy's initial reaction to discount the thought but after being around Clarissa for five days, she could visualize the woman doing just that. "I won't."

"Don't worry about Clarissa trying to fire you. I won't let that happen. She has no say."

Maggie looked at her until Amy nodded. "Jake has the final say, and he will side with me, especially on this."

Amy felt a twinge of unease but nodded again.

"Good. Now here's the combination to the security system and a key to the house in case Jake forgot to give you one. I'm sure Clarissa hasn't."

"Thank you." Amy took the key, sliding it into her pocket.

"Now do you have any questions?"

"None left that I can think of. This list is what I was coming to ask you about."

"Excellent. I wanted to speak to you about something else while I have you."

Amy felt a twinge of dread and didn't know why.

"A week from Friday, we will be having a social here. It will mostly be friends and neighbors, but a few business associates will also attend. I would like you to plan on joining us. Chance will be making a brief appearance, but I'd like you to attend the whole evening."

Chapter Six

Amy felt her chest tighten at just the thought of the place being full of elegantly dressed people. She didn't know why she knew it was that kind of party; but Maggie's next words confirmed it as Maggie continued before she could utter a word.

"I'm sure you don't have anything to wear, so you'll need to go into town and find a suitable evening gown. Here is a list of places for you to look at." She handed her another slip of paper. "Just tell them what it is for, they'll help you find something that is suitable and they will send the bill here. I put an authorization on the paper."

"I–" Amy started to protest but Maggie cut her off.

"Now, none of that. You will be just fine. You are going to become an important member of this household, and I want you there."

"Maggie–"

The older woman placed her hand over hers and squeezed. "Please do this for me."

Amy looked at her and was lost. "I've never been to anything like this."

"It's just like any other party but the dress is just a touch more fancy."

Amy couldn't keep back the groan that slipped out.

Maggie McCarron laughed knowing she'd won. She patted her hand again. "Don't worry. If I can get used to them, you can. I remember my first one. I spilled punch on the mayor."

Amy groaned again, and Maggie leaned forward. "It wasn't entirely an accident," she said confidentially.

"What?"

"The man was a pompous prig." Maggie waved her hand through the air.

Amy started to laugh. "You really did?"

"Of course. The man insulted my husband."

"I bet he never did again."

"No, in fact, we became quite good friends. Though, he was always a touch pompous. Now don't worry about this. I just wanted to give you some warning. You can take this week to get settled. Then Monday or Tuesday you can go into town. You can take Chance with you. He hasn't had any experience shopping with a woman. It is something he should learn so he doesn't complain overly much when he gets married."

Amy wasn't sure she was the one to teach him. She didn't mind shopping but this was out of her normal league. All she could do was nod.

"Excellent. Now, I also wanted to let you know Ruth said your boxes arrived before we got here. She didn't know what they were or what to do with them so she had them put in storage room three. That's in the basement, third door on the left, the one before the food storage. There should be plenty of space on a shelf if you want to store your art supplies there, but I'm sure you'd like to bring your other belongings up. We'll have to think of someplace you can use as a studio." The woman looked thoughtful.

Amy felt warmed by her thoughtfulness but a little embarrassed. "That's not necessary. I can paint on the patio, if that's all right?"

"Well, certainly some of the time that would work, but when weather is not permitting, you'll have to have somewhere else to work. Well, we can worry about that later. I think I'll get back to my book."

Taking that as a dismissal, Amy stood, still feeling a little shocked. She was only halfway across the patio when something else disturbed her senses. It took a second of looking around to spot the woman under the deck awning that ran along the far wing of the house. The swimsuit she wore exposed plenty of toned, tanned skin.

Clarissa hid her age well. The only thing that marred her perfection was the scowl on her face. Amy had no doubts it was directed at her. She expected the woman to call her over and berate her for something but instead Clarissa turned in one fluid motion and stalked away.

Amy started forward when she caught sight of another person watching her from the shadows of the awning. A chill went through her which was silly. She blinked against the sun, and shifted to get a better look, but he was gone. There one moment, then he was gone, like some figment of her imagination. But she knew he was real, just as the brief glimpse was enough to recognize him. Though, she hadn't seen the chauffer, Knowlton, since they'd been back, there was no mistaking him.

Unease spiked again in her but she shook it off, telling herself that he wasn't watching her, just out there to talk to Clarissa. Stressing that firmly in her mind, she continued to the kitchen to talk to George about lunch. He assured her he'd have it when they were ready to leave. Amy stopped to check on how Chance's practicing was going then headed down to find her boxes.

They were just where Maggie had said she'd find them. She opened the box with her paints to make sure everything was all right. Luckily, none of the tubes had split in transport and her mediums were okay. What made her pause was the pouch containing her brushes.

The brushes were fine, but the ties on the pouch were undone. It wouldn't have bothered her but she was always very careful about doing it up. Some of the brushes were expensive. She took very good care of them. Obviously, somehow, during the trip the tie must have worked its way undone. It was the only possibility because nothing else was disturbed, and the box had still been sealed.

Her mind remained on the pouch as she picked up her clothing box. She'd taken two steps into the hall when a clattering sound around the corner made her freeze. There was no sound, then a faint skiff. Amy forced a swallow to clear her throat.

"Hello," she called out, then listened. There was no answer. She had just relaxed, thinking again how foolish she was being, when a click sounded, like the lock on a door catching. Heart pounding, she rushed to the cross hall but it was empty. Shrugging it off, she headed upstairs.

ᘔᔐ

Amy was relaxed again by the time she and Chance took the short walk out to the stables. She was surprised at the size of the building. Everything on the McCarron ranch seemed to be built on a grand scale. As they entered the stable a late middle-aged man came out of what looked like an office.

"Hey there, Chance," he greeted then turned to Amy. "You must be the new governess. An improvement on the old ones, I'd say." Smile lines creased the sun-wrinkled face.

"This is Amy." Chance took over the introductions as she reached out to shake the hand that was extended to her. "This is Ben. He's our foreman."

"Nice to meet you, ma'am." He tipped his head to her.

"And you."

"Jake said you'd be down." Ben turned his attention back to Chance. "That you'd be showing Amy, here, around. Said I was to put her on Shasta." He glanced back at Amy. "I'm thinking Jake's right. They'll suit each other. I already moved her and Dusty into number three. Your tack is there."

Amy caught him looking at her backside, but wasn't offended, realizing it wasn't personal. He was checking her out so he could pick out a saddle that would be best for her. As if to affirm the thought, he just grinned at being caught.

"Just give me a second, and I'll get you a saddle."

Chance headed to a stall. She followed him. Inside were two horses. Neither was very tall. She guessed the first one, a little dapple gray, would have been pressing it to reach fifteen hands. The other, a roan, with black stockings, mane and tail might have been a half hand taller. Both had beautiful lines and a proud hold of their heads. When the dapple saw Chance, it nickered a greeting, coming right to the gate.

"This is Dusty. He's my horse. My Dad broke him. He gave him to me when I turned five. He said I was ready for my own horse then."

"He's beautiful." Amy slid her hand through the bars, letting the horse smell her fingers before she tried petting him.

"We have some of the finest horses in the nation," Ben said coming up, carrying a bridle and a blanket.

Another man followed him holding a saddle. He set it down just inside the stable and turned away but not before Amy caught him giving her the once over. She shifted uneasily at his attention and looked back to Ben.

"Several have ended up as National champions," Ben was saying. "John always worked hard to make them the best, and Jake has continued in his father's footsteps. This one," he flicked the brim of Chance's hat, "seems to be right in step."

Chance beamed proudly as Ben continued. "Shasta here can pull a cow out without anyone on her back. Just point her at the calf you want and she'll get it. She's got a real nice gait too, a pleasure to ride." He opened the gate, stepped in, and started to saddle the mare.

Amy picked up Chance's saddle while Chance took the

blanket and started on Dusty. Ben glanced over his shoulder and when he nodded, she understood that he was checking the job they were doing. In just over a minute, they led the horses from the stable. Chance climbed immediately on the horse while Ben fastened down the saddle bags holding their lunch.

"Do you need a hand up?" He looked at her.

"I think I can manage." She placed a foot in the stirrup and swung up. It felt a little different being on a horse after so long, but it faded when she wiggled into the saddle.

"How's the stirrups?"

Amy stood in them, testing the length. "Good."

"All right, have a nice ride." Ben stepped away.

"Thanks. All right, Chance, lead the way." A feeling of déjà vu hit her as she turned and caught a glimpse of a man beside the corner of the barn watching them. He turned and walked away before she had an opportunity to get a good look at him. Being a new comer to the ranch sure seemed to draw a lot of attention, she decided as she urged her horse into stride with Chance's.

They talked as they rode down a lane with hay fields on either side. Amy sighed, tilting her face up to the sun and took in a deep breath of fresh air. After about twenty minutes, they shifted directions heading toward a small hill that stood in the distance. Amy could see Black Angus cattle spread out over the hillside. Another fifteen minutes and the hay field ended, and they went through the gate into the pasture.

"So where's the old homestead?" Amy asked.

"At the bottom of the hill by those trees. The stream goes right by there."

Amy could make out the trees but no buildings. "So why did it get moved?"

"My great-great, I think, grandmother didn't like being so far from town so when my great-great-grandfather was building them a new house, he moved it to the edge of the property closest to town. At least, that's what I was told. Jake knows more than I do."

Amy smiled. Chance was such a smart boy and always seemed so grown up, she had to remind herself how young he really was. She looked back toward the house. They were a couple miles away now and she could no longer see it. She was impressed the man would move the house that far just so his wife could be closer to town. It was a different time back then. People didn't go to town that often, but it was a big social event when they did.

She was still looking back when a flash of light caught her attention. It was there and gone. At first, she thought she'd imagined it like she had the person watching earlier, but when it came again, she knew it was real. She studied the area, trying to decide what it was, when she saw the glint a third time she understood what she was seeing. Someone was looking through binoculars. Her first thought was studying the cattle then it hit her, someone was probably checking on her and Chance.

It made sense she guessed.

"Want to race to that bush?" Chance asked, pulling her attention back around.

She looked to where he pointed and hardly got the yes out before he took off. "Hey," she nudged her horse. Shasta took off, reacting immediately as if she had just been waiting for the signal.

Amy leaned forward in the saddle. The wind rushed over her face bringing a charge of excitement with it. Ben was right; Shasta had such a smooth gait she felt like she was flying.

She almost caught Chance before he reached the bush. He let out a loud whoop. Amy followed the motion of pulling up beside him.

"I won." He grinned.

"I want a rematch."

He laughed happily leaning down to wrap his arms

around his horse's neck.

"Happy?" she asked, seeing the pleasure on his face.

He smiled up at her, he eyes bright. "Yes, I don't want you to ever leave."

Amy felt the tug at her heart. The thought of leaving him hurt. She knew she had fallen for the little boy but she didn't know it was so strong. It had only been a week. What would it be like leaving in a year?

She didn't want to think about that. "I'm not going anywhere," she said firmly. "I'm happy, too. Though you know, there will be times when I'll probably have to be the mean, old governess that makes you do things." She dropped her voice into her best wicked witch imitation.

Chance wrinkled his nose and laughed.

"Hey, I'm serious." She tried to act offended.

"I know. Jake has to sometimes, too. He doesn't like to, so I try not to make him. I'll try to do the same with you."

Amy felt tears threaten. "Thank you. But you know, even if I ever have to get after you, it doesn't mean I don't love you."

He nodded. "Jake said the same thing."

"Okay, shall we head for the homestead?"

They rode in silence for several minutes before Chance spoke up again. "I love you, Amy."

She looked over at him, choked up at what she felt. "I love you, too, sweetie."

"Do you want to have another race? This time to the trees?" He pointed to some big cottonwoods up ahead.

"Start together?" She tilted her head and looked at him.

"Okay, one, two, three." He exploded forward on the three like out of a gate. This time it was a longer run, and she really got to see what kind of a rider he was. He leaned out over the horse's neck just as much as his small body allowed. With a good grip on the reigns she had no doubt he was in control. Amy had to admit Chance was a better rider than she was. He was a natural. Still she didn't think she made a bad showing.

Chance was whooping again when they pulled up.

"Okay, you beat me fair and square," she conceded, gaining another hoot. "So where do you think Jake is?" She turned in the saddle, looking around them. The words where hardly out of her mouth when she caught sight of him riding down the slope toward them.

Chance saw him too and took off. "I beat Amy," he shouted in way of a greeting.

"I saw." Jake looked past his brother, and Amy felt her heart jump.

His black cowboy hat was tipped up framing the chiseled planes of his face. He sat as easy on his horse as his brother and, though he was totally relaxed, his biceps bulged under his T-shirt sleeve. The horse he rode was amazing. The whitish-gray coat had a dappling like Chance's horse, black stockings, mane and tail like hers. The combination was extremely striking.

"It seems like you're doing fine on Shasta."

"Yes, she's a wonderful horse." Amy leaned forward to stroke the mare's neck.

"I like her." He swung down as he reached her. Chance did the same so Amy followed suit, running her hand again over Shasta's neck, admiring the horse. The next thing she knew, Jake was standing next to her making the same motion.

"How are you beautiful? Have a nice run?" he talked to the horse. It reacted much the same as it had to Chance's greeting.

Amy was impressed. "Do all your horses act like that around you?" She tilted her head to the side to look at him.

"Quite a few. Shasta here is special though. She's the first horse I trained myself, and I just bred her with Beau here a couple weeks ago."

"Oh, is it okay I ran her?" Amy felt a twinge of worry,

though he didn't seem upset.

"It's fine. She can use a lot of good exercise this summer. It's just the last couple months that you won't be able to ride her. Don't worry, I'll let you know."

"Okay."

"I get to help Jake break a horse this summer?" Chance spoke up.

"That's the plan. You ready to eat?" Jake asked.

"Yeah." Chance's ever present enthusiasm was in his voice.

"So what's to eat?" Jake asked as he led the way to where they could tie the horses.

"I don't know," Chance was the first to answer. "Amy?"

"I don't know either. George just handed it to me when I went in. I figured he knew what you like and didn't worry too much about it."

"Well, let's go see what we got." Jake handed her a blanket and led the way to a spot under a tree, not far from a small stream.

Opening the bag, they found thick roast beef sandwiches on sesame seed rolls, a bowl of pasta salad for each, a bag of cookies, and bottles of fruit juice and water.

"Umm, okay, he knows how to pack a picnic," Amy commented as she bit into the sandwich and was met with the tangy taste of whatever George put on it.

"This is his working man's picnic. We'll have to get him to pack us an evening basket sometime."

"Oh." Amy looked over.

He didn't pull back from her obvious interest.

"Yes, I can always tell what he thinks of my date by the baskets."

"You take a lot of women on picnics?" Amy couldn't believe she asked the question. It wasn't her place to pry, and she wasn't interested in him that way. Even as she thought it, she knew it was a lie. She was interested, just realistic enough to know nothing was ever going to go that way.

"A few, if I really want to get to know someone, I can learn a lot more about a woman on a picnic than I can in a movie or fancy restaurant."

Amy had to admit that was true.

"So," he turned to Chance, "how did the tour go?"

"Great, and I got my piano done."

"Good." He tossed his brother a cookie.

"I was telling Amy about the homestead that was here."

"Really?" Jake looked at her.

"I'm not sure who moved it," Chance said around a mouthful of cookie.

Jake gave him a slight frown and he swallowed. "It was great-great grandpa, the first John."

"Chance said that it was so his wife could be closer to town."

"That's right. The story goes he loved his wife a lot. She was from a titled family back in England and gave it all up to marry him. They struggled there for a while before they came to America, all the way out west. Their first cabin was small with two rooms. It stood just over there. All that's left is part of the chimney."

He pointed about twenty feet away. "She worked right beside him making the ranch work and it did. My grandfather was a savvy man, and they'd picked a good location. The ranch grew right from the beginning but it was rough on them. She had three babies that were stillborn or died within a day of the birth."

"Oh," Amy couldn't keep in the exclamation that tugged at her heart. She knew it happened a lot back then, but it would have been so hard.

He smiled at her but continued. "The ranch was becoming quite prosperous, and they also found some mineral deposits that ended up being very profitable. He was already thinking of building her a larger, grander house, so when Emily, his wife, told him she was expecting another baby he decided to move it closer to town so she would be closer to the doctor and mid-wife."

"That is amazing," Amy said.

"More like a miracle. She ended up having trouble again. The doctor arrived just in time and fortunately was not a quack. He was barely able to save her and the baby. History has it if he'd had to make it all the way here, she would have probably lost the baby and bled to death before he reached her. That was our great-grandfather. She was never able to have any other children."

"That is a miracle. So where was that house? It's not part of the house now?"

"No. It was closer to where the stables are now. It had been added on to several times. It was a grand house with a big wide front porch."

"What happened to it?" she couldn't help ask, knowing by the nostalgic warmth in his voice, that it wouldn't have just been torn down.

"There was a fire when I was a senior in high school." Pain flickered over his face. Everyone made it out and we were able to save most of the house but structurally, it wasn't feasible to rebuild it. Besides, the old house was three stories so it was difficult for grandma. This house is much easier."

"It's a beautiful house."

"My father had it designed. He wanted to keep the family together, but still give me the privacy he figured I'd be needing."

"It does that."

"We do pretty well, huh." He reached over and ruffled his brother's hair.

Chance's head bobbed up and down. "I'm glad I'm down by your room instead of by Clarissa. My room was next to my Dad's until he came back with her."

Amy didn't miss the stress on her.

"Clarissa thought they needed more …" he looked to Jake for what he was meaning.

"Space."

Chance nodded. "I'm glad."

"Me, too." Jake dropped his arm over his shoulders.

They continued to eat and talk a few minutes more before Jake announced, "I need to get back to work."

Amy and Chance cleaned up the meal while Jake headed back up the hill. With the horse packed up, Chance led them home across the meadow around the hay field toward the house.

⊂ℨ℞

Amy wrapped the elastic around her hair then piled the mass on top of her head catching it there with a clip. Grabbing the towel, she headed out into the hall, stopping long enough to look in on Chance. The boy was deeply asleep. They hadn't even read three pages tonight before he had dropped off.

It had been quite a day. She was tired, but decided a few minutes in the hot tub would feel great before bed. She walked down the hall. The house was quiet. A light shown under the door to Maggie's room, hinting that the older woman was still awake. Amy smiled, she really liked her. Maggie made her feel comfortable, but Amy wished Maggie hadn't insisted she go to the social. That was something she would just as soon miss, but she'd face that later.

Amy went straight to the hot tub. She sucked in a breath as she stepped in, dipped down, and then came up before settling on the seat.

"Oh my." Amy tilted her head back and sighed. "That feels so good," she murmured to herself and relaxed, letting her mind drift. She guessed she shouldn't have been surprised her thoughts went right to Jake McCarron. He seemed to have captivated her.

His image came clearly; Jake sitting next to his brother, leaning over and ruffling Chance's hair. It had been such a move of unconscious affection, it pulled at her heart. There was more to him than she had first thought.

She got that he loved his brother and his grandmother by the look in his eyes when he'd talked with her the night before. She also got that he was a hard worker. That surprised her the most. He didn't lead the pampered life. The image of his car came to her mind. He did like nice things, but wasn't shallow, and as nice as his car was, she knew it wasn't that outrageously expensive.

Amy tried to pull her thoughts away, but they went right back to him. The picture of him on his horse came clearly to her. Both were so magnificent. Painting people was not her thing but she'd be so tempted to paint him on his horse. A brush over her senses said there was someone watching her. She opened her eyes to look up at the very man that kept slipping into her mind.

Jake McCarron stared down at her, his lips kicked up in a lopsided smile. "Feels good after a busy day doesn't it?" He didn't wait for an answer as he stepped down into the water.

Chapter Seven

Amy's breath caught as Jake settled down across from her. Water lapped at his shoulders. He had great shoulders, all sculpted muscle that begged for her fingers to trace them. There was a sprinkling of hair across his chest, not thick just intriguing. She ripped her thoughts away, steadying herself before she did anything foolish.

She used the action of raising her hand to wipe moisture from her brow to regroup her thoughts. "It does feel good. I'm afraid to say it's been a couple of years since I've a chance to do any riding."

He chuckled. "A touch sore?"

"Just a touch. Better than I figured, though it wasn't a hard ride. It was a lot of fun." She met his gaze then glanced away.

"Do I make you nervous?" he asked directly.

She looked back at him then lowered her eyes.

"A touch," she repeated in honesty. "But, it's not just you. I'm not real good with people."

His brow arched, and she hurried to clarify. "I used to be extremely shy. I tried to hide it and worked really hard to get over it when I went to college. I was never one of those peppy, popular girls." She couldn't believe she'd just admitted that to him.

He nodded in acceptance. "No, you were one of the hard workers that hid in the background." The warmth of his words surprised her, especially when he added, "You are also artistic. That puts you a touch out of step from everyone else because you see things in your own light."

"I'm not an off-the-wall type."

That brought a laugh from him. "No, you're the practical type, an odd combo, a renaissance woman. You can do anything."

Amy thought he was teasing her but when she looked into his eyes, they were filled with seriousness.

His lips twitched as if picking up her train of thought. "It's all right. You fit in well here."

That did surprise her. "I want to be Chance's nan ... governess."

"Good. He likes you, but what I was referring to was the artistic thing. I can't say I have much of it but I grew up around it. Maggie used to do pottery and a little sculpting before her accident. There are still a few of her pieces around, though most of the pottery was lost in the fire."

That piqued her interest. She'd noticed several pieces on the tour of the house but hadn't really had time to look. "I didn't know that. Why'd she give it up?"

"Dad always told her he'd get someone to do the bronzing for her, but she kind of lost her drive for it after my grandfather died."

Amy was about to ask about her accident and what happened to his grandfather when he continued. "My mother was a jewelry designer. That was how she met my father. A section of our land has black fire opals on it, and she came to him for permission to collect some. That was a long time ago, before my father even knew what opals really were and what they were worth. He did recognize my mother as she was the one for him." He smiled again.

"What happened?" Amy was intrigued.

"He insisted on taking her out there. He used to say he courted her over a pile of rocks. He gave her the property where the opals are for a wedding present."

Amy felt a tug on her heart. The light coming up from

under the water seemed to intensify the sharpness in his eyes, and she had to fight the urge to shift under his gaze. She decided to change the subject. "Chance said you were named after John Wayne characters."

He tipped back his head and laughed. "Nice move. Yes. Our father's name was John, as was his father. They had an old ranch hand that instead of calling him Johnny, like everyone else, started calling my father the young duke. Soon it was just Duke and everyone picked it up and it stuck. Later, John Wayne westerns were his favorite movies. The night I was born, the movie Big Jake was on TV. They watched it during my mom's labor. I came not long after it ended."

"And they named you Jake or Jacob?"

"Jacob."

"Chance was from Rio Bravo?" she asked.

"That's right. That and also he was a chance in a million. They'd given up on having more children. My mother had miscarried several times, then nothing. The odds of her carrying Chance were not good. So when they found out she was expecting they got a specialist. He kept a real close eye on her and that's how he discovered her cancer."

Amy gasped. "I'm sorry. I lost my mother to cancer." She realized they had to have been about the same age. She was surprised when he reached over and caught her hand giving it a squeeze.

"I'm sorry, too. It's rough."

She nodded.

"It kind of helped that we had Chance."

Amy could hear the tenderness in his voice. "How old was Chance when your mother died?"

"Just over a year. She got to see his first tooth, first steps and his first birthday. She said those were important miles stones. For me—"

"Oh, Jake darling, I'm so sorry to keep you waiting."

Amy had to look up to make sure the honeyed voice really did come from Clarissa McCarron. She'd never heard such a sweet, sultry tone out of her.

The woman came around the side of the hot tub into the light. With a dramatic flair that seemed rehearsed, she dropped her filmy cover from her shoulders back onto a chair, revealing a swimming suit that Amy would've been surprised if it had taken a foot square piece of the metallic material to make, but undoubtedly cost quite a bit. Amy had to admit the woman had a toned body. She was evenly tanned and proportioned to the point that Amy figured she had quite a bit of help, or nature was being real generous.

Clarissa slipped her foot out of one high heel then the other and stepped down into the water. Letting out what sounded like a purr.

Amy wasn't even aware of Jake still holding her hand until he released it as the woman glided down between them.

"It is so nice to be home," Clarissa said, her attention was focused solely on Jake. "I'm sorry I didn't join you last night, I was just so exhausted. You will forgive me for leaving you alone, you can forgive me can't you? I'm sure we can make up for it this evening," she continued without giving him a chance to answer. "I'm quite reinvigorated now."

Amy almost choked at the unsubtle innuendo. The faint sound escaped her.

Clarissa shifted and gave her a look as if she'd just realized she was there. A flicker of anger flashed over the woman's face. "Miss Mathews. What are you doing here? You should be keeping an eye on Chance."

"He's asleep. I checked on him right before I came out."

Amy could see the woman was building up for another waspish remark but before she could speak Jake cut her off.

"I told Amy she was welcome to use the hot tub

whenever she liked."

The lines tightened around the older woman's eyes then faded when she turned back to Jake. She reached out and placed a hand on his bicep. "You are so kind to the help but I must caution you. The way you treat them, they start to act like part of the family. Mr. Davidson and Mrs. Jeffers take way too many liberties. Mr. Davidson can be forgiven because he is an excellent chef and so is bound to be eccentric, but Mrs. Jeffers ..." She let it hang.

Amy decided she didn't want to wait and see what came next. "If you excuse me, I don't want to impose on your time anymore." She stood.

"You don't have to leave," Jake said as she made her way up the steps.

She glanced back over her shoulder. "I'm tired and have had enough for tonight. Thank you for the conversation. It will help me in understanding Chance better. Goodnight." The image of Clarissa's manicured hand lying on his hard muscle lingered in her mind as she snatched up her towel and headed in.

What was she thinking? That Jake might actually like her. He was being kind to her for his brother's sake. She was so foolish but what she had trouble believing was that he would be interested in Clarissa. Yes, the woman was beautiful but, then again, maybe he couldn't see past her body.

ᘓᘔ

Chance knocked on her door as Amy was just about ready to leave.

"Morning," she said opening it to him.

"Ready for breakfast?" he asked with a big grin.

"Yep." She smiled, stepping out into the hall.

"What are we going to do today?" he asked excitedly.

Amy realized the newness of her hadn't yet worn off. She hoped it would be a long time in fading.

"Well, first I have to see what your brother's schedule

is. He was going to give me a driving lesson on his car. Remember?" Amy tried not to cringe. She'd worried about it all night.

Amy wasn't sure she wanted to be around Jake. He made her as nervous as the thought of driving his car did. She didn't know what to do about the feelings he evoked in her. They were so unfamiliar. She certainly wasn't going to pursue them. He was her boss, and if there was something going on between him and Clarissa, she didn't want to be anywhere near that. That really confused her because the more she thought about the way he talked, the more she'd swear he didn't care for Clarissa much.

"Can we have a tennis lesson today still?" Chance's question pulled her back from her thoughts.

"I'm sure we can fit that in," she answered as they stepped into the kitchen.

"Good morning," George greeted robustly.

"Morning."

"And what are you up to today?" The man turned his attention to Chance.

"Amy is going to teach me how to play tennis depending on when Jake takes her driving."

"On that," George turned back to her. "Jake flew through here about a half hour ago and asked me to tell you he had to take care of some business."

"Oh, okay." Amy felt relieved at the reprieve.

"He's not on the ranch?" Chance asked obviously disappointed.

George smiled, reaching out to ruffle the boy's hair. "I'd say not. He was wearing a suit and tie."

Chance scuffed his foot on the floor. "That means he'll be gone all day."

"That's what he said," George affirmed. "Why don't you two sit down and eat?"

"Well, I guess we're clear to start your tennis lesson right after we eat and you do some piano."

"All right." Chance brightened.

George looked at her and winked as if saying nicely done. Amy smiled and shrugged. Chance was an easy boy to figure out what would work.

An hour and a half later they stepped into the building down at the park, as Amy thought of it. She stopped and looked around, impressed. It had a pretty good supply of sports equipment, balls of all type, badminton, croquet, lawn dart, Frisbees, even a couple sets of golf clubs, and at least a half dozen bikes. Basically, it looked like any sport a person wanted to play was there.

"First we have to see if we can find a racquet that will fit you pretty well." She'd been concerned about it on the way there, but now as she looked at the rack attacked to one wall, she realized she shouldn't have been. There were easily a dozen and a half tennis racquets with various sized hand grips.

It said a lot about the people on the ranch that they didn't worry about leaving all this there for anyone to use. She guessed it also said something about Jake.

She shrugged it away. "Okay." She looked at the numbers on some of the handles that looked small. "Try this one." She lifted one down and had him take a hold of it. "Not bad. You want your fingers a little more around the handle if you can." She took another one down and handed it to him. "That's better," she said then looked for one for herself.

Out on the court, she showed him how to hold and swing the racquet, then she had him practice hitting the ball at the backboard for a while. Once he was hitting pretty regular, they started volleying over the net.

"You're doing great," she encouraged him when he hit the ball, then she hit it back.

"Are you about done yet?" The sharp demand startled both of them, and Chance missed the ball jerking his swing to the side.

Amy tried not to frown as she shot Clarissa a glance before looking back at Chance. She knew it wasn't a question. "Yes, we were just finishing up then going to go swimming before lunch," she said in a way to appease Chance.

His frown faded instantly.

"What about his lessons and work?" The woman scowled.

"I have everything scheduled. He's already done his piano, and we just finished his tennis." Amy smiled pleasantly and started picking up the balls on her side of the court. Chance followed her example on his side.

"He needs time reading and other school work."

"I'll make sure he spends time on academics. Do you want the balls?" Amy held out the ball basket.

"No, we have our own." The woman actually tilted up her nose as if the idea of touching the balls was repulsive.

Amy finally let her gaze drift past the woman to her tennis instructor. The man was extremely good looking with chiseled features. He had dark hair and the trim well-muscled body of a tennis player.

What bothered Amy about him was the look of speculation in his eyes. It was as if he was calculating if it was worth his time flirting with her. The thought was confirmed when he glanced at Clarissa. He reached out, laid his hand on Clarissa's arm, and gave her an adoring smile.

"Are you ready to start?" His tone was smooth and coaxing.

With one last glare her way, Clarissa turned with such a quick action that it caused the little skirt of her tennis outfit to flare out.

Chance fell in step with Amy as she headed for the equipment shed. He glanced back over his shoulder then leaned toward her. "Do I have to spend the rest of the day doing homework?" he whispered with a look that was so miserable Amy couldn't help smile.

"No, at least not the whole afternoon, but it wouldn't hurt to spend a few minutes on math. We read together before bed, so we can count that." Amy went for a thoughtful look. "Up in the library I noticed a lot of interesting books. How about we find one on someplace cool and then see what we can find on the internet?"

His look went to as thoughtful as she hoped for. "Okay."

"Good, after we're done with that, we can download the pictures from my camera and start on your slide show."

"All right." He bounced up and down with excitement at that.

෧෨

That evening Amy returned to the loft library, this time to find a book for herself. With Chance asleep and the house quiet she decided reading on the patio held more appeal than watching TV. She'd just reached for a book when she heard what sounded like the door coming from the garage close. She didn't think much about it until she heard the voice call out from down below.

"Jake, oh Jake." Clarissa's voice was back to its purr. The sound was really getting annoying. "I'm so glad you're home. I've been waiting to talk to you."

"What is it Clarissa? It's been a long day, and I'd like to go change and relax."

It sounded like he was right underneath her. Quietly, Amy stepped to the railing and looked over but couldn't see anyone.

"Oh, I'm sorry you had such a hard day. I don't know why you trouble yourself with all those meetings. It's just like those foul cows. You should hire someone to handle all that for you so you can enjoy life."

"It's my responsibility, and I enjoy handling it." His words were flat out direct.

There was a cooing sound. "You poor daring, what can

I do to help?"

Amy heard a loud sigh.

"Nothing. Now what is it I can do for you?"

"I'm sorry to bother you but I figured you'd want to know. I have no idea what your grandmother was thinking. I guess it's just a slip of her mind, but Maggie has invited Chance's governess to the social."

Amy felt her breath catch in surprise. She waited but heard no reply.

Clarissa's voice finally came again, escalating an octave. "Did you hear me? Your grandmother invited the governess to our big party with all your friends and important contacts. Can you imagine?"

"I don't see a problem with that."

Jake's reply took her by surprise.

"You don't?" Clarissa burst out, losing some of her composure. "For one thing, it just isn't done. More importantly, it could be a fiasco. If she made a major faux pas, just think how it would reflect on the family. It could be disastrous."

"I hardly think anything she could do would be disastrous."

There was a snort that Amy didn't think sounded very lady like.

"Just look at her. She's so plain. And you can hardly believe she would know how to act properly. And heaven knows what she will pick to wear. It will probably be something totally garish."

"I doubt that. Amy's an artist. She probably has a very good sense of style. I haven't seen anything wrong with what she's been wearing so far."

Amy was again surprised by his defense.

"She's been wearing jeans or just cheap, ordinary shorts, even to play tennis." Clarissa made the last sound like some kind of crime.

"That sounds reasonable with what she'd been doing,

but if you're so concerned, why don't you talk to Maggie about it."

"I've tried. You know she won't give me any say here." Clarissa's pouting reached up to the loft.

Jake moved out into the family room, and Amy caught her first look at him for the day. She pulled back by the center row of bookcases hoping not to be seen but couldn't take her eyes from him. He looked devastatingly handsome in a charcoal suit. His burgundy and blue tie had been loosened. Still, he looked as natural in the suit as he did in jeans.

Clarissa stepped forward and Amy almost gasped at what she wore. A thin, ruby-colored, silk robe draped over her body not even reaching the middle of her thighs. It was questionable if she had anything on underneath. If there was, it wasn't much. If Jake was shocked at seeing her clad that way, he'd already recovered from it. In fact, he didn't seem to even notice.

Clarissa sidled closer, laying a hand on his arm similar to how she had the evening before at the pool. Her nails matched the robe. "Won't you help me on this?" Her purr was back.

Amy couldn't tell but thought Jake's head pulled back slightly when Clarissa raised her other hand to stroke one glossy nail along his cheek.

"Oh, you look so tired." The woman's voice dropped, and she moved closer, edging her body up against his. Amy couldn't make out what she said and was extremely embarrassed to be watching. She just wasn't sure how to get out of there without making herself known.

Jake stood stiff for a minute then raised a hand to brush Clarissa's away. "Why don't you talk to Amy?" he asked abruptly.

"Your grandmother forbade it." Her hand dropped.

"Then it's simple, she comes." He started to turn away.

"But you must talk to your grandmother or tell the

bumpkin she is not allowed to come. I don't want her making a spectacle of herself." Clarissa's voice went shrill.

"No." He turned back, his face set firm. "If my grandmother wants her there, she will be there, even if I have to go pick out a dress and put her in it myself. Is that clear? Goodnight, Clarissa." He turned again and stalked down the hall leaving the woman no room to object.

A shiver went through Amy at the thought of his threat. It hadn't really been directed at her, but she knew she didn't want to tempt it, because she really thought he might actually try to carry it out.

A small shriek from below made her jump and hold her breath to keep from making a sound. Silence stretched out for a full minute before Clarissa stormed from the room, her footsteps hard enough even the soft slippers made a sound on the hard wood floor.

It took a second for Amy to still her thundering heart. She hadn't realized she had her hand covering her mouth until she went to rub her arms to ease way the shivers going up and down her.

Her hands trembled. She didn't know why she was shaking. She had already come to terms with having to go to the party. Well, one thing was certain, she was not going to let Clarissa's prediction come true. She would get something appropriate and show Clarissa she knew how to act.

Amy looked back at the book shelf. The idea of sitting on the patio reading had lost its appeal but the need to escape in a book had intensified. She quickly found a thriller to lose herself in and snuck back to her room, praying she wouldn't be caught.

⋘⋙

Jake stripped out of his clothes and pulled on his swim trunks. He hoped Amy would be out at the pool but doubted it. He was sure she'd been up in the loft. He didn't know how he knew she was there. There was only one faint sound that might have been an indication that someone was up there, certainly nothing definitive, but he was positive.

He wondered what she thought of the discussion. He hoped she got his message that she was to come. First, he didn't want her to be intimated by Clarissa. But more, he wanted her there, because he wanted her with him.

Truth be told, he also wanted to see her all dressed up. The way she looked in normal clothes, he'd bet she'd be a vision to take his breath. There were no doubts in her ability to hold her own in the situation. He thought about what she had said about being shy and felt a twinge of concern. Well, if there was a problem he'd be there for her.

A faint click down the hall pulled his attention up. Amy had made it back to her room. Jake looked at the door and thought of going to see if she would join him. He really would like to see her. Though everything had gone well, it had been a long day. Just the thought of Amy there had been comforting to him and made him wish he could hurry home. It was an odd feeling.

He started for the door then stopped, deciding it might not be a good time to approach her after Clarissa's scene. With a sigh, he headed alone out to the pool, as his thoughts went to their driving lesson. Anticipation hummed through his body.

Chapter Eight

Amy stepped into the garage fighting a wave of apprehension. At least she'd almost finished eating when Jake came through and told her it was time for them to go for a ride. She wished she could've come up with a reason to postpone but knew she couldn't.

He was her boss. She wished her silly mind could just come to grips with the fact. It had been another night where he plagued her thoughts and stole into her dreams. Why did he have to disturb her so?

"Ready?" The low voice rumbled in her ear.

Amy spun to face the man she hadn't seen in the shadows and felt a touch lightheaded. His lips tugged up at the corners as if he knew he'd startled her or maybe had even planned it.

His arm brushed hers as he stepped past her. Her heart jumped. She swallowed hard. "This really isn't necessary. I hate to take up your time."

"It is necessary if I'm going to be putting my brother in your hands and you on my insurance. I want to know what kind of driver you are." He opened the door of the sports car and motioned for her to get in.

Helplessly, she moved past him. "I'm a good driver," she said a little defensively.

"And that's the reason I'm letting you drive my car." He looked down at her as she settled in her seat. "But, I want to make sure you can handle this car." His eyes seemed so intense for a moment before he closed the door and walked around to get in.

He didn't say anything as he started the car and pulled out of the garage. Instead of turning onto the road to town he went the other direction.

"Where are we going?" Amy asked after a couple minutes of studying the interior, familiarizing herself with it. It was nice but the only thing that seemed the least bit fancy was the navigation system, and those were beginning to be common place it seemed.

"I thought we'd take a short drive, enjoy some scenery, and find a place that is somewhat deserted. At first, I was thinking about taking you out into one of the fields, but I think this will be better."

"Okay." She tried to relax. The leather seat hugged her. Jake had the roof open. Just a touch of breeze caressed her. Still, she was glad she had pulled her hair back into a ponytail that morning.

"So, how are you getting along? Are you feeling at home, yet?"

His question surprised her.

"I'm feeling quite comfortable. Everyone has been wonderful."

"Everyone?" He glanced her way, his eyebrow arched, one side of his mouth cocked up.

Amy felt her own lips twitch. "Well, almost everyone."

"That's better. I'm under no delusions about Clarissa. Do not let her intimate you. If you have any problems, feel free to come to me or Maggie."

Amy wasn't sure what to say to that. Maggie had said much the same thing to her but for some reason it sounded more powerful coming from Jake. "Everything is fine."

He glanced her way again. The arch of his brow had changed and she wasn't quite sure what he was looking for in her. "Good," he said after a second. "I want you comfortable here. I hope…." He broke off abruptly. "Here this looks like a good place for you to take over." He pulled over to the side of the road.

Amy had forgotten why they were out there, and her chest tightened as she stared down the road. Her hand shook as she reached for the door-handle.

Jake's hand caught her arm, bringing her attention back to him. "I'll be right there to get the door." He reached up and brushed a finger over her cheek in a light caress. "It's okay."

Amy was so stunned nothing registered in her mind until the door next to her opened. Jake offered her his hand. She swallowed. Taking it, she let him help her out. The next instant she found herself standing just inches from his body. Her heart pounded, and she became unsure if it was from nerves over driving the expensive car or being so close to Jake McCarron. She drew in a breath and realized it was a mistake as the scent of him filled her—the touch of spicy aftershave mixed with the clean masculine smell of him was heady to her senses.

"Amy," he said her name softly like a reminiscences of the caress.

She looked up and got caught in his hazel eyes. The color seemed to shift and hold her. His head lowered toward her, blocking the sun so it haloed around his head. Her heart beat faster. A loud honk had her jumping back as a car sped past them. When she looked up again, Jake stood several feet away. The expression on his face was as hard as stone and just as telling of his feelings.

Amy rushed around the car and settled into the driver's seat with a combination of nervousness and excitement. Jake got in beside her, and his arm brushed her shoulder as he reached for his sunglasses. He slid them on shielding himself further. She wished she'd thought to bring sunglasses unfortunately they weren't something she often wore.

Amy adjusted the seat to give herself time to regain

control. She looked over the console familiarizing herself again with it, then laid her hand over the shift. The leather top of it was warm.

"It's like any other car, with just a little more power." Jake startled her. "Clutch in, shift, let out the clutch nice and easy as you give it some gas."

"What if I kill it?"

He laughed. "You start it and try again. Just try not to grind my gears."

Amy took another deep breath and pushed in the clutch. She was surprised how easy the car started out. She watched the RPMs come up and shifted.

Jake let out a whoop, and she shifted again smiling at how the car responded.

"Good. Why don't you stop and do it again," Jake suggested. They did it three more times, each one a touch smoother.

"I don't think there is anything to worry about." He grinned and relaxed back into the seat.

Amy was enjoying the feel of the car. It was unlike anything she'd ever driven before, and she had to admit, as she relaxed, it was a lot of fun. She looked over to say so and found Jake staring at her. There was such intensity in his eyes it was all she could do to force her gaze back to the road.

"I think we'd better head back now." His voice was sharp, at odds with the look on his face.

He gave her directions. It seemed like no time before the house came into view.

"I've got to get to work," he said as she pulled into the garage, hopping out of the car before she brought it to a complete stop. "Keep that set of keys and drive it anytime you want." With that he got into his truck and drove away.

Amy sat still, not quite sure what had happened. She still didn't have it figured out before Chance came bounding out of the house.

"Hey. How'd you do?" He slid into the passenger seat.

"I guess I passed. I got the keys." She held them up and jangled them.

"All right. Can we go for a ride?"

"I guess a short one. I don't know my way around yet. Besides, if we take too long, we'll have to hurry to get our tennis lesson in before Clarissa shows up."

‿❀‿

Jake stopped his truck next to the stables, tilted his head back and groaned. *What was I thinking?* The words almost came out aloud. He knew what he was thinking. The vision of Amy came instantly to his mind. Excitement had lit her face. Pleasure beamed in her eyes. Enthralling, intoxicating, bewitching were all words she brought to mind.

The sun on her had made her tawny hair shine with gold and red streaks. Her face was clean of makeup but the light remains of gloss on her lips tempted him to steal a kiss. The light purple, V-neck T-shirt she wore was plain and sexy at the same time as were the jean shorts she wore. They were not overly short, not like a lot of women's. Still, they showed off an incredible amount of long, lightly tanned legs.

He had been doing well keeping his thoughts reigned in until he noticed her legs as she shifted gears. How that motion was sexy he didn't know, but it put his thoughts back to wanting to kiss her. Not that his thoughts were far from it anyway, since the car came along and pulled him back to his senses a second before he would have hauled her up into his arms.

"What was I thinking?" This time the words did come out aloud.

When the truck that had passed and honked, he'd recognized the driver. He knew when he ran into Alex again, Alex would question him about the woman that had been driving his car and that he'd been kissing, not that he actually had kissed her, yet.

He pushed his hand up through his hair. How would he explain Amy, besides that she was Chance's governess? That made her an employee. And that made her off limits. "What was I thinking?" he repeated again. It took a second more to set his resolve to stay away from Amy Mathews, Miss Mathews. He corrected in his mind.

☾☽

"Jake told me the barn cat is about to have kittens," Chance said as they walked to the equipment shed. "He said he'd let me know when they come."

"Cool, I didn't know you had a cat. I love cats." She ruffled his hair.

"I do, too. I like dogs also. I think that Jake might let me get a puppy. There's a couple cattle dogs on the ranch but they're Ben's, so they live with him."

"What kind of dog do you want?"

"A big yellow one. We used to have one. We got him when Jake was about my age," he said as they went through the door. "I'll get the racquets."

"Okay." She reached for the ball basket as he picked up a racquet. Out of the corner of her eye, Amy saw the board with all the gear mounted on it shift.

"Chance," she yelled diving for him as the whole wall came loose. She hit him, knocking him across the room. Chance's cry was followed by one from her as a barrage of sporting equipment came down on her followed by the rack.

Silence settled over the building for several seconds.

"Amy?" Chance was the first to speak, pulling her out of the stupor she'd fallen into.

She held in a groan. "You okay, sweetie?"

"Yeah, I scraped my knee."

She pushed up on her elbows to see him. Chance sat a couple feet away, one leg tucked up with blood trickling from the inch round scrape. Pain bit into her as she tried to push up farther and a groan slipped out.

"Amy?" Chance reacted.

"I'm okay." She tried to shift again, but was hit with another stab of pain. "My legs are trapped."

"I'll help." Chance got to his feet and grabbed a hold of the corner of the rack. Amy tried to push up at the same time, but there was only a slight shifting. She tried to keep in the wince of pain that came with it.

"I can't lift it." Panic flooded into his voice.

"It's okay. Can you run up to the house and get George?"

His head bobbed up and down.

"It's okay, sweetie. I'm okay. You just need to get someone to get me free."

"I'll be right back." He took off running obviously not concerned any longer about his knee.

Amy let out the groan she'd been holding back. She didn't think anything was broken; prayed nothing was broken; but bet she'd have some real big bruises. Not able to do anything else, she lay on the floor and tried to relax.

CB80

Jake had just finished going over the weekly logs with Ben when his phone rang. He was surprised to see the house number.

"Jake," Chance yelled his name before he even finished getting his hello out. "Amy's trapped. She pushed me away but it fell on her." He gasped a breath. "I couldn't get it off. I tried but–"

"What? Slow down, Chance." He tried to calm his brother as his own worry rose. "What fell on her?"

"The rack. It just fell." Chance started again.

"What rack?"

"The one with the racquets on it. In the shed. The whole thing just came down."

"Is she awake?"

"Yes, she said she was okay but I couldn't move it.

And no one's here." Panic again filled his brother's voice.

"It's okay. We're on our way. Ben and I will be right there. You did great." He was already moving to the truck with Ben, the foreman, following right behind.

"I'm going to Amy." Before Jake could call him back, the phone went dead. He knew Chance was running out of the house and wouldn't come back even if he heard the phone ring.

"What happen?" Ben asked once they were headed down the road.

"Chance said a rack in the equipment shed fell over and pinned Amy." His heart pounded at the thought. He hoped his brother was exaggerating, but Amy wasn't there, and that bothered him.

"Pinned?"

"He said trapped but−" Jake drove passed the house taking the road down to the park. The tires screeched as he stopped. Ben ran with him toward the shed. He could see Chance running down the hill. The door stood wide open. Jake caught the doorframe and swung around to a stop. Ben halted just behind him.

Balls and other gear were spread all over the floor. The floor to ceiling rack stretched across a large portion of the room. Barely visible on the far side was Amy laying half hidden under it.

Fear hit Jake at her stillness then he saw her shift slightly as if trying to look back. Her hiss of pain made his heart hurt.

"Stay still," he barked out.

"Jake." Her voice was tight but strong

"Right here. We'll have it off you in a minute. First, are you injured?"

"No, I don't think so. I just can't get out from under it." She pushed up to turn her head to look at him and gasped.

"Stay still." He crouched down beside her. "Relax." He touched the back of her head then looked over at Ben. The other man positioned himself opposite to him as he gripped the rack. "Okay, straight up, on three."

Ben nodded.

"One, two, three."

The rack was heavy but nothing that was hard for them to handle. They brought it straight up, about three feet off the ground then moved it to the side, tipping it up against the wall.

As soon as they released it, Jake was back at her side while Ben stayed to secure the rack so it couldn't tip again. Amy started to shift up, but he stopped her with a hand to her back.

"No, stay still until I check you out." He kept his voice gentle and calm though it was at odds with what he was feeling as he looked at the red stain forming just above the lower edge of her right short's hem.

It wasn't bleeding excessively so he forced his attention from it and laid his hands on one arm, running his fingers over it, probing lightly. "Any pain here?"

"No."

"What about here?" He continued checking down the other side.

"No, I'm fine really. Just a few bruises and feeling slightly battered."

"Just stay still until I make sure," Jake said gruffly, all too aware of the blood on her pants that declared differently. He moved to the other arm to satisfy himself then to her head. Burying his fingers in her mass of hair, he loosened it from its ponytail. A small gasped escaped her but it held no pain and he felt no bumps. Slowly, he probed her neck trying not to notice her satin soft skin under his touch.

She made another little sound that was more of a purr than a whimper. He froze, his eyes going to her face. Her eyes were closed, her lips slightly parted. Forgetting what he was doing, he stroked again.

"Oh." The sound escaped out of her with pleasure.

He was about to do it again when Ben moved bringing him back to what he was doing. Continuing down over her shoulders, he tried to force his thoughts to a clinical assessment. She jerked and started to sit up as he traced the first rib.

"Stay down."

"I'm alright," she rushed the words out.

"You don't move until I've made sure nothing is broken. Now, don't move," he reaffirmed when she started to object again.

He felt several flinches as he probed each rib but no sign of excessive pain. Her breathing seemed to quicken to match his own, or his to match hers, he wasn't sure which, but his heart pounded in his chest.

"How is she?" Ben came over by him.

"Feels fine so far." The words rumbled out of him.

"I didn't ask how she feels," the man said with a touch of humor.

Jake sent him a glare. "Will you get me the first aid kit?" Starting on one long leg, Jake tried to ignore the feel of warm, bare skin and toned muscles under his hands. Finding a scrap, he pulled his thoughts back to where they should be when they started to slip.

"Amy!" Chance burst into the room, just as Jake started up her right leg. "You're bleeding," he cried out.

Chapter Nine

"What?" Amy tried to turn and sit up.

Jake dropped his hand on her rear, keeping her down. "Stay."

"But," she still arched and tried to curve around to see.

He splayed his palm out and pressed her down hard. "Let me take a look first."

She still squirmed a second more until she must have realized she couldn't see it and settled back down with a frustrated huff.

There was a hole in the material but it didn't let Jake see where the blood was coming from. He tried to lift the material.

"Oww," Amy cried out.

"Sorry. I owe you a pair of shorts," he said as he pulled his pocket knife free.

"What?" She got out as he slipped the blade under her shorts about two inches from the tear and sliced through the material.

"Hold still," he said as she gasped and repeated the action on the other side, careful not to cut her with the sharp blade. He dropped the knife beside his leg and lifted the flap of material he'd made to reveal an inch long gash at the base of her derriere. He couldn't help but notice how it curved so delightfully into one shapely globe.

Jake wanted to swear at the mark but held it back aware of Chance standing just over his shoulder.

"Well, that's a shame to mar such a beautiful piece of flesh." Ben remarked.

Jake sent another glare back at his foreman for the comment.

Ben just gave him a look to say, weren't you thinking the same thing? "Here." Ben's lips twitched as he held out a gauze pad from the first aid kit.

Jake accepted it, aware of the urge to shift to keep the man from seeing the exposed portion of Amy's anatomy, which was foolish because she was plenty covered. He forced himself to clean and examine the area.

It was a shame, he thought repeating what Ben had said, as he traced around the edges of torn skin. It really was beautiful, soft skin; smooth, firm, perfect, except for the appalling puncture.

He glanced at the rack and saw the hook that probably caused the damage. He wanted to growl at it, but it wouldn't do any good. Forcing his mind back to the subject at hand, he continued to clean away the blood. The area was starting to swell and bruise.

"You're going to need at least a half-dozen stitches in this." He tried to be matter-of-fact, but the knowledge bothered him.

"What?" She tried to turn again. Amy was like a skittish filly that was always checking to see what you were doing around her. Well, skittish fillies were his specialty he thought with a wave of satisfaction. He reached for another swab to clean the area better.

"You're not going to do it!" she demanded, panic causing her voice to raise.

"Nope." He almost laughed at the horror in her expression. "I could in a pinch, but I think we'll get someone with a little more skill so we don't mess up this attractive area of your body."

She let out a soft snort then gasped as he ran a finger over the soft skin just under the cut to let her know he was serious before covering it with a pad until they could get to the doctor.

"Okay, that will do. Are you sure you're okay, no pain or numbness in your legs, hips, or back?" The worry didn't seem to want to leave him.

"I'm fine really. I just feel a little sore."

"Okay, up slowly. Any pain at all, we stop and get the paramedics in."

He helped her to her feet. She groaned but showed no signs of serious pain. Once she was steady, Jake turned to Ben.

"I'm going to take her to get stitches."

"Do I really have to?" Amy broke in.

"Yes, and don't be a pain in the ..." he looked down at her rear and smiled, "about it."

She gave him a sour expression and turned from him to Chance. She reached out and touched the boy's cheek. "You okay?" Her voice softened.

Jake heard the question and swung back. "Chance, did it hit you?" Jake felt another stab of panic, looking his brother over for any sign of damage. There was nothing he could see but a skinned knee.

Chance was shaking his head. "Amy pushed me out of the way. I didn't even realize it was falling. I just took down my tennis racket. Honest," he added.

"It's okay. It wasn't your fault," Jake said hurriedly to assure him. "It was just an accident."

"Jake," Ben called his attention, and he tilted his head to the rack.

Jake followed his motion, stepping over with the foreman. He was about to ask Ben what he wanted when he followed Ben's gaze and saw the bolt. The sheared off end was shiny but only a sliver of the metal looked to have been snapped. Instead the rest showed obvious scratch marks, as if it had been sawn through.

He looked to the bottom bolt. It looked normal. The

threads didn't look dug up or worn and there were no signs of the nuts anywhere on the floor. He shifted to see the ones on the far side. They looked like the one on the bottom, totally unmarred.

His gaze went back to the one that looked like it had been cut. He tried to reason out an explanation but none came. He started to turn back to Ben but found himself staring at Amy, her eyes fastened onto the same bolt that disturbed him and Ben.

He looked over her to Ben. "You want to see about getting this fixed up so no one else gets hurt?"

"Sure."

"I don't know how long I'll be gone." Unable to stop himself, Jake reached out and took hold of Amy's arm. Her eyes shifted to him. She looked more shocked now than when they'd first reached her and she'd been trapped.

He wondered if it was his touch that disturbed her or if she understood the significance of the bolt. He just couldn't figure out why anyone would cut through a bolt. It looked like it had been cut recently, but when? Was whoever did it really trying to cause an accident? If so, who would it have been intended for? There were a lot of people in here on a regular basis. Had whoever done it even cared who was hurt?

"I'll drop you off at the barn," he said to Ben. "Is it all right if Chance hangs out with you until someone gets back home?"

"Sure." The man winked at Chance.

"Can't I go with you?" Chance pleaded.

"We're just going to be sitting in the doctor's office," Jake answered, but could see the desire in his brother's eyes and knew he wanted to come.

"Please, I won't be any trouble."

Jake didn't even consider that he would. Chance was seldom trouble. If anything ever worried him, it was that. Oh, he had his moments, loved to be out on the ranch, to run and play, but Chance was quite serious for his age. Jake glanced at Amy. "All right, if you're sure? It would probably be more fun with Ben."

"I want to make sure nothing happens to Amy."

Amy laughed and laid an arm around his shoulders, hugging him to her. "Nothing is going to happen to me, but I'm going to get a shot and stitches in my backside, and there's nothing you can do to stop that. And, I won't let you watch even if you are there."

"I can't be with you?"

"Nope. This is one of those things that's going to be done in private."

He looked torn. "I'd rather stay with Ben then."

"Good decision." She kissed the top of his head.

"Great." Ben said, rubbing his hands together. "Grunt labor, my favorite kind. I may even tie him to the back of a horse." Ben gave a wicked grin that made Chance laugh and Jake relaxed knowing his brother wouldn't worry.

Together they walked to the truck. Jake kept his hand on Amy's elbow but she didn't seem to be having any trouble until they reached the four-wheel drive vehicle. When he opened the door for her, and she started to get in, a flash of pain crossed her face. She bit down on her bottom lip, and he knew that it was to keep from crying out. Before she made another attempt, he slid his arm behind her legs, well away from the cut, and scooped her up. She gasped, but he had her on the seat resting her on her uninjured side before she could object.

Ben was already climbing into the truck bed instead of the back seat. Chance followed him and Jake didn't say anything about it because they were just going to the barn. Still, he took the road back to the barn at a much slower pace than he had getting there. He stopped to let the two hop out. Chance came up to Amy's window.

"You sure you don't want me to come?"

"No, have fun and be good until I get back. I don't

think we're going to get our tennis lesson today."

"That's okay." He shrugged. "I'm going to see if Ben will let me ride Dusty."

"I think that can be arranged." The man came up behind him. "Come on, so they can go."

Jake put the truck in drive as the two stepped back. He almost brought it to a stop again when he heard a groan beside him. He glanced over as Amy pressed back on the seat. She grimaced, hissing out with pain.

"You okay?"

"Yeah," she groaned out. "I just feel a little battered all over. Don't worry, nothing serious. You really don't have to take me to the doctor."

"Yes, I do. You need stitches."

"You know how embarrassing this is?"

The thought of it made him want to laugh, but she looked too uncomfortable for him to do it. "Thank you," he said instead. "It sounds like you saved Chance, again."

Her shrug ended in another hiss.

"You know, you'd do better if you stayed still." This time, he let the corner of his lip creep up.

"I'm trying. It's just kind of hard. How long to the doctor's office?"

"About twenty minutes."

"You think they'll take my insurance?" There was a touch of unease in her voice.

"I know they take it. You're on our insurance. It wouldn't have mattered though, I'd cover this anyway. It happened on the job."

She was quiet a minute. "I didn't know I was on your insurance."

"I did it the first night. A woman who plays with poisonous snakes needs good insurance." He tried to make it sound like he was teasing but the idea still bothered him.

She fell silent again. "The one bolt–" she started then left the sentence hanging, but he got the drift of where she was going.

"Can you tell me what happened?"

"I'm not really sure. Chance went to get down the racquets while I reached for the ball basket. I saw the thing shift."

"You knocked him out of the way." The words sat heavy in his chest.

"I didn't think."

"Just like you didn't with the snake," he observed. "You may want to think about thinking more. Though I'm grateful you didn't."

"I ..." she broke off.

After a couple minutes, he broke the silence. "I really am thankful, Amy. I don't know how it happened, but I will try to find out."

The rest of the trip was made in quiet contemplation as his mind went over that possibility that the accident was planned. He didn't like the possibility, especially where it involved Chance. It didn't make any sense that anyone would want to hurt him. Chance was a kid and a great one at that. The family didn't have any enemies that he knew of. There might be a few disgruntled old employees but none came to mind, though he would talk it over with Ben and Russ, his mining chief.

He was almost surprised to realize they'd reached the doctor's plaza his mind had been so locked on his thoughts. He pulled into a parking place and glanced over at Amy. Her head was back on the seat, turned toward him with her eyes closed. She looked peaceful, but he didn't think she was asleep. A lock of hair curved along her cheek. The temptation to reach over and stroke the spot pulled at him. Instinct told him her skin would be unbelievable soft. It seemed to invite his touch just as her lips beckoned to his.

He jerked his eyes away, forcing his hand to the key to shut off the engine. The action brought her alert, and she started to sit up straight, then froze with gasp of pain.

"Stay put," he instructed. "I'll be right there to help you out." He was almost surprised when she did. She also made no objection when he slid his arms under her lifting her up against him.

He caught the scent of her and had to keep from tightening his hold, but couldn't make himself release her. He could feel her heart pound against his chest. The blue of her eyes wrapped around him, bringing him into a world of their own. Her mouth parted slightly in startled invitation. He was just about to accept it when a car pulled into the slot next to them. Her head dipped, breaking eye contact. Jake lowered her to the ground, conscious of every inch of her.

When he was certain she had her balance, he stepped back. "I guess we better go get this over with."

She turned from him, looking at the building dubiously. "Easy for you to say," she said sourly.

Two hours later, Jake drove up to the front door to let her out instead of into the garage. "Hang on, I'll be right there." He cut her off when she automatically reached for the door handle.

Amy wanted to assure him it wasn't necessary, especially where she was his employee, but she understood that opening doors for a woman was part of who Jake was. He was used to treating a woman with that courtesy, and if she had to admit it, Amy would say she liked it. She just had to get used to it because she was used to doing things like that herself.

She tried to wait patiently but she really wanted to get out. Her hip hurt like crazy as did most of her body, but sitting at the odd angle so she wasn't directly on her stitches irritated it more. She almost groaned at the thought of how long it would be before she could sit down comfortably.

The first couple days she couldn't because it would be to sore and just when that was getting better, the stitches would start to itch terribly with healing, and then it would be time to get the stitches out and that would make it tender again for another day. "Oh." The groan did slip free just as Jake opened the door.

"You okay? I better lift you down."

Before she could object, he had her in his arms again and her heart took off like a bronco out of the chute. Trying to take a deep breath to steady herself backfired, bringing in his heady male scent.

Amy fought for control. She tried to tell herself her reaction was because she had never had a man lift her like that before, but knew that didn't account for the mesmerizing feel of his arm muscles running around her back and his shoulder under her fingers. Amy stopped herself before giving into the urge to run her hand over his chest. She could still picture his chest from the evening in the hot tub.

Jake's hold on her seemed to linger, before he lowered her feet to the ground. He held her tight while she got her balance, though the whole reason she felt unsteady was because of his touch.

Amy was trying to think of something to say when she heard Chance call her name. He ran toward the house from the barn. It helped pull her back to the reality of why she was there. She stepped back.

"Thank you," she said politely and glanced beside her into the truck. "Sorry about the blood on your truck seat. I should have thought."

"I didn't give you time to think and it's no big deal. Besides, it's not the first time." He shrugged it off. "We're a working ranch, accidents happen. The seat's leather, so it will wash right off."

"If you wait a minute, I'll clean it."

"No," he cut her off. "You'll go in, lay down with an ice pack like the doctor said. Either watch a movie, or I suggest, go sit on the patio, or maybe even both. Just take it easy."

"I–"

This time it was Chance who interrupted her. "Amy." He reached them, slightly out of breath. "Did you get stitches?"

"Eight of them. I'm afraid no riding for me for a few days."

"Wow. Can I see them?" He tried to look at her rear.

"Sorry they're under a bandage. I have to keep the area clean and dry a couple days while it starts to heal."

"She got some cool bandages that are waterproof though so she can soak in the hot tub later," Jake spoke up for her.

"Cool."

"Yeah," Jake continued. "She's supposed to spend the day resting. So why don't we grab something to eat then you can come with me."

"All right!" he exclaimed then looked at Amy. "You don't need me; do you?"

"No." She smiled at his concern for her, though he was so excited to go. "I'm going to try to take a nap after we eat."

Chance looked relieved. "All right," he repeated as they started into the house. "Can I see your stitches later?"

"We'll see. They're kind of in an embarrassing spot."

"Maybe when you go swimming?" Chance came up with an idea.

"I don't know if I can wear my swimsuit. It will go right over the area and it's kind of sore." She paused in the entry. "Why don't you go eat with Jake? I'm going to change my shorts and I'll be right there?"

"Okay," he nodded.

Amy tried not to limp as she walked away, aware Jake was watching her. She wondered if she should have asked to be excused then shook the thought away. She just didn't know what to say to him, and it was frustrating her.

After the brothers left, Amy refilled her ice pack and stretched on the couch to watch one of her favorite action movies, then, deciding to follow Jake's advice, she moved out to the patio by the pool. Stretching out under the awning on one of the lounges, she let out a groan and willed her muscles to relax.

Her leg, hip, back and shoulder were killing her. The shot the doctor had given her before the stitches had worn off and her backside throbbed. She hated the thought of taking a pain pill but gave up and took one of the ones the doctor had given her.

She knew she probably should have taken it earlier because now her body had to play catch up with the pain. She just hated how she reacted to pain medication. They hit her like a ton of bricks. The thought was hardly through her mind when the world slipped away into a haze of sleep.

"What do you think you're doing?" The irate words ripped Amy back to consciousness, but she still had trouble assimilating what was going on.

"Where's Chance?" Clarissa's demanding voice pierced through the fog.

"What chance?" she said as the image of a little boy with the sweetest smile came to her mind. Amy locked on it, pulling more alert. "With Jake." She managed to get out.

"You're drunk."

"Don't drink," she mumbled. She was just so tired, and the dull ache in her body was threatening to erupt.

There was a loud huff and the lounge jerked setting off the first tremors of pain that was enough to bring tears to her eyes.

"You're not paid to lie around the pool while others watch the boy. You're fired. I knew it was a mistake to hire you. Get your things packed."

There was another jolt on the lounge. Amy groaned under her breath.

"You have a half hour. Anything you leave will be

shipped to you later. I want you out of here now." The voice was shrill.

Amy wasn't sure if she tried to move or not, even thinking of it was beyond her.

"Knowlton will take you to the airport. No, that won't work, that hick town of yours doesn't have one. He'll take you to the bus station."

Amy raised her head. She wanted to say they had an airport but not a bus station, but Clarissa was still carrying on.

"Get moving. Didn't you hear me you're fired. You lazy–"

"No, she's not!" The voice that boomed out rattled Amy senses, but it also brought a wave of comfort despite the anger it held.

Jake was there. Amy lowered her head back to the cushion.

Chapter Ten

"Jake." The shrewish voice faded back to honey. "You cannot condone this kind of behavior in an employee. It's obvious she's drunk or something worse. Think of Chance."

"I am. And I don't only condone it, I ordered it along with the doctor. Amy was in an accident. If you'd bothered to ask, or even look, you'd know that. But, that makes no difference. She is not on duty every second of the day. She is allowed free time."

There was a sharp silence. Amy peeked but couldn't see anything then there was another huff and Clarissa whisked by with the click of heels. Her beautiful body barely covered by another minuscule bikini and a filmy cover up that covered nothing.

Amy relaxed with another groan.

"I guess I don't have to ask how you're feeling." The words were said as almost a caress.

"I hurt everywhere." The words slipped from her before she could stop them.

"You have several bruises visible." There was a shifting on the lounge. "On your elbow." There was a light touch to the area mentioned. "I can see one under the edge of your T-shirt, up on your shoulder." The touch went from her elbow up to slip under the edge of her sleeve then up to her neck.

Amy couldn't hold back a whimper, but it wasn't from

pain.

"You have bruising visible here coming down from your hip." His other hand caressed along the edge of her shorts. "Besides around your stitches." The touch stayed away from the damaged area. "These are just the edges. I wonder what the real bruise looks like."

"I don't want to know." She held back a sigh at his lingering caress. Instead, she rubbed her cheek against the cushion.

"Are you always this mellow on pain medication?"

"They put me out."

"That's good to know."

"I don't like it, I'm afraid I might say something I wouldn't regularly say." The sigh made it out as his fingers found a wonderful, sensitive spot.

"Like what?"

"I don't know." She groaned as he pressed down on a sore muscle in her back then immediately stroked it to wipe away the pain. "Oh, my."

"This may hurt a little but it should feel better when I'm done." His words were low and husky.

"Oh, it already does. That feels wonderful. Ohh." She was aware of a purring sound coming from her but didn't care. All that registered in her mind was the feel of his hands running over her. "I like your hands on me."

She let herself drift. Once she thought she heard a groan from behind her. She tried to shift to look up at him but his hand moved to the back of her neck, stroking. "It's okay, stay still."

She floated in pleasure until a niggling in her mind slipped in. "Where's Chance?"

"Probably changing into his swimsuit. He stopped to tell George all about what happened. Sorry, this is going to hurt." That was all the warning she got before his hands shifted to her shoulder and bit down. The languid feeling in her disappeared. She arched in pain. "Easy," he urged her back down.

"Ow, I liked what you were doing before better."

"Agreed, but you reminded me it would be better to be done before Chance gets out here." He splayed his fingers over her shoulder again, and it didn't hurt nearly as much. It was just beginning to feel real good when Chance's voice reached them.

"Are you okay?" His feet made a pattering sound as he ran to them.

"Yes." Amy forced herself back to being alert. "Jake was just working out my muscles for me." She shifted suppressing a groan.

"Jake said you would be real sore just like he was when he got thrown trying to break Lucifer. He hurt for days."

Amy started to laugh then glanced at the man beside her, the one who had just been running his hands over her. She swallowed hard. Jake wore a swimsuit, and he was gorgeous. He had magnificently sculptured muscles she longed to trace. His skin was well tanned too. Amy guessed it was as much from working outside with his shirt off as sitting in the pool. But it was the intensity in his eyes that made her insides quiver.

Amy forgot what she was going to say. Luckily, Chance was on a roll. "Jake's going to swim with me a minute then climb into the hot tub with you before dinner."

The last part of that got her attention. "I can't get my stitches wet, yet." She stumbled over the words again as thoughts of getting into the hot tub with him filled her.

"It's okay. We have those water-proof bandages. He'll put one over it," Chance answered.

"I'll be right back to do that, come on Chance." Jake added before she could form an objection.

After the massage, the thought of his hands on her so intimately made her already sensitive body tingle even more. She was in so much trouble where he was concerned.

She didn't know what to do. Unfortunately, using the excuse of having something else to do wasn't an option. Between the sore muscles and the lingering effects of the pain pill, Amy wasn't sure if she could get up on her own if she tried.

She listened to the brothers having fun in the pool. Chance challenged Jake to a race with a half-length head start. She smiled hearing Chance cheer that he won. It was followed by a loud splash, and Amy could picture Jake picking him up and throwing him out into the water.

Amy closed her eyes but the image of Jake filled her mind with her artist's detail, down to the slight scar on the right-side, lower ribcage. She wondered what happened. Behind her the laughing and splashing continued. Amy drifted contentedly listening to the sounds.

When the noise stopped, it pulled at her consciousness. She opened her eyes to see a pair of corded muscled adult legs, lightly covered with hair, standing next to her. There was another scar, this one just over the knee cap. The thought slipped through her mind. She started to reach out to trace it but the movement hurt.

Amy took a deep breath before she tilted to the side to look up at the man standing over her. The grin on Jake's face stole away the breath she'd just managed to get.

"Ready for your soak?"

"I don't know if I should."

"The doctor said it would be okay. It will probably make you feel better."

"I …." She was too embarrassed to admit she'd like to, but there was no way she could reach to put on the bandage.

"Amy?" He waited.

She shook her head, feeling heat color her cheeks.

His lips quirked up on one side. "Roll over so I can put on this covering."

"What?" She blurted out just before the hand landed

firmly on the middle of her back and forced her to lie flat. "I ...." Her protest ended with what she was going to say being forgotten at the feel of his fingers easing up the material of her shorts.

"Come on, Amy. It's all right. You can't do this yourself. I don't think you want Chance trying. I guess Maggie might manage it but it would be hard for her. I definitely don't see Clarissa volunteering—you're not male. George could do it but he's busy with dinner."

"What about Ruth?" she managed to find her voice.

"She's busy. I'm right here, and it's all done," he said, wiping all thoughts from Amy's mind as he stroked a finger over her skin in a final movement.

"I really shouldn't. The meds."

"It's all right. I'll be there by you. Come on." His hand appeared in front of her face. She stared at it a second while gathering her thoughts then pushed up. She had to grab his hand to steady herself as everything blurred around her.

"Easy."

The word caressed her along with his breath against her temple. His chest glistened a scant inch from her, and Amy was tempted to lower her head to the tanned skin. Pulling her mind from the direction that it had taken, she raised her gaze to find him looking down at her. A smile crested his lips as if once again he knew where her thoughts had been.

His hand came up and caught a lock of hair that lay against her cheek. To her surprise, he wrapped it around his finger, testing the feel of it with his thumb. "So soft," he said huskily. "Are you as sweet as you appear?"

She was mesmerized by his eyes. "Sweet?" she managed to get out.

"Yes. I've longed to taste you since you arrived."

Amy's heart thundered in reaction to the words.

"Doesn't that frighten you?"

"Yes." The answer slipped from her honestly.

His lips quirked up a little more and the back of his hand moved over her cheek bone in a light caress. "Truth. So, I will admit, it does me, too. I don't know what I'm to do with you. Though I didn't hire you, technically, I'm your employer. Which means you are under my protection, and you are off limits to me." His words deepened as if he was repeating them to himself.

They were hardly out of his mouth when he stepped back. "I was going to join you in the hot tub but I think it might be best if you soaked on your own. I'll go see if Maggie can sit out here with you so you aren't alone. I really don't want you to fall asleep and drown in the hot tub." He turned and stalked away.

Amy stared after him trying to understand if what she thought she'd just heard could be right. Could Jake McCarron be interested in her? She shook the idea away. The pain killer had her loopy.

⊗⊗

Amy went in and changed into her swimsuit and was getting settled in the hot tub when Maggie wheeled her way out to her. "I heard I missed some excitement today while getting my hair done."

"Quite."

"How are you feeling?" the woman asked in sincerity.

"I'm fine, just sore. I don't know how well I'll be sitting down for a couple days. I presume Chance has told you about my stitches."

"Of course. I got all the gory details."

"I didn't think it was that gory."

"Oh, but to hear Chance tell it." The woman laughed. "I'm sure it gets bigger and bloodier with each time."

Amy joined in the laughter. "Chance is in with George."

"Yes, I know but I wasn't worried about him. You are doing an excellent job with him." She turned serious.

Amy fidgeted a second in the silence. "I'm not sure, I

113

...." She broke off wondering how to bring up what was nagging her in the back of her mind. When the woman's eyes turned piercing on her, Amy wished she hadn't brought it up.

"What is it?" Maggie pressed, not giving her a chance to drop it.

"I was just concerned about the accident today."

Maggie waited.

"It's just ... I don't know if Jake has mentioned anything to you about it." Amy glanced away to break eye contact.

"No." The woman had an amazing way of demanding with silence.

"One of the bolts holding the rack to the wall had been cut, and the others ... the nuts were missing."

The air in the woman's silence shifted. "You're certain of this?"

Amy swallowed, "Yes. I saw them."

"You're saying you don't think it was an accident?" Maggie asked directly.

Amy nodded. "Ben noticed it. He showed it to Jake. That's how I saw. It bothered them."

"That doesn't make sense." Concern tinted the woman's words. "Who would want to cause such an accident? Anyone could have been hurt. And there was the rattlesnake." Maggie's mind went right to what had been bothering Amy, but she hadn't voiced it yet.

It was shocking hearing it said aloud. It made the danger seem more real and focused it right on Chance. Amy felt as if her chest was constricting. How could anyone want to hurt him? He was a sweetie, a touch lonely, but the little boy tried so hard to please.

"You think someone is trying to hurt Chance?" Maggie said plainly.

Amy took a deep breath as everything ran through her mind once more. It just didn't make sense, yet it seemed obvious. "I don't know. It could be just a coincidence."

The older woman remained quiet for a full minute. Amy didn't know what else to say. Finally, Maggie broke the silence. "A coincidence is what it has to be. No one would gain if something happened to Chance. The estate is already locked in a trust. Jake and Chance are the main partners in it. After that, it would go to me and as they are my heirs, with several charities to receive it if all three of us were to be killed. Clarissa gets nothing. Something she didn't find out until after John died. All she received was what was in his personal bank account. The rest of the holdings are all incorporated."

Amy noticed how Maggie's suspicion had gone right to Clarissa. Hers had done the same. Though, with what Maggie said, the only one to gain sounded like Jake and there was no way she could see him harming his brother.

"I'm sorry to mention anything. I think it's the pain medication making me loopy." Amy used the first excuse she could think of so the woman wouldn't think she was a paranoid nut case and fire her. She'd already been fired once today. That brought her back to Jake and what happened after. She tried to push the thoughts of him away, thinking if Maggie fired her it would stick.

"Don't worry about it, dear. It's sweet of you to be concerned, and I must admit it has bothered me, too."

Ruth stepped to the door to say dinner would be in twenty minutes.

A half-hour later, Amy was wishing she had begged off eating as Clarissa continued to drone on about the accident.

"You really shouldn't allow everyone access to the building. Things could be stolen out of there at any time. Look at the malicious destruction they have caused. Chance could have been hurt," she said for at least the sixth time. "Or someone else. Then we could be sued."

Amy wanted to roll her eyes as Clarissa turned her

attention on to her.

"Are you going to sue us?" the woman demanded scathingly.

Amy was stunned at the thought of it. "No," she stumbled getting the word out.

Clarissa glared at her a second then tilted her nose up. "Good. We'd fight it and you'd lose. How do we know you didn't set it up yourself?" There was no missing the waspishness in her voice.

"Clarissa, really." Maggie got out at the same time Chance and Jake started to protest but Maggie continued. "How can you say such a thing? I will hear no further discussion on this. Do you hear?" Maggie challenged.

The area around Clarissa's lips tightened as did the spot between her eyes but she just looked away. She was still sitting stiffly when Ruth came in to clear the plates before bringing in dessert.

"I think I would like mine served in my room." Clarissa stood and stalked away to Amy's relief.

Amy couldn't help thinking that Clarissa went over the risk of Chance getting hurt just a little too strongly but shrugged it off since Jake and Maggie didn't seem to be concerned.

CB⳹

If Amy thought she hurt the first day, it was nothing compared to the aches that plagued her body the next day. Chance was wonderful about sitting down and having a movie fest letting her relax. Later, she stretched out by the pool and watched him swim. By afternoon the next day, she felt better, but was getting bored with sitting around. So at lunch, she hit George up for letting them take over the kitchen for a while to make cookies.

They were just taking the first pan out of the oven when Jake walked in.

"Look what we made." Chance greeted his brother with a big grin.

"Wow, it looks like I have good timing." He leaned back against the counter and watched as Amy took the cookies off the pan and put them on the cooling rack.

Amy jumped when his arm brushed hers as he reached around her to snatch a couple of cookies. She looked back, and found herself staring right into his eyes. The gold in the hazel seemed to sparkle with challenge. Her breathing hitched with excitement.

"This is a definite plus to hiring you." He leaned a touch closer.

"You haven't even tasted them yet."

His eyes dropped to her lips. "I'm planning to, but first I think I will try a cookie." The words slid over her as his eyes did the same with her face, lingering on her lips.

Unable to stop herself her gaze went to his mouth just as he bit into the warm cookie.

"Umm," the sound came provocatively from deep within him. His tongue slipped out to catch a smudge of chocolate left on his bottom lip. "And what are you thinking?" he whispered to her. Amy was so lost in awareness of him she couldn't get a word out before he spoke again. "If I'd left it there, would you have done that for me?"

She flicked her eyes to his, then back down to his mouth as the thought exploded in her mind. For an instant, she pictured herself doing just that.

"Maybe you'd like a taste." He lowered his head.

Unconsciously, Amy eased forward.

"Ew," Chance's groan ripped her back away.

Heat flooded Amy's face as she realized what she was about to do.

Jake didn't seem to have any such reservations. "Thanks a lot, little brother." Jake shot him a glare then swooped in to lift him from the chair tipping him upside down in the same motion.

Chance erupted in laughter even before Jake started to

tickle him with one hand. Chance squirmed in the air roaring in pleasure, even as he yelled for Amy to help him.

Amy joined the laughter, staying back to let the brothers have their fun.

"What in heavens is going on here?" Clarissa shrieked as she burst into the room then stopped when she saw Jake. "Oh, Jake. Just the person I wanted to see." She recovered quickly.

The fun broken off, Jake swung Chance up in the air, catching him and setting him on his feet. "What can I do for you?"

"I wanted to change the menu for the party. I thought—"

"The menu was set weeks ago and the party is in three days." He cut her off. "It's too late to change it."

"If you called and pressed it, I'm sure they would do it."

"No. I'm not going to do that. I'm sure they've already purchased everything and started to prepare."

A pouty look crossed her features. "But, I thought—"

"No," he said firmly.

Stormy was the only word to describe Clarissa's next look. Amy saw the challenge coming, then Clarissa glanced at her and with a toss of her head, Clarissa turned and blew from the room with the same arrogance with which she had entered.

Tension lingered in the room after her, until in a sudden movement Jake swooped on Chance once again, throwing him up, catching him and then putting him back down. "I need to go." He reached over and grabbed up a hand full of cookies. "These are great. By the way, have you got your dress yet?"

"Ahh, no. I really haven't had a chance." She glanced away uneasily, not wanting Jake to see she had been putting it off.

"Accident or not my grandmother won't let you out of

it. Will you go get it tomorrow, or do I have to take you?"
He arched an eyebrow.

"No," she said quickly, embarrassed at the thought of
him taking her shopping. "Chance is going with me to help.
We'll go in the morning.

"Good. Get the dress you want," he said firmly. "Don't
worry about the price."

"You know you could get in trouble saying things like
that." She arched an eyebrow.

"Somehow, I don't think so with you."

"You never know." Amy felt a little mischievous after
his bossiness.

"Go for it." He met her challenge.

Heat rose again. She got he was challenging her for
something more. When she didn't say anything he popped a
cookie in his mouth, then picked up one more and
sauntered out.

Chapter Eleven

Amy pulled the car up into a parking place in front of the address the navigation system had led her to. She looked at the upscale shop. A feeling of being overwhelmed hit her even before she got out of the car. She didn't have to walk in to know she had never in her life shopped in a place like that before. She glanced at Chance. "Ready?"

He grinned impishly. "Are you?"

She shook her head. "No."

He laughed, and Amy knew he thought she was teasing.

"Remember, honest opinions. Nothing hideous." It hit her she was relying on a seven-year-old boy for fashion advice. She wondered if the woman in the shop would turn her nose up when she stepped in the door.

There was a slight chime that could barely be heard over the soothing music that greeted them. A mid-aged woman in a soft yellow summer dress appeared with a warm smile. If she found anything lacking in Amy's white shorts and aqua, French-cut T-shirt, it didn't show on her face. "May I help you?"

Amy forced a smile. "Yes, I'm looking for something for a social this weekend at the McCarron estate."

"Oh, yes." The woman clapped her hands together. "Mrs. McCarron, the matriarch was in here just a couple weeks ago, and we have been busy with many other women getting ready for the event."

"I'm afraid I'm a little late in looking." Amy shifted as the woman openly looked her over.

"No worry, with your shape you should be easy to fit without modifications. Oh yes, I can think of several things that would look spectacular on you." The woman clasped her hands in front of her again. "Actually, that color you're wearing makes me think of the perfect dress, though let's try a couple other things first, just to see. My name is Ellen."

"Amy." She smiled, feeling more comfortable.

Chance was settled on a couch with the controls to a TV while Amy was led around the shop so Ellen could judge what she favored. Amy wasn't sure what she liked because the last formal gown she'd bought was for her high school prom, and these weren't quite in the same category. She didn't know what she wanted, just something not flashy. In fact, she didn't want to stand out at all, but she also didn't want to be an embarrassment to the McCarron family.

"First, I have a dress I think you should try. Then you'll want to try on a classic little black dress. After that, why don't you see if anything catches your eye?"

Amy had just started looking at dresses when the chime sounded again.

"If you'll excuse me a minute?" Ellen said.

"I'm fine." Amy waved her away, continuing to look at the gowns.

They were all beautiful but she had a hard time picturing herself in most. The black seemed to stark for her, some were way too bright. Others were so short, she was afraid her stitches would show. That led her to another thought. The bruises on her shoulder meant she'd have to have something with at least a cap sleeve, maybe even a little longer. That helped her eliminate a lot of dresses from serious consideration.

Amy pulled an ivory colored gown off the rack as two women about her age joined her.

"Oh, what about this one?" A brunette, with her hair in a short bob, pulled out a peach colored dress for the blonde to see.

"No. I told you I want something that really stands out."

"But you'd look beautiful in this."

"But I want mind blowing. After all this work, I want something so Jake McCarron won't even notice any other woman exists."

The comment caught Amy's attention. Amy shifted to get a better look at the woman with a cascade of light-blonde hair. She was as tanned as Clarissa, and her bust pushed up almost as much. Her smoky gray eyes were lined by lashes, extra-long, with thick mascara.

"I told you, it won't do much good. I heard Clarissa myself in the spa the other day and none of her hints were cryptic, which was totally disgusting since she's his stepmother. She was pretty blatant that things were beyond just close between her and Jake."

"Until there's a ring on her finger, he's fair game and even then ..." The woman smacked her lips. "He is quite delicious."

Amy pulled back in shock. She glanced toward Chance but if he heard the remark, he showed no reaction.

"Have you found anything else you're interest in?" Ellen asked coming back to her. Amy looked down at the dress she was holding and handed it over then forced her attention back to the dresses.

She thumbed passed the next half dozen when a squeal made her jump. A hand shot past her shoulder to grab up the red dress in front of her that she was about to pass-by.

"What do you think?" The blonde bubbled with excitement.

"That should get his attention," her friend agreed. "Try

it on." The two dashed off.

Ellen met her look. "Sorry about that," she apologized for the pair.

"It's okay. I wasn't interested. It wasn't really my type."

The woman nodded. "I didn't think so. You are a softer, more classical stylish look, with a little free flowing thrown in."

Amy was surprised at the comment and wondered if the woman really saw her that way or was just being a good sales person.

"Why don't you go check out the dress I put in your room? I just got it in. I hadn't even had time to put it out yet. Save it for last, though," the woman suggested for a second time.

Amy followed her to the room. Her gaze went to the light-aqua lace, over a white cap-sleeved shift, hanging to one side. It was simple and elegant at the same time. The soft color was accented with a silver metallic thread woven in. The sleeve would come almost to the elbow. The length would be mid-calf.

Turning away, Amy tried first the black cocktail dress. It fit nice, clinging to all her curves. The only thing was it just didn't seem like her. Shrugging her shoulders, she stepped out to see what Chance thought. He looked up and wrinkled his nose.

"Thanks." Amy wrinkled her own nose.

"You said to be honest. Too … black."

She laughed. "I agree."

She turned, just as the other woman stepped from the room. The little red dress looked even smaller stretched over her body. There was only one strap, and it teased at releasing the top of the dress at any minute. Even when the blonde took her pose and stood still, the dress flowed with motion. It was covered by a fine layer of fringe that danced with her every breath.

"Well what do you think? Perfect," she announced to her friend as if challenging her to object.

"Yes," the other woman squealed, and the blonde echoed it, jumping up and down in a pair of extremely high red heels.

Amy was afraid any minute the dress would explode, but luckily Chance had turned his attention back to the animated movie he was watching. Amy started back to her room but not in time to miss the woman looking her over and smirking.

She decided it was a good thing she hadn't really liked the dress. Still, she didn't think it was that bad. Next she tried the ivory dress, then a light yellow that wasn't too bad. Fortunately, she heard the other women purchase the red dress and leave before she came out.

Ellen echoed her opinion. "Not bad." She looked thoughtful.

"Pretty. I like that." Chance gave her his opinion.

"I don't know." Amy hurried back to the dressing room, anxious to try the aqua dress. Even as she slipped into the dress she felt her excitement rise. "Perfect," she let out airily, using the same word the blonde had chosen. The dress hugged her but it wasn't too tight. It flowed and moved with her, like it had a life of its own. Amy studied her image in the mirror. She felt like she was wearing an art form, or maybe she was an art form. She smiled and stepped out.

"Chance, what do you think?"

He looked up and his eyes went wide. "Wow, now that's pretty."

"Yes," Ellen said, clasping her hands together as Amy realized was her habit when she was pleased. "Just as I thought, and if you pull your hair up so only a few wisps hang down it will be stunning."

Amy tried to contain her excitement. "There's no price on it," she said hesitantly, afraid of the answer.

The price the woman said made her wince but it was cheaper than the yellow or the ivory. She'd never paid that much for a piece of clothing in her life but she knew it was acceptable. "Okay, I'll take it. Maggie McCarron said she would contact you about sending the bill to them."

"Yes. It's no problem. She talked to me last week. Now, will you need some shoes?"

Amy looked down at her bare feet and thought about what she had. "I guess so."

The woman laughed. "I have something that will be just perfect." She showed her a pair of silver strap high heel sandals. They weren't as high as most but Amy was used to more casual wear.

"Oh, they are pretty if I don't kill myself in them."

The woman laughed again, her pleasure really showing through. "Why don't you try them?"

A few minutes later, Amy walked across the room. "They feel great."

"You have a natural grace. You know, next month, I'm one of the shops involved in the charity fashion show. I'd be honored if you'd consider being one of my models."

The question took Amy by surprise. She'd been asked to model for art classes quite often in college, but this was so totally different the request stunned her. "I'm not a model." She stumbled over the words.

"Few are. Most are from families here in the area, but, as I said, you have a natural grace and a perfect body to make clothes look good. A trim, muscled body that isn't too thin to not be womanly. The proceeds of the show go to the children's hospital." The woman tagged on just as Amy was about to refuse.

"I'll think about it." Amy found herself saying.

"Thank you," Ellen said as if she had already agreed. "The McCarron's are always so wonderful to support it."

Amy's thoughts went immediately to what Jake had said about his mother's difficulty having children. She looked at Chance and nodded. "If you wish, when the time comes you can reach me at the McCarron's."

"Thank you." Instead of clasping her hands together as she seemed to do normally, Ellen grasped Amy's shoulders and stepped forward to brush an air kiss on her cheek.

Amy fought not to wince, not from the kiss but her shoulder was still sore.

"What do you think, that was pretty painless wasn't it?" she said to Chance a few minutes later as they walked out to the car. Chance carried her shoes while she had the dress bag.

"Yep."

"Well, we have extra time. What would you like to do today before we go home?"

He was quiet a minute. "Can we go to the zoo?" he asked hopefully.

"Sure that sounds like fun. I haven't been to a zoo for a long time."

୧୫

Amy twisted in front of the mirror checking to make sure she was ready from all directions. If anything, the dress seemed more amazing on her now. Ellen was right about piling her hair up. It was the perfect style to accent the dress. Fortunately, none of her fading bruises showed. She probably should've thought of jewelry but had spent so much already, she figured her little silver studs would do.

Amy blew out a breath. She was as ready as she would ever be, and people would be arriving soon. The whole day had been a buzz of activity. Between people setting up tables, chairs and decorations, then caters and entertainment, it had been a crazy day. It was time to check on Chance and see if he was ready.

She crossed the hall and tapped lightly on the door. It opened a second later.

"I can't get the tie on straight," Chance groaned in frustration.

Amy smiled. "Let's see if I can do it." She took the offending item from his hand. "Head up." She didn't have much experience helping men with ties but after a few seconds she managed to get it in place. "There, now let's see. Wow, you look pretty spiffy."

"You look beautiful," he said in return.

"That she does."

Amy turned to the sound of the deeper male voice, and her throat went dry. Jake McCarron in a tux was devastatingly handsome. She had no breath to get any comment out, even the simple 'wow' that burned in her chest. She swallowed hard fighting for her composure. "Thank you. You look rather ... amazing yourself."

The corner of his lips twitched up as he started down the hall toward her. His hazel gaze seemed to flick with flames as it ran over her body from head to toe and back up again.

"I hope this is suitable," she fought for something to say.

"Extremely," the word rumbled from him. "But there is something missing, I think." Jake stopped in front of her, raising a finger to touch the hollow at her throat. "What do you think Chance? She needs a necklace, doesn't she?" He glanced at his brother and then lightly touched her earlobe. "And some earrings."

"Yes," Chance bounced excitedly. "Come on, Amy." He caught her hand and drew her down the hall.

Amy was aware of Jake following right behind them. She was surprised when they reached the stairs. Chance released her hand and headed down. Amy glanced back over her shoulder, but Jake just nodded for her to go on.

"This way," Chance said, heading down the hallway before she even reached the bottom. She was about to follow Chance when Jake took her hand. She froze in surprise and looked up.

"Allow me." He wrapped her arm around his and laid

her hand on the back of his hand. He escorted her down the hall like they were entering a grand ball.

Her heart pounded so loud she was surprised it didn't echo off the walls. Chance shuffled in anxiousness as he waited for them at the end of the hall by a large metal door. Amy realized they hadn't gone in this room on their tour. She also hadn't noticed the key pad. Jake stepped forward, punched in the combination and opened the door.

The room they stepped into was concrete lined and to her surprise there were two more doors inside. One with a combination pad similar to what they'd just entered, the other looked like a door to a bank vault.

Jake made a slightly twirling motion with his finger. She followed it and turned around.

"This really isn't necessary." She let out, her self-consciousness rising.

"Oh, but I think it is," Jake said.

She heard a light whooshing behind her and started to turn.

"No, stay still," Jake ordered. "What do you think? This one?"

Beside her, Chance's head bobbed.

Jake's hands came around her but before she could see what he held, his fingers brushed her neck wiping out all thoughts. Her eyelids drifted down. His breath caressed her neck setting off a quaking deep within her. There was a slight groan. She didn't think it came from her but couldn't be sure. She felt faint when he touched her earlobe and knew the whimper that sounded was from her.

Amy fought to steel herself, remembering Chance was standing right there, and she couldn't be falling for his brother, her employer. She forced the thought forefront in her mind. He's my employer, she repeated. She managed a deep steadying breath, only to have the spicy, tantalizing scent of the cologne he wore fill her senses. Still, she managed to stabilize herself just as a final brush on her lobe threatened to sweep her away.

"Now, let's see." There was a shifting around her and his hand slid under her chin tilting it up. "Oh, yes. Beautiful."

Amy opened her eyes to find herself staring into Jake's. The flickers she'd thought she saw in them earlier now burned so hot she could feel the heat rise within her as time seemed to freeze around them. Amy didn't know how much time passed before he spoke shattering the hold.

"Chance." He looked to his brother. "Why don't you escort Amy upstairs? I'll lock up and be right there."

"Come on, Amy." Chance took her hand, drawing her out of the room.

"Like a gentleman," Jake admonished. Chance slowed and placed her hand on his arm. They reached the stairs before Amy cleared her mind enough to try to look at the necklace. She could only get a glimpse of silver and a flash of aqua, blue and green. Then she had to concentrate on the steps. Falling on her face didn't seem like the thing to do right then.

Chance had her in the living room before she knew it. Catching her image in the mirror, she froze for a whole different reason than before.

For an instant, she couldn't believe it was her, then her gaze locked on the fire of the opal hanging around her neck. It was like none she'd ever seen before. It wasn't just colorful. It radiated color. Small diamonds were scattered around the opal and a single tiny perfectly round, iridescent pearl hung just over the top edge all entwined delicately in bands of what she guessed was white gold instead of silver. Matching earrings dangled from her ears."

They were exquisite. Amy swallowed hard. Her first impulse was to reach up and remove them. She didn't even want to contemplate their value, but she couldn't bring herself to. She felt like a princess in a dream.

"Chance, will you run and check with George, if

everything is set?" Maggie's voice called Amy out of the trance she'd slipped into. "Now, let's see, dear. Oh, yes. Yes indeed, and the jewelry, perfect accents."

"I ... I don't think I should be wearing these." Amy brought her hand up to the pendant.

"Nonsense, I say it's where it should be. Jake had to have given it to you to wear if you have it."

"But, it's so ..." She lost the words to describe it.

"Yes, it is. It was one of Jessica's favorite pieces. John wouldn't even let her consider selling it, though several galleries offered her a lot of money for it," Maggie explained.

"It was Jake's and Chance's mother's?"

"Yes. She made it. She would love to see it worn tonight. She loved for all her work to be enjoyed, and you do it such justice."

"But—"

"Not a word of objection." Maggie cut her off, fire of her own filling her eyes. "They stay where they're at."

Chapter Twelve

Jake fought to catch his breath as he watched Amy walk away. The sway of her hips beckoned him to follow. He wanted to pull her back. No, not just pull her back, but pull her into his arms and kiss her–to claim her. But, wasn't that what he did in putting the necklace on her? She might not know it, but he did. He wondered who else would understand the significance of the necklace. His grandmother would.

He wondered again if that wasn't his grandmother's plan, that she had picked Amy for him, not Chance. He didn't care if it was or not. If things worked out like he hoped, he would thank his grandmother for bringing Amy into their lives. Jake knew it was too soon for thinking such thoughts, but the woman called to something deep within him, something he'd kept buried, protected, for a long time. His reaction to her was almost animalistic, like a predator claiming his mate.

Jake closed his eyes, but the vision of her filled him. It was so clear he could trace every line of her. He could remember how soft her skin was to his touch and the way she had reacted. He knew now, Amy was as aware of him as he was of her. He could still feel the quivering in her and hear her slight moans. If Chance hadn't been there, he would have kissed her and probably would still be kissing her, because he didn't think once would be enough. Forever might not be enough.

He wondered if that was what it was like for his father with his mother. He remembered the love in his father's eyes when he looked at her. He'd seen it every day of his life until his mother had passed away, and then he'd seen the lingering tender sorrow.

His thoughts went back to the manhood talk his father had had with him. He'd said, "If he'd only had one day loving her, it would have been enough for his lifetime." That was before they knew of her cancer. When they found out, the words became even more significant to him.

Smiling, he pulled himself from his thoughts, turned and locked the safe. He was going to figure out a way to win his governess.

He found his prey in the entry talking to his grandmother. His heart jumped again at the sight of her. He went forward and leaned down to kiss his grandmother's cheek. "You like?" he asked, noticing her arched brow.

She eyed him a minute, a smile cresting her lips. "I do."

They didn't get to say more because the doorbell rang, and it was like the opening of a flood gate. People poured into the house.

⋈

Nervousness threatened to swamp Amy as she was introduced to an array of elegantly dressed people. After the first couple minutes, she gave up trying to keep their names straight because she knew she never could.

Chance appeared at Amy's side and stayed tight. To her surprise, Jake took up her other side and remained just as close, always returning when someone drew him away. She lost count of how many times Jake took her arm, his fingers lightly touching her skin just below where her lace sleeve ended. The thing that really surprised her was never once was she introduced as Chance's governess. It was always just Amy Mathews.

They stayed in the entry for a good half hour before

both Maggie and Jake's attention was needed elsewhere, and she and Chance took their semi-escape. They made their way through the family room, and were about to go out onto the patio where the food was set up when Clarissa made her grand appearance, sweeping down the hall like royalty. Amy had to keep from shaking her head at the spectacle she made, but the sound Chance made in his throat was a good approximation of what she thought.

When she looked down at him, he grinned up innocently.

"We both better learn to be good," she leaned over slightly and whispered.

"I like your dress better."

"Thank you. I do, too." She looked back at Clarissa and knew she could never pull off that dress. The shear, black material hugged her body. The halter top barely held in her bust that threatened to spill out of the neckline then plunged to her navel. The slit that ran up one leg came almost to the top of her thigh. Her heels easily had Amy's by two inches in height.

As a seductress, Amy knew she wasn't even on the first rung of the ladder next to Clarissa. She wondered where that thought had come from. She wasn't trying to be a seductress or catch anyone's eye, but when Clarissa walked over to where Jake was talking to a group of men and slid her arm into his, Amy knew it was a lie. The man who interested her was so far out of her league she shouldn't even be teasing herself with the thoughts of him falling in love with her.

She tore her gaze away and looked back at Chance. "Let's go out and get something to eat."

"Yes." He showed more excitement than he had all evening. He'd been a good sport with the whole affair. She knew of no other seven-year-old boy that could have handled it any better.

Even though Amy had seen the setup earlier, with the

lights shining on it, she still had to pause and take it in. The ice sculpture of a peacock in full fan glisten with colored lights. She figured the peacock wasn't Jake's idea, or even Maggie's. It almost screamed of Clarissa, but it was stunning, as was the food. There were pawns that were larger than Amy had ever had in her life, chicken and beef kabobs, with an array of other delights.

They got their food and settled on the small table outside Chance's room to eat and listen to the music. The singer had a beautiful voice with a very soothing quality.

"Gran'ma said I could go in at nine," Chance said after inhaling several of the little canapés.

"She told me that, too. After we eat a little, we can walk around a bit. Be seen." She grinned at him. "Then I'll take you in and get you settled. I have to come back after that."

"Do you not like the party?" He tilted his head to the side.

"Actually, I do. It's nice. I've just never been to anything like this before. It makes me kind of nervous."

"It doesn't show."

"Well, I've had you to help me." She reached over and tickled him.

He laughed. "I'm really glad you're here."

"Me too, sweetie." She smiled back.

"I imagine you're like my mom would have been."

His words caught her by surprise and choked her up so fast she had to hurry to blink back the tears that threatened to rise. *Of all the times to be wearing mascara.*

"Jake told me what she was like." There was a wistful quality in his voice, but he smiled at her.

"That was a wonderful thing to say." She reached over and cupped his chin.

"So this is where you snuck off to."

Startled, Amy jerked around to the older McCarron male. "We decided to get something to eat."

"Excellent idea. How is it?" He reached down and picked up a shrimp off her plate and placed it in his mouth.

"Excellent." She used his word back to him.

"I was just checking on you, don't hide too long."

Amy was aware of his gaze on her and fought to tamp down her response. "We won't."

He nodded and slipped down the path back toward the party. Five minutes later, Chance finished his snacks and they went back out amongst the people. She didn't see Jake but Maggie was at one of the tables visiting with friends.

"There you are, darling." Maggie held out her hand for Chance who went to her side. "You all know my grandson, Chance, and this is Amy." She introduced the people around the table.

"A pleasure to meet you," Amy said politely.

"Amy is a budding new artist. You may be seeing her work in area galleries in the near future," Maggie continued.

Amy almost choked in response. "I don't know …"

"Nonsense, dear. Don't be so modest. You forget I've seen your work. You are very talented. She prefers painting outdoor and wildlife scenes. Has an excellent eye for detail."

"Really?" one of the gentlemen said. "I look forward to seeing your work."

"Mr. Jameson runs one of the galleries here, dear." Maggie patted her hand.

Amy got what Maggie was doing. She was giving her contacts, important contacts, and Amy was grateful enough not to lose the opportunity. She slipped into a chair, with Chance settling on the corner, and joined the conversation for several minutes before moving on and letting them get back to what they were talking about.

They had made a circlet through the house when Amy glanced at the clock and noticed that it was past Chance's bed time. "Time for bed. Are you ready to turn in?"

He nodded. "Can I say goodnight first?"

"Sure, let's find Jake, then your grandmother."

They actually ended up finding Maggie first. It only took a minute for him to give her a hug and say goodnight. They found Jake in the family room amid a cluster of people. Amy hesitated approaching when she saw Clarissa there, though the woman was across the circle, on the arm of another man. Chance had no hesitation sliding in next to his brother.

"There you are." Jake looked back and extended his hand, drawing Amy to his side.

"Hello," the man standing next to Jake said with interest as he made room for them. "I don't think we've been introduced yet."

"Oh, this is—" Clarissa started to say loudly but Jake cut her off.

"This is Amy."

"Amy, sweet and pretty." The man raised an eyebrow, and she wasn't sure what he was getting at. "Are you from around here?"

"No, Wyoming," she said easily.

"What brings you here?" The man leaned in. He was in his early forties, good looking, but a little too self-assured and pushy.

Amy didn't like it. "I'm here as Chance's governess." She met his gaze squarely.

"Really, I don't think I've met a governess before," a woman on the other side of him said.

"We're a dying breed." Amy shrugged and gave her a smile.

"So what does a governess do?" the man asked as his eyes drifted over her. There was no missing his interest.

"Spend time with him. Watch out for him. Teach him things." Amy felt another set of eyes on her and ventured a glance at Clarissa. The woman glared. Amy could see a snide remark coming. Clarissa let her gaze run over her as if to find fault, then her gaze snapped back up, locking on the necklace Amy wore. Her eyes widened slightly then tightened. Venom poured from her.

Amy wondered for a panicked second if the necklace and earrings were hers, then discounted it. Jake wouldn't have her wear something of Clarissa's. In fact, she was certain Clarissa would've been wearing them if they were hers. They would've looked just as stunning with her gown. Better than the plain diamonds.

Instinctively, Amy reached for the necklace, but Jake caught her hand. He intertwined their fingers and brought her hand to his side. His thumb ran over her knuckles in a soothing motion.

Amy was shocked at the action and saw all in the circle had noticed it. There were several that smiled as if they were just let in on a secret and were pleased. Clarissa's eyes narrowed with restrained fury.

The man next to her edged back. "Oh, so that's how it is."

Before Amy could comment, Chance spoke up. "I just came to say goodnight."

Amy became aware Chance had taken her other hand. She squeezed it.

Jake looked down at his brother. "Goodnight." He turned back to her. "Will you come join me when you're done?"

Slowly, Amy raised and lowered her head.

Jake released her hand.

Amy was relieved to make it to Chance's room. She turned down the covers while he went to change.

"Do I still get a book?" Chance asked as he came back into the room after brushing his teeth.

"Of course."

He grabbed a book off his shelf and climbed up on the bed, sliding under the covers.

"Did you like the party?" He looked up at her.

"Of course. What about you?" She settled down beside him.

"Yes, but I think Mr. Harris wants to steal you way."

Amy was about to ask him who that was but he continued and she knew.

"But he doesn't have any kids. He just got divorced. I heard Gran'ma mention it to Jake. She said it was too bad he didn't pay as much attention to things at home as he did to business. She told Jake, home always needed to come first."

Amy wondered if there was anything Chance heard and didn't remember. "Well, I'm not going anywhere. And your grandmother's right. Home and the people we love always come first." She leaned over and kissed him on the top of his head then started to read.

Music muffled the commotion going on outside causing a kind of pleasant background hum. Chance slid into sleep a few minutes later before they had even made it a quarter of the way through the book.

Amy brushed her fingers over his brow. She stood looking around the room. A feeling of unease about leaving him alone settled over her. Amy figured it was silly, still she went to the French doors and pushed the curtain aside to look out. Lights flooded the area. She could see people moving around on the other side of the shrubs.

Amy flipped the lock on the French doors. Crossing the room, she paused to look back at Chance. Since she had a key, Amy engaged the lock as she stepped out into the hall. There was a temptation to go to her room instead of returning to the party, but with a sigh she headed to the family room. She'd hardly stepped into the room when Jake broke free from the people he was talking to and headed her way.

He was about ten feet from her when a blonde in a very short red dress moved between them. Amy recognized her immediately as the blonde from the dress shop, the one who wanted to make a play for Jake.

Amy thought of retreating back down the hallway, not wanting to see the drama and how it played out, but Jake caught her eye just an instant before the woman moved between them and cut-off her view. The single look was enough for Amy to see the plea in Jake's eyes. He knew what was coming and didn't want to be trapped.

⋐⋑

Jake was relieved when he saw Amy come back down the hall. He was afraid she'd disappear into her room instead. He was surprised at how much he wanted her to return. He started toward Amy when a woman moved into his path. He was so focused on Amy it took him a second to acknowledge the woman. He fought back a grimace.

"Hi, Jake," the woman said airily. Her perfume reached him before she did.

"Ashley," he said her name in greeting, but looked beyond her for Amy.

"I'm so sorry I'm late getting here. I hated to miss a second." She gushed, shifting closer.

Jake knew her timing was on purpose. It gave her an excuse to be late leaving, and she was hoping to get some one-on-one time with him. Maybe use the excuse her ride left so he'd have to take her home. He wasn't going to fall for any of the excuses she employed.

"You're in good time. I don't think many have left yet." He pulled back and made a move to go around her, relieved to see that Amy remained.

Ashley rested her fingers on his forearm, squeezing briefly into the muscle, before running her well-manicured nails over the area in small circles. "I was hoping you could show me around. It's been so long since I've been to your house."

Not long enough, Jake thought. The woman might have been the daughter of one of his father's friends, but she was always throwing herself at him even before it seemed she was old enough to. He wanted nothing to do with the gushy, flirty piece of fluff who didn't have any goal in life except marrying a wealthy man who could continue to give her anything she wanted.

"I'm sorry, Ashley. I've been trying to catch a few minutes with someone else." He sidestepped and this time made it around her. Jake reached his hand out to Amy and to his relief, she took it.

Ashley turned just as he wrapped Amy's arm through his. Ashley lips came out in a slight pout then tightened. Her eyes burned into a glare of what Jake would term as pure hatred.

It was the second time that night he's seen that look directed at Amy. The first time had been Clarissa. Until that moment, he didn't think Clarissa had really seen Amy as someone who could compete for his attention. Seeing Amy dressed in a gown that accented her classical beauty, and the natural elegance which Amy exuded, changed that. Amy was now more of a threat to Clarissa, and he'd have to watch out for her.

Jake knew what really irked Clarissa was seeing the necklace on Amy. Clarissa had recognized it as one of his mother's. She had never been allowed access to his mother's jewelry. His father had made it clear when Clarissa first arrived that the jewelry belonged to Jake and Chance, and the other stones were in trust. That didn't mean his father couldn't have given Clarissa some of them. His father just hadn't cared to. As far as Jake knew, his father hadn't even shown her the vault.

Jake focused his attention back on Ashley. "Have you met Amy yet?" He tried to direct the hostility away from her.

Looking back to him, Ashley's expression changed abruptly as she realized what she was doing. "No, I haven't, but I saw her the other day. We got our dresses at the same little shop."

Jake wasn't sure what he was supposed to say about that.

"She was with a little boy," Ashley said as if it was some kind of naughty secret. Her eyes went to Amy, waiting to see if she got a reaction.

Amy smiled. "I was with Chance."

"My brother," Jake supplied when Ashley looked blank.

"Yes, that's the day we went to the zoo," Amy said.

Ashley's mouth actually dropped open. "You took his little brother to the zoo?"

"It was a great day. After all, he was good enough to go with me to find a dress," Amy said with such innocence, Jake wanted to laugh.

Ashley was stunned silent for several seconds. Unfortunately, it didn't last. "I suppose he helped you pick your dress?"

"Of course. It was his favorite of all I tried on."

"And you would wear it?" Ashley looked and sounded like she wouldn't be caught dead in something like what Amy was wearing, then again, looking at the dress she was wearing, she probably wouldn't.

Jake decided to step in. "I like the dress. It's perfect for her. She looks like a water nymph." Jake wasn't sure where that came from but as he looked over at Amy that was just what she reminded him of. "Magical and sexy." The words slipped from him.

"And what do I remind you of?" The woman purred, shifting close to give him a view of her cleavage.

"I don't think I should answer that."

He tried to pull back, but Ashley came forward bumping Amy away, sidling closer.

"Oh, come on," she whispered in his ear while glancing brazenly at Amy.

Jake didn't even pause in his answer. "Show and sex for anyone to have if their willing to pay the bills and be at your beck and call."

Ashley jerked back, her mouth dropping open again. Jake figured she was about to shriek or yell something like she'd never been spoken to like that before. Instead, just a loud humph escaped her as she spun around on her impossibly high heels. Her hair whipped out across his face.

Jake watched her go, sad that he'd offended her. He'd never spoken to a woman like that before.

"Jake?"

He winced when Amy said his name. "Sorry," he said as he turned back to her. "I shouldn't have said that. It wasn't well done of me." He wanted to say more, explain that he didn't normally treat women that way. It was just the continual plays Ashley made whenever she was around him that drove him crazy.

"I understand." Amy laid her hand back on his arm, the way it was before Ashley had bumped her aside.

He relaxed, smiled and placed his hand over hers. "I'll call her father tomorrow and apologize. Do you want to go outside and get a breath of air?"

She nodded.

They started to move to the open patio doors but never made it as people continued to snag Jake, everyone wanting just a moment of his time, though much of their attention seemed to be focused on Amy.

Jake wondered if she realized what the speculation in the room was. He could almost read the people's thoughts because never once had he had a date at any of the family socials. He even made sure he didn't spend significant time with any one woman. On his part, it had been totally intentional. Gossip always ran rampant, and he didn't want his interest in a woman to be misconstrued.

By taking Amy's hand, everyone there was wondering if it was a statement of intentions. Looking over at Amy, conversing so amiably with an old friend of his grandmother's, he knew it was. He was interested in her and didn't care if the whole world knew it.

Chapter Thirteen

Amy smiled at the gallery owner as he took her hand.

"Remember, I look forward to seeing your work," Mr. Jameson said.

"That is sweet of you. As soon as some of my pieces arrive, I'll bring them by for your opinion. That is if you promise to be brutally honest."

"Brutally?" He arched his brow.

Amy let out a little laugh. "Okay, so maybe not brutally, but I do want you to be honest."

"That, I'll do. If I think I can sell them, I'll tell you."

"Thank you, I should be in to see you sometime close to the end of the week."

"I look forward to seeing you. Good evening." He kissed her cheek before catching Jake's attention to say goodnight.

It was Jake's turn to lean down as the man and his wife left. "It seems you've won over Mr. Jameson."

"Your grandmother introduced us and told him I was an artist. He requested to see some of my work."

"I'd like to see some of your work, too." He looked serious.

Amy was surprised to realize he hadn't. It seemed like they'd known each other for a long time. "I'm going to call my cousin tomorrow and arrange for her to send me some."

"Good. That reminds me, how'd the painting lesson with Chance go?"

"Actually, pretty good, he does much better than the same old stick figures."

"What do I have to do to get a lesson?"

Amy didn't get to answer as another person came to bid farewell. For the next half hour they were inundated by people. Amy soon felt like she was in a crush of people vying for her and Jake's attention. It didn't seem to matter which. They mainly just wanted to talk. Most were extremely pleasant. A few made her think they were just looking for little tidbits to be repeated, and there were several that reminded her of Ashley, trying to snag Jake's attention.

Amy was having a pleasant time until she looked across the room and saw Clarissa staring at them from the entry to the music room. Displeasure was easy to see on the woman's face. Clarissa had never hid the fact that she didn't like her, but at that moment, Amy knew it was much more. Clarissa loathed her.

Nerves made her stomach clench. Her throat tightened up, and she realized she was afraid. She needed to get out of there now.

"Jake," she squeaked out. "I want to go check on Chance."

He looked at her. "Is something wrong?"

Amy shook her head, fighting not to show the fear that blossomed in her. "No, I ..." She wasn't sure what more to say. Fortunately, though, he didn't probe further.

"Okay."

Amy nodded, forced a smile and slipped away. Reaching the hall, she had to make herself not run. She stopped at her room to get the key. She was only planning to just peek in, but when she opened the door she stepped through. Chance was sleeping peacefully. Amy didn't know why she expected differently.

She noticed his suit pants on the floor just outside the closet and went to pick them up. He must have dropped them and not noticed. She stepped into the closet to hang them up. It was when she came out Amy noticed the water trickling in the sink. She smiled. He'd been more tired than he let on.

Amy stepped over to turn off the water and found herself looking at her reflection in the mirror. The glint of color around her neck caught her attention. The nightlight gave only a faint glow, but it was enough to ignite the fire of the opal and give spark to the diamonds. She stared at it transfixed by its beauty. As she shifted, the pearl glowed with a luster that was not to be out done by the sparkle of the diamonds.

Raising her gaze from the necklace, she caught her image in the mirror. What she saw took her breath away. What Jake had said came back to her and she saw herself as a water nymph. Sexy and magical, was that really how he saw her? Her heart pounded. Then self-doubt slipped back in. She was in good shape but far from sexy, and there was nothing magical about her. It had to be the lure of the necklace. She was normal boring Amy, who babysat kids, played sports and was more likely to be covered in paint than satin.

She raised her hands to take off the necklace but couldn't seem to undo the clasp. After a second, she lowered her hands and stepped away from the mirror. Once more she glanced at her young charge, and her thoughts went to his brother.

Chance was so much easier for her to figure out. He was a little boy that just needed love from her. But what did Jake need? Love—the word came to her mind, but she shook it away. She was not going to fall in love with him. She almost said it aloud.

Still, disquieted she went to the French doors, letting herself out into the night. She paused long enough to check the lock before turning, and tipping her head up to the night sky. There was too much light from the patio to see many stars.

The party had quieted down. A good portion of the people had already left. She wasn't willing to go back yet. She felt too mixed up inside. At her first step onto the grass, her heels sank in. Stepping back, she slipped out of her shoes and left them there.

The grass felt cool and welcoming to her bare feet. She went over the rise, past Jake's patio and down off the small hill. Instead of turning to the sports court and playground area, she went straight out almost to the fence where the fields started. There she tilted her head again, closing her eyes letting the calm of the night wash over her.

Amy opened her eyes to be welcomed by a myriad of sparkling stars overhead. The night sky was glorious. She just stood there.

ை

Jake was relieved as the last person left. It seemed that when Amy disappeared everyone else took it as a signal to do the same. Though Clarissa had taken Amy's spot at his side to play dutiful hostess, few lingered to talk with her like they had Amy.

As the door closed behind the last person, Jake started to make his break, but before he could get away, Clarissa's hand tightened on his arm. "I want to speak with you." Sharpness she normally controlled around him slipped into her voice.

Jake wanted to say he didn't want to speak to her, but knew that would just lead to a blow up. He turned back. "Yes?"

"The governess was given far too much latitude this evening. People were thinking she had a place in the family far above that of an employee."

"Several people that work for me were here tonight. I don't see the problem."

"She was thought of as an eq …" Clarissa wisely broke off as his eyes tightened.

"Amy is part of this family at this time, and I will have her treated as such," he said sternly.

"You never showed any concerned for any of the other governesses," Clarissa snapped.

"None of the others would have stuck their toe past their perceived responsibility to help Chance. Let me make this clear Clarissa. Leave her alone or it will be you who is forced to leave." With that he broke away. Fury burned through him that matched the look on Clarissa's face though again she wisely kept quiet.

Jake turned to find his grandmother watching from just inside the family room. She nodded to him, looking satisfied. He walked to her and leaned down, placing a kiss on the top of her head.

She caught his hand and patted it. She was smiling when he met her gaze. "Good night, dear. I think I'll turn in now."

Jake thought the idea sounded like a good one but went into the kitchen to see if everything was okay there. George and Ruth waved him away, assuring they had everything under control. Too worked up to turn in, he walked out onto the patio. He watched the band pack up their gear for a minute and went to thank them.

He thought of changing out of his tux and swimming for a few minutes but rejected the idea, needing more peace. Still, he reached up and removed his tie, dropping it on the table outside Maggie's room where it wouldn't be in the way of anyone cleaning up. Jake released the top button on his shirt then after only a slight hesitation, took off his jacket leaving it with the tie. Rolling his shoulders to loosen the muscles, he let out a sigh and followed the path away from the house.

Jake stopped at the crest of the knoll looking over the lawn to the pasture beyond and froze at what he saw. As if pulled from his heart's desire, Amy stood below him dressed in moonlight and delicate lace. Silently, he started toward her, drawn by threads of need. He let his gaze run over her, taking in every detail. When he got to her bare feet, he smiled, but when she lifted her face to the stars he almost groaned at the vision she made.

His need to kiss her was strong. Quietly, he made his way down the slope. He had almost reached her when her eyes drifted closed, and he heard a gentle sigh escape her. It had the opposite effect on him. His heart leapt, thundering with desire in his chest.

He halted to get himself under control. Once before he had likened her to a skittish filly, and he knew that assumption hadn't changed. If anything, his mystical nymph was even more of a challenge. Instinct told him if he moved too fast, he would frighten her and she'd disappear in a flash of magic. She would take time and a gentle hand to coax her to be his.

"I might have been wrong about a water nymph. There in the moonlight ..." he broke off as she spun to face him, her hand going to her throat.

"Jake."

His name reached him in a whisper and pulled at him. He closed the gap between them.

"I didn't hear you." She stumbled over the words, sidling just out of his reach.

"Sorry. I didn't mean to frighten you. I'd just come out for some air when I saw you."

She gave a half nod signaling her understanding. "Is everyone gone?"

"All but those cleaning up, but Ruth will oversee them." He eased a step closer.

She was quiet a moment. "It was a nice party."

"You weren't uncomfortable?"

The question seemed to catch her off-guard. She thought a second before answering. "No, I wasn't. Everyone was extremely kind."

"Everyone?" He couldn't help asking, edging in.

She gave a little laugh. "Well, maybe not everyone." Her fingers came up to the necklace. "You really shouldn't have let me wear this." She fingered it with a light, loving touch.

"I wanted to see it on you." He was near enough that he reached out and closed his fingers over hers on it. He felt her breath catch.

"Maggie." She swallowed. "Maggie said it was your mother's. Her favorite."

"Yes. She called it Earth, Moon and Stars. My father gave it to me after she died. He said it represented her—his whole world."

She gasped. "You really shouldn't have let me wear it."

"Yes, I think it is where it should be." He ground the words out low and husky. He drew in nearer. His eyes caressed her face then he let his hand follow the motion.

Her eyes drifted close. She turned into his touch. Raising his other hand, he cradled her face in his palms and lowered his mouth to hers. The first touch was just a bare whisper. He followed it by another.

She still didn't pull back so he came in fully, drinking of her lips, capturing the flavor of moonlight off them, fresh, mysterious and intoxicating all at once. A little whimper escaped from deep within her followed by his name.

Her hands came up to rest on his chest but made no effort to push him away. Her touch was soft. Tender and timid came to mind at the same time. It took all his will to rein in the kiss. He wanted to pull her tight into his arms and devour her but, for her, he kept himself in check letting her learn of him and instigate more.

When her fingertips came up to brush the hair on his neck, he almost lost his control. He tightened his hold, and she didn't pull back. He let his tongue brush her lips and savored the tremor that answered the action. She kissed him back harder, following him in the dance he was leading her in.

Suddenly she jerked back and broke from the kiss, and he was afraid he'd moved too fast and lost her, but instead of pulling away, she lowered her head to his chest. He felt every inch of her as she fought for air.

His heart pounded in rhythm with hers. He encircled her with one arm and slid the other hand around her to bury it into her hair. She sighed against him as he made little stroking motions. Her fingers picked up the movements, repeating them on his back.

They stood together in the moonlight.

Time passed. Jake finally eased back so he could look down at her. He started to lower his head again to kiss her, but she shook her head and pulled out of his arms.

"No," she said turning her back to him.

"Amy?"

"I can't love you."

A wave of panic hit him with her words. "Why?"

"I can't. You're my employer, my boss."

"I said I might have to fire you," he said under his breath in jest, but she didn't take it that way.

"No, please, Chance."

"Amy, stop. I'm not going to fire you."

She took a breath and nodded. "I can't fall in love with you," she declared again. He was about to argue but what he saw in her eyes stopped him. She might say she couldn't love him, but, unless he read what he was seeing wrong, she already did.

His first instinct was to challenge her on it, but instead, he let it drop. "All right enough for now." He stepped back and held out his hand. "Shall we go in?"

He watched her catch her bottom lip in between her teeth as she decided. It was almost a full minute before she reached out and took his hand. They walked together up the hill. Silence greeted them when they reached the patio. The lights in the house were out. The light from the pool gave a glow that filled the area.

"You can come in through my room," he said in a hushed tone that fit the calm of the evening.

"My shoes are just outside Chance's. I need them," she whispered back.

"I left my tie and jacket outside at Maggie's table. I bet Ruth already got them but I should check." He wasn't worried about them. He just didn't want to leave Amy yet. He wanted to walk her to her door and maybe get to kiss her goodnight, though from what she'd said before, he wasn't sure he'd get that. He knew he was right when they reached where the small path cut off to Chance's room.

She stopped and shifted to him. "Goodnight," she said softly and turned away. He watched her take the half dozen steps to where the path curved behind a small pine tree.

She froze. "Hey," she cried out.

Jake sprang forward. He rounded the curve just in time to see a shadowy figure disappear behind a tree.

"Stay here," he ordered as he passed in pursuit.

Jake dodged around the tree. The man in front of him only had a small lead and was fast, but Jake was gaining on him. A few more feet and he could make the tackle.

They raced past his room. The man went around the corner of the house. Jake put on more speed. Intent on the man, Jake sped around the corner catching a blur of shadowy movement. Jake threw up his arm to block the blow that would have caught him right across the neck. His momentum still took him to the ground, laying him out flat.

Breath slammed from his body. It took a second before he was aware of what had happened and the sound of heavy fleeing thuds were replaced by softer foot falls that almost disappeared in the soft grass. Then Amy reached him.

"Jake!" She dropped down beside him, one hand going to cradle his face, the other to his chest. "Are you alright?" Panic filled her voice.

"Yeah," he swallowed, suppressing a groan. He started to get up.

She pushed back on him. "Maybe you better stay down."

He caught the hand on his cheek, pulling it away. "I'm all right, just not happy." He sat up, fighting back another moan. He looked to where the man had disappeared around the house. Jake knew the man would be gone, but still he stood and walked to the front, surveying the area, aware of Amy behind him.

"I thought I said to stay there?" He turned back to her.

"You might have needed help," she said in defense.

"You might've gotten hurt," he answered back, feeling the fear of the possibility rise within him.

"And what about you?" she demanded right back.

He couldn't argue that, so didn't. "Did you see who it was?" he asked instead.

She shook her head. "No, he was in the shadow. Did you?"

"No, his back was to me and he had a hood. All I could tell was it was a man and in pretty good shape by the way he ran and clotheslined me."

"Are you okay?" she asked again, reaching up to touch his face.

He caught her fingers bringing them to his lips to brush a kiss across them. "Yes, we better go back and check on Chance."

"Chance!" Her concerned flared.

"It's okay," Jake said immediately. "It didn't look like he got in. The door must have been locked." Still, he hurried as he led her back.

"I locked it when I left. I didn't want anyone going in there by mistake and disturbing him."

"It's a good thing. I wonder why they just didn't go in another door. I don't think mine's locked and the patio doors are probably open. Maggie's may be locked because she already went to bed but ..." He left it hanging as they reached Chance's door. He took the knob and twisted. It was locked. Behind him, Jake heard a sigh of relief. He was thankful she'd locked it. He hadn't thought about it but should've with all the people there.

He pulled his keys from his pocket. It had been an automatic thing to pick them up and put them there when he'd dressed. He opened the door slowly. Amy pressed to his side to see into the room. Relief filled him. Chance was asleep on the bed. He hadn't even been disturbed.

Amy brushed by him going to the bed to check closer. He saw the smile cross her face when she was satisfied Chance was all right. She looked back at him and nodded before returning to the door.

They stepped back out and he closed the door.

"He's okay."

Her concern touched his heart. She really cared for his brother.

"What do we do now?"

"Why don't you go to bed and try to get some sleep. I'm going to call the police. I don't think there is anything they can do. He was wearing gloves, but I want to at least make a report."

She nodded again, and studied his face a minute, her eyes coming to rest on his lips. He wondered if she was going to kiss him, and felt her start to draw near, but she pulled back. "Goodnight." She turned and hurried away.

For the second time that night, he watched her go and was about to follow her when he noticed her shoes. Cinderella lost her slippers, he mused through all the turmoil going on in his mind.

He looked around the area, not that he hoped to find anything before going to his den to call the police. They took a report over the phone and said they'd have a car come around and check the area but figured whoever it was, was already long gone.

The 'whoever' part, bothered him. Who had tried to break in? He had no doubt that was what the person was doing, but was it Chance's room by accident or was it on purpose? Was it someone trying to use the cover of the party to sneak in and steal something? He wished he knew the answer. He leaned back in the chair with his feet up on the desk for a long time before he gave up and went to bed.

ରଧ୍ୟ

Amy laid back in her bed, her mind trapped on what happened. Had it been a coincidence that the man had gotten Chance's room or was it more? Thoughts of the snake and the rack falling bothered her. There was no doubt the snake was in Chance's room, but how had it gotten there? Did it have help? Yes, the rack had landed on her, but it could've as easily been Chance. In fact, it would have been if she hadn't pushed him out of the way. She was really becoming paranoid, but wondered what the police had to say.

Amy thought of going to find Jake to ask what he thought, but wasn't ready to see him yet. Her mind flipped to kissing him. She shouldn't have done that or let him do that. Her heart pounded at just the thought of his lips on hers. Never had she felt that way before.

It was all the fault of the necklace and earrings. She shouldn't have ever put them on. Amy stopped – let him put them on her. Earth, Moon and Stars. His whole world. The words were addling her brain but, when Jake looked at her, she could have sworn he meant it.

She pushed the thought away and willed herself to sleep.

The next morning being Sunday, they all slept in. It was declared a lazy day. It was supposed to be Amy's day off but without anything else to do, she hung out with them. The late breakfast on the patio consisted of her, Jake, Chance and Maggie eating eggs-ala-George, fresh fruit and George's famous cream cheese Danish.

Afterwards, they moved to the grassy area to play croquet. Amy was in the lead until Jake knocked her ball a good fifty feet out of play, and Maggie won instead.

"Pool next?" Chance asked looking around at the adults.

"Why not?" Jake answered and they headed back to change.

Amy almost groaned when they reached the patio, and she saw Clarissa there on one of the lounges. To her surprise, Clarissa didn't say anything, even turning away from Jake but not before Amy caught a look of pure fury in her eyes. Amy wasn't sure what happened, but the woman was definitely not happy.

They split up to go change. When Amy came out a few minutes later, Chance and Jake were already in the pool.

"We're going to play keep away," Chance announced to her. "You're in the middle first."

"Hey," she exclaimed.

"That's what you get for being the last one out," Jake returned letting his eyes drift over her.

Amy felt the heat rise in her as a slow smile spread over his face. She dove into the pool to break the contact between them.

The rule was set that, to make it fair, they had to get Chance with the ball three times to get him in the center. Twenty minutes later, they had Jake in the center. He was going for Chance who got the throw off to Amy. The ball went over her head, and it was a race between her and Jake to get to it. She made it to the ball, grabbed it and threw it to Chance but Jake kept coming.

"Too late." She laughed just before he caught her.

"I don't think so." His arm snaked around her, pulling her up against him.

"Hey, foul."

He tightened his hold.

"Jake," she gasped out, looking into his eyes, seeing

his intent. "No."

"Chance, look away," Jake said over his shoulder.

"Why?" Chance asked back.

"Because I'm going to kiss Amy."

"Eww, yuck," Chance said but laughed.

"We …" Amy was cut off as his mouth captured hers. She tried to pull back, but it was only half-hearted. "But …"

He settled more firmly over her mouth, deepening the kiss. Amy gave over to it with a little groan, getting lost in the feel of his warm muscles under her fingertips.

They broke apart at the sound of applause coming from above them.

"That was nicely done." Maggie looked down at them.

Color flared in Amy's face but Jake seemed to have no reservations.

"Thank you," he said cheekily.

"Now, if you're done ravishing her, do you want to come help me get into the pool?"

"Glad to."

To Amy's surprise, he turned back to her and gave her a quick kiss before placing his hands on the side of the pool and pushing out.

"Show off." Maggie laughed as he came to help her in.

Amy wasn't sure what to say, but fortunately no one mentioned it and Jake didn't make any other advances the rest of the day.

CঝৎৎৡৢD

"I'm doing pretty good, aren't I?" Chance said three days later as they walked away from the tennis court.

"I'd say better than just pretty good. I'd say you're doing great." Amy looked down at him.

He really was. He could return the ball with consistency now. True, she wasn't trying to make it difficult for him. "You want to swim before lunch?"

"Yeah," he said eagerly.

It felt wonderful to have the stitches gone and be back to full activity. The new week had been going pretty well, mainly because she hadn't seen much of Clarissa. She would almost say the woman was avoiding her which was a surprise because Jake wasn't around. He had flown out for meetings Monday and wasn't expected back until later that afternoon.

"Can we make cookies this afternoon for Jake?" Chance asked, pulling her attention back from his brother, where it continually wanted to shift. "He liked the last ones we made."

"I don't see why not. We can even take a plate out to the barn for the crew when they come in," she suggested as they reached the rise.

"Yeah, I bet they'll like that." He beamed with excitement. "Gran'ma." He looked up and saw Maggie sitting outside her room. "We're going to make cookies again."

Maggie lifted her hand then it dropped, going to her chest. Amy realized something was wrong immediately and started running even before Maggie went limp in the chair. She passed Chance, reaching the old woman first, dropping down by her wheelchair.

"Maggie!" Amy called her name but got no reaction. "Maggie," she repeated, not liking her coloring. Maggie's hand was clammy and limp when she picked it up.

"Gran'ma?" Chance said behind her.

Amy reached up to check her pulse and couldn't find one. "Chance." She tried to remain calm. "Run in and tell George to call 911 and to tell them you grandmother's having a heart attack."

Chapter Fourteen

"Gran'ma." His voice cracked with fear.

"Go, Chance," Amy ordered, lifting Maggie from the chair to lay her flat on the ground to start CPR. She heard Chance running, yelling for George and Ruth as she check Maggie's airway and for a pulse one more time.

Ruth came running out a second later. "George is calling." She stopped a few feet away.

Amy nodded concentrating on what she was doing, setting a rhythm in chest compressions. She heard Chance return, then Ruth take him back inside. She lost track of everything else until two men rushed onto the patio.

"Can you continue?" one of the men asked as he opened up a case beside her. Fatigue screamed in her, but Amy nodded. It seemed like forever but was only a minute later when he returned. "Taking over," he said shifting in next to her. On the count of three, she moved aside as he took over.

Amy scrambled back, sagging to the ground, gulping in air, watching the men work.

Time stood still then one of the men announced, "We've got a pulse."

Tears spilled down Amy's cheeks. She hadn't even realized the ambulance people had arrived until they wheeled the gurney up next to them. They got Maggie loaded and were gone.

Amy started to climb to her feet. George extended a

159

hand to help. She accepted it.

"Well done." He wrapped an arm around her.

She leaned into him, her body shaking with the suppressed stress.

"You did well. She's going to make it." George squeezed her shoulder.

Amy prayed it was true. She stepped away, going to the paramedic picking up gear. "Thank you," she said when he looked up at her.

"You're welcome. You gave her a good chance. They said you started immediately. That's important."

Amy nodded realizing George had probably given them all the information. "I didn't have any aspirin," was the only thing that came to her mind.

The man grinned. "They'll take care of all that."

She nodded again and looked up to see Chance standing by the doors. She stepped toward him and opened her arms. He ran to her, wrapping his arms around her, burying his face into her stomach. She hugged him to her, taking as much comfort as he was from the contact. When she had herself under control, she eased back.

"Let's get ready to go to the hospital, okay?"

"I can go?" He looked like he was afraid she'd say no.

"Yes." She wiped the tears from his cheeks. "If you want."

He nodded.

"I just need to get hold of Jake." Amy touched his cheek.

George laid his hand on Chance's shoulder. "I already tried. He must be on the plane or his phone is off. I left a message and sent a text. I'll drive you."

"Okay, just let me grab a couple things." She looked down at Chance. "You stay with George. I'll be right back. I just need to get my purse."

When they reached the hospital, they were told Maggie was doing well but the doctors were still with her. They'd been in the waiting room for about an hour when Jake strode in. Amy saw him immediately. Relief poured through her, even as she felt the tension in him.

She nudged Chance, who was leaning against her side playing half-heartedly on the tablet she'd brought for him. He looked up, saw his brother and jumped for him. Jake caught him, lifting him into his arms. Chance wrapped his arms around Jake's neck and hung on as Jake hugged him.

Amy stayed back, giving the brothers time.

"How's she doing?" Jake asked when he finally raised his head.

"The last they told us … good," George answered first.

Jake settled on the couch next to Amy with Chance in his lap.

"Do you need anything?" she asked.

He caught her hand and squeezed it. "I have what I need. Can you tell me what happened?"

Everyone joined in with the details. When they finished, he leaned over and kissed Amy on the cheek.

"Thank you."

"I just did what I could." She felt the tears rise in her again. Fortunately, the doctor chose that moment to walk in.

After introductions with Jake, she said, "Mrs. McCarron's stable. No signs of prolonged damage, but …" She raised her hand in caution. "We still need to wait to know for sure. Some of the levels were off in her body. I want to figure out why. You said she doesn't take any heart medication?"

"No," Jake answered and looked to the others.

Ruth took over the answer. "I gave the complete list of everything she takes. Maggie is very healthy, at least, until today," she added.

The doctor talked with them a minute more before she left. It was several more hours before Maggie was settled into a room, and Jake and Chance were allowed to go in and see her. After, Jake stayed behind while the others took Chance home.

Amy kept Chance close to her. They had a light meal then watched a movie until time for bed. Jake wasn't back yet, but called several times to give them updates. When it was time for bed, Amy laid down by Chance until he fell asleep.

She had just stepped into the family room when she heard the garage door open and close. She wondered if it was Clarissa, not having seen the woman all day. Jake walked into the room. He looked haggard. His suit coat was slung over his shoulder, his tie hung out of a pocket and the top two buttons on his shirt were undone.

She froze when he walked toward her. He stopped a foot short. Amy closed the distance, wrapping her arms around him. He hugged her to him, burying his face into her neck. Neither said anything. She just held him.

When Amy felt him sigh, she moved back.

"She woke up and was alert for a while," he said with a hint of a smile coming through.

"That's wonderful."

He brushed his knuckles over her cheek, his eyes studying her face. "How can I ever thank you?"

"I think you have several times today." She remembered the fear she'd felt as she'd tried to be calm and do what was needed.

He made a slight shake of his head. "It's not enough."

"Are you hungry?" She changed the subject. "George and Ruth have both turned in, but I can fix you something."

"I would love something." He released her and followed her into the kitchen. "It doesn't need to be anything fancy. Just an egg or sandwich will do or if there are any leftovers."

Amy pulled out the leftover chicken George had been fixing for lunch and fixed the salad to go with it. She placed it on the counter in front of him and took the stool next to him. "Did the doctor say anything more?"

"Just that she was doing well. A lot better than was expected. Maggie seems to be very strong. The doctor's running more tests. She can't figure out what happened. My father was the only other one in the family that had a heart problem, and we didn't even know until he had his heart attack."

"I didn't know your father had a heart attack."

Jake raised and lowered his head. "Maybe if someone had been around, they could have saved him." He reached over and took her hand. "I'd left the house early to get to work. We were supposed to meet at the barn at noon and go talk to the mine manager. He wasn't there when I got there and didn't answer his phone. He'd left it in the truck, which was common for him."

"A half hour passed and I got worried so I drove out to where he was working to check on him. I figured he'd just lost track of time, which also wasn't uncommon for him when he was on the ranch. I didn't see him when I pulled up to the truck. He was on the ground about thirty feet away. He was already gone. I couldn't do anything. I'm first responder and rescue trained. Being on the ranch that made sense, but I couldn't do anything."

Amy stood and wrapped her arms around him.

"The hardest thing was knowing he was alone." He leaned in, taking her comfort. They were still standing like that a few minutes later when they heard the front door open and the sound of heels clicking on the hardwood floor. A second later, Clarissa stopped in the doorway to the hall.

She glared at Amy before she turned her attention at Jake. "Jake, thank goodness you're home." Clarissa came over and kissed his cheek.

Amy was surprised at the genuine distress that poured off her.

Then Clarissa continued. "You can't believe what has

been happening while you were away. No one has been doing any of their duties. You have to talk to George and Mrs. Jeffers. I know it's all because of ..." she glanced at Amy again, "her, and the leeway you've given her, but as you started it, you need to rectify it. You can't let the others get away with their slothful behavior."

"What?" Jake blinked at her, shaking his head.

"It's like today. Everyone just disappeared. When I came back there was no one here and no lunch. I finally had to have Knowlton take me to the club, but when I got home, there was still no one around. I had to change and go back into city for the evening. Otherwise, I would have starved."

Amy wasn't sure who looked more shocked, her or Jake.

Jake stood and paced across the room before he turned back. His jaw clenched as he fought for calm. "Maggie had a heart attack. They were all at the hospital," he ground out. "She wouldn't have survived if it weren't for Amy."

"Well, no one told me." It sounded like an accusation. "She survived then?"

The way Clarissa said it got to Amy. She knew Clarissa didn't care for Maggie much, but she expected at least some reaction of concern for another person.

"Yes, she's doing well. I just left the hospital."

"Uh, oh well, then everything is all right." Clarissa looked more put out than remorseful. "I'm sorry." She went to give him a hug. He stepped back.

"What is it, darling? I was just trying to comfort you." Her voice was heavy with mock confusion and she looked at Amy again. "Then again, maybe you don't need any more comforting." She made it sound like another accusation.

"Not tonight, Clarissa. I'm not in the mood for any of your games," Jake said.

"Games? I was just concerned. What do the doctors

say?"

Jake paused as if for some unknown reason, he didn't want to tell her. "She's still in guarded condition, but the doctor thinks she'll be fine in a couple days. The doctor wants to know what caused it before they release her."

"Caused it? Surely her age and being in a wheelchair is enough. They ought to just be making her as comfortable as she can be. I've said it before, we should get her a nurse. She's far too frail to be on her own."

Amy thought Clarissa better not let Maggie hear her say that.

"She's not on her own, and she's as healthy as a horse." Jake used one of Maggie's favorite idioms.

"Yes, and that's what your father said before he was taken from us so suddenly." Clarissa made a poor-little-me sniff.

Jake fell silent. Amy wanted to smack the woman for bringing up his father's death at a time like this.

Clarissa sniffed again and stormed away, but Amy saw no sign of tears or even remorse on her face.

Jake had turned, looking out the window toward the pool. When he didn't move after a minute passed, Amy went to him.

"Jake." She laid her hand on his arm.

He looked down at her, so sad again it hurt. This time it was him that reached for her, pulling her into his arms.

"He shouldn't have died." The words came from him full of sorrow. "He seemed so strong and healthy. He shouldn't have."

Amy wrapped her arms around him and held him with all the strength she possessed. Tears slipped from her eyes for the man and boy who'd lost his father. Jake had loved his father and it hit her, she loved him. No matter how many times she told herself she couldn't, it did no good because she already did.

He leaned back and raised a hand to cup her face. It

seemed like he was always doing that and she liked it. He studied her face for a moment then brushed his mouth over hers very lightly. "We should get to bed. It has been a long day."

Taking her hand, he led her out of the kitchen and down the hall. Amy was just starting to wonder what to say when he stopped in front of her room. Again he faced her, lowered his lips to hers briefly then left her watching him walk way.

The next morning, Jake took Chance with him to go visit their grandmother. Amy found herself free to wander through the house. She was up in the loft library when a book caught her attention because it was sticking out farther than the others on the shelf. She was about to slide it back in when she noticed the title. It had to do with medications.

She wondered who'd been reading it or why they would even have it, and then remembered Jake said he'd taken training. It would made sense he would refresh himself on care for Maggie so he'd understand better what the doctor was talking about. Amy opened it to the section on heart attacks, but since she didn't know what the cause was, she really didn't know what treatment they were looking at. Amy put the book back and decided to use her free time to go out and paint.

03&0

"You ready?" Amy stuck her head into Chance's room. This morning, she was taking Chance to the hospital, since Jake was out in the barn with the vet and a sick horse.

"I'm ready." He hurried to her, excited to go see his grandmother.

They headed to the garage to Jake's car.

"Gran'ma told me yesterday that she thinks she will get to come home by the weekend."

Amy had already heard it all but let him ramble as they drove down toward town.

"Jake's worried about the horse. He doesn't know why it's sick." Chance changed topics. "He knows a lot about horses."

"Well, hopefully the vet can figure it out." Amy slowed to make the bend as the road started to wind down the hill.

"Jake says Dr. Harmon is very good."

He'd have to be if Jake let him near his horses, Amy thought. One thing she'd picked up already was Jake had special feelings for the horses. It wasn't that he didn't like handling the cows and other stuff, but the horses were his love.

The car started to pick up speed. Amy pressed on the brake and shifted into a lower gear. "George asked us to stop and get a few things for him after visiting your grandmother."

"Okay," Chance said easily.

"We never got to make our cookies the other day. Maybe if it's not too late when we get home we can make some this afternoon."

"Okay." That answer came more enthusiastically.

The car was picking up speed again so Amy pressed down on the brake. This time the pedal went right to the floor.

Chapter Fifteen

A flash of panic hit Amy. She had no brakes. She squelched the panic down, going back over what her father had told her when learning to drive. She shifted into a lower gear. There was a loud vroom. The car jerked and slowed some.

"Chance, hold on. I'm going to down shift. It's going to throw you forward. Now!" She put the car into second.

The engine whined, and the car jerked violently, throwing Amy forward even though she was expecting it.

"Amy?" Chance cried out.

"Hang on!"

The sharp curve at the bottom of the hill was coming closer. She gripped down on the wheel with one hand and pulled the emergency brake with the other. The car bucked and skidded, angling toward the side of the road. They were almost on the curve. Amy was sure they weren't going to stop in time; then they weren't moving except for the shaking in her body.

"Chance!" she cried out, her hands still locked on the wheel.

"I'm okay." His voice was high with fear. "What happened?"

Amy sat a minute more, before she could work her hands off the wheel and reach down to turn off the car. She turned to Chance, wrapping her arms around him. She fought to keep back tears, but there was nothing she could do about her trembling.

"Amy?" he asked after a minute.

"The brakes failed, but it's okay. You're okay." She kissed the top of his head then sat back, running her fingers through his hair. She blew out a breath and tried to still the tremors that shook her body. It took another second before she felt like her legs would hold her if she tried to stand.

Amy undid her seatbelt and got out, walking around the car. She stopped. Placing her hand over her face, she took another big breath. Fifteen feet directly in front of the car, the edge of the road dropped off into a ravine. It was only a twenty to twenty-five foot drop, but she didn't want to think of the possibilities if they hadn't made the curve and had gone over. She walked back to the car.

"I'm going to move the car off to the side of the road so no one comes around the corner and hits it. Why don't you hop out while I do that?" She really didn't worry about going over the edge now, but was not willing to risk Chance. He got out as she got in. Instead of starting the car, she just released the emergency brake and let the car roll forward, steering it to the shoulder, then reset the brake.

"I guess we better call up to the house and see if George knows who your brother uses for towing or who we should call." It was hard to keep her voice from shaking while she told George what happened and where they were.

He told her to sit tight, and he'd have someone right there.

Amy leaned back in the seat and looked over at Chance who had slid back in beside her. "We wait. I'm sorry about not going to see your grandmother, but we'll try to get there later."

"It's okay. You okay Amy?"

"Yes, but your brother's going to kill me." She groaned.

"No, he won't. It wasn't your fault, was it?"

"No, I don't know what happened. Just suddenly the

brakes were gone. There was nothing." Fear crept into her thoughts. She looked over at Chance, how odd another accident happened around him.

It hit her hard. It was too unbelievable that someone really could want to hurt Chance, but the way things were stacking up, it was the only conclusion. Brakes didn't just fail like that. At least, not on a car as new as Jake's, and she had already figured out that Jake took good care of his vehicles. The big questions were; who was it and why?

"Amy." Chance's call for attention came just as she heard the car approaching around the bend.

Instead of a tow truck it was a sheriff's vehicle. Relief spread through her. The car pulled over to the shoulder, its nose facing the nose of her car.

Amy got out as the man did. He was easily in his late fifties, over six foot tall and weighed about two hundred and fifty pounds.

"Looks like you had some trouble," he said in way of greeting as he walked toward her.

"The brakes went out coming down the hill."

He looked shocked at first then, as he looked over the car, it changed to obvious doubt. "The brakes went out," he repeated, tilting his head to the side, studying the car again. "Isn't this Jake McCarron's car?" His gaze shifted back to her.

"Yes. I'm Chance McCarron's governess, Amy Mathews." She held out her hand, deciding it was better to be forthcoming with information. "Jake gave me permission to drive it. We were going to visit their grandmother in the hospital."

"I heard about Maggie. How's she doing?" The man relaxed slightly after glancing at Chance in the car.

"Good. We were fortunate."

He was quiet a second before he started again. "The car's a clutch." He gave her an assessing look as if trying to see if she understood that.

"Yes." Amy got the feeling he was trying to decide if she was a dumb air-head. "I'm familiar with clutches, though I've never driven anything quite this fancy before coming here. It's not the first time I've driven it."

"But, it is an unfamiliar car," he said pointedly. "It's possible you got confused. If you were going a little fast and put in the clutch, the car would pick up speed going downhill." There was a logical tone to his voice that Amy found patronizing. Amy could tell where he was going though.

"I understand, but the clutch wasn't in. The brakes went out. To stop, I had to downshift and pull the emergency brake." She met him straight on.

"Maybe–" he started, but she cut him off.

"Why don't you check?"

He eyed her a minute then stepped by her and climbed into the car. He glanced at Chance.

"Chance." Amy said his name.

Chance got out and came around the car to her. Together they watched as the sheriff tried the brakes. Amy was satisfied when she saw the brake pedal go all the way to the floor.

"You don't have anything here." He got out of the car. "I wouldn't have guessed it. I'll call you a tow," he offered.

"I already called up to the house. They were going to send one." Getting up her nerve, Amy tried to figure out how to broach the subject of the multiple accidents. "Chance, will you wait in the car for a second while I talk to the sheriff?"

He nodded, but looked curious.

The sheriff got her point and walked back to his car.

"You wanted to talk to me about something?" he asked as she approached.

"Yes." She took a second to decide what to say. "Are you aware the other night someone tried to break into the McCarron house?"

"I saw the report," he said slowly, studying her once again.

"It was Chance's room the person was breaking into."

He eyed her suspiciously.

Amy knew he got what she was saying, but wanted it out loud. She didn't let it stop her now that she'd started. "These are not the only things that have happened around Chance lately. Just over three weeks ago, the night I got here, there was a rattlesnake in Chance's room."

"It's unusual, but it does happen."

"Two weeks ago, a wall rack that holds sports equipment almost fell on him. The nuts were missing from three of the bolts. The other looked like it had been cut away. If I wouldn't have knocked him out of the way ..." She broke there.

"What exactly are you getting at?" His gaze intensified.

"It's just so many accidents. I was wondering what you thought?" She reached up, running her fingers through her hair in attempt to let off some frustration. "I know what I'm saying sounds farfetched, but it's just too much for coincidence."

"Well, I get what you're saying, miss, but it doesn't hold water. This is Jake's car."

"But, it's the one I'm driving." She tried to object.

"Are you saying you think someone is after you?"

Amy wanted to groan. Now he thought she was paranoid. "No. I'm never without Chance."

"Has Jake been driving it, too?"

Amy thought about it for only a second. "He took Chance to the hospital yesterday in it."

This time it was the sheriff that looked thoughtful. "Any other incidences around Jake?"

His words hit Amy hard. "Not that I'm aware of." Jake hadn't said anything, but he was the type who would keep trouble to himself; not wanting to worry anyone else, and figuring he had to handle everything all by himself. Was Jake in danger? She couldn't help asking herself the question, not liking the possibility.

When she looked up, the sheriff was still staring at her in silence.

The sound of a vehicle reached them. They both turned to see Jake's truck speeding down the hill toward them. He pulled up behind the car and hopped out as Todd Wessex, one of the hands, climbed out the other side.

"Amy, Chance," Jake said, relief heavy in his voice.

Chance ran to him as Amy said, "We're okay."

He scooped Chance up, not breaking his stride as he walked to them. "What happened?" Jake looked from her to the Sheriff. "Ralph." He extended his hand.

"Looks like they lost their brakes. She did real well. Didn't panic and got them stopped," the sheriff answered.

"Lost their ..." Jake's gaze went to Amy, then the car.

Amy was ready for doubt, even accusations, but instead he simply said, "Are you all right?"

She nodded, feeling the first touches of panic rise in her. She wanted to run to him like Chance did and have him hold her, but she couldn't do it in front of the other men.

Jake seemed to wait for more, but when she didn't say anything else just nodded. "Okay. We'll tow the car home, and I'll take a look at it. "You want to—" he started to talk to Todd, but the sheriff cut him off.

"Jake, can I speak with you a minute?"

This time Jake met with him over by his vehicle and Amy was cut out. She went to stand by Chance at the back of the sports car, wrapping an arm around the boy's shoulder, holding him to her. Her feeling of protectiveness seemed to grow by the minute.

She guessed the sheriff was asking about what she'd said. She wondered what Jake was thinking. There was a scowl on his face, and he nodded several times during the low-toned conversation. By the time they were done, Amy figured she was about to be fired for all the trouble her very active imagination had caused. When they turned, Jake looked grim but, at least, there was no anger in his face.

"The sheriff's going to bring in a tow truck and have the car taken into a garage to be checked out. So we'll just give you a ride back to the house, and I'll take you to visit Grandma this afternoon." He directed the last part solely at Chance.

"May I get my purse?" Amy asked.

The sheriff nodded, but beat her to the car, reaching in to get it and the tablet, handing them both to her.

"Thank you." Amy smiled in gratitude. Just maybe he was taking her seriously.

"You're welcome." He tipped the edge of his cowboy hat at her.

Chance and Todd climbed in the small back seat of the cab, leaving the front seat by Jake for her. Amy settled in beside him and relaxed, but she couldn't let go of the niggling hints of fear that slithered through her.

Two hours later, Amy wandered about the house still antsy. She wished Jake and Chance would get back from the hospital though they hadn't been gone an hour. What the sheriff said still bothered her. Could they both be in danger? The possibility was driving her insane. The McCarron men had both buried themselves in her heart.

She should have talked to Jake about her concerns. As soon as he got back, she would. Needing something to keep her busy, she went to find Ruth. Amy found the woman in the laundry room folding clothes.

"Hi," Ruth greeted her.

"Hi. Looks like you got a lot of work to do."

"Just trying to get ahead of things. With Maggie in the hospital, I decided to go visit my daughter's family for a couple days. I talked to Jake about it this morning. I'll be back Friday before Maggie gets here."

"That sounds great. So what can I do to help you?"

"That's not ..." Ruth started to say something then really looked at her. Whatever she saw must've changed her mind. "You can put these towels in the bathrooms. These are Maggie's, Chance's, the hall bathroom and Jake's." She motioned to each pile. "I'll take care of Clarissa's." She grinned.

"Thanks. I don't think Clarissa would like me in her room."

"She has taken a disliking to you."

Amy rolled her eyes. "She'd have me out of here if Maggie would let her."

"Jake wouldn't let her."

Amy felt a flicker of shock that the woman would say that. She wondered if she knew Jake had kissed her. Her thoughts went right to him as they'd been doing the last couple of days. There was no doubt about it, Jake had wedged his way into her heart.

"Hang in there," Ruth continued. "It's nice having you around."

"Thanks." Amy forced her attention back to the housekeeper. She picked up a towel, folded it, and added it on top of Chance's pile.

"You're welcome. You know, you might get dumped on the next couple of days. George is also going to take off. I think I gave him the idea. He's going to Sacramento to visit an old friend of his. He made up a few meals and put them in the freezer to cover you while he's gone."

"No problem, we'll get by," Amy assured her.

"You and the boys will, but I don't know about Clarissa." Ruth arched her brows. "Constance is going to come in to serve dinner, see to the beds and tidy up."

"We'll be fine." Amy picked up the first load of towels.

She started with Maggie's room and worked her way down the hall with Jake's room last. She hadn't been in

Jake's room before and paused just inside the door, glancing into his private domain.

It had an opulent, high ceilinged room like the family room with a wide fan window over the French doors that seemed to bring the outside in. It was easily the size of any apartment she shared with five roommates at college. The room was a combination of tan, rust and blue that was entirely masculine but pleasing to her at the same time.

She felt a quiver of trepidation as she stepped inside. She didn't want to intrude but she was curious, too. The bed was a large four-poster, with several rows of pillows. Amy guessed Ruth came in and made it in the mornings to get it looking that good. Still, as much as Jake liked the outdoors, she could see him enjoying the touch of plushness. She couldn't resist peeking into the large walk-in closet.

"Wow." The exclamation escaped her. The closet was bigger than the bedroom she grew up in. Jake had suits, shirts and pants all sectioned out, and he still only used a third of the space. She went through it into the side entrance of the bathroom. Her breath caught, bringing with it a touch of sandalwood and musk. She tried not to think of him as she looked around the room.

Amy didn't know why she should be surprised after living in the house for nearly a month, but his bathroom was amazing. A large Jacuzzi tub sat in one corner with windows that reached the ceiling on two sides so it would be almost like being in the outdoors.

The marble tile was tan mixed with sienna, and had fine bluish and black lines running through it. The enclosed walk-in shower had three showerheads. It wasn't a surprise to her that there were two sinks in the vanity that ran along the opposite wall.

"Wow," she said again. Pulling her attention back to what she was doing, she opened a cupboard and guessed right on the first try to where the towels went. As she laid them in, Amy heard something tip over behind them. Quickly, she pulled them out and to her relief it wasn't anything liquid.

She reached in and retrieved a prescription bottle. The prescription was for Maggie and was dated ten months earlier. From the label, Amy had no idea what it was for, but it seemed odd to be there. She started to put in back, then hesitated. It wasn't a smart place to leave a prescription. She doubted Jake remembered it was there.

Amy slipped the pills into her pocket, put the towels back on the shelf, and went to find Ruth. "What's next?" she asked.

"Nothing at the moment. The clothes in the dryer are Chance's, but they won't be done for a half hour at least. Just take it easy," the woman said.

"Not in the mood to." She shoved her hands in her pocket, felt the prescription bottle there and traced it with her finger. "I'll be back to put them away." Amy hurried down the hall and up to the loft. Going through the books, she quickly found the one she wanted on medications. The way drugs changed, she wasn't sure it would be there, but she found it in the index and turned to the page. It was already marked.

Chapter Sixteen

Amy froze.

Both George and Ruth said Maggie hadn't had any previous heart problems. Jake had also said that. Amy checked the name on the prescription one more time to confirm she'd gotten the right drug, then started to read. When she reached the warning that 'an overdose could lead to heart failure', she felt faint and had to sit down. She backed up and re-read it again. It didn't change.

She stared at the page then the bottle. She picked it up with trembling fingers and opened it. Of a count of thirty, only four little pills remained inside. There had to be an explanation, but for the life of her, Amy couldn't come up with one. Why was nothing said about Maggie having a previous heart problem and why wasn't it on record with her doctor?

The pharmacy was in Las Vegas. That didn't seem right. She couldn't see Maggie going to Vegas just to see a doctor, unless she wanted to hide her condition. But, why would the bottle be in Jake's room, correction, hidden in Jake's room? A shiver went through her.

With more questions than answers, she went to close the book again when she noticed the slip of paper marking the page. It was a one by two and a half inch sticky note.

Nora, need info tonight. Don't forget.

There was no signature. Who was Nora? A study partner? Old girl friend? She didn't know and it didn't matter, but for some reason something in the note felt ominous to her. Amy placed the note in her pocket along with the prescription bottle, placed the book back on the shelf and went to find Ruth.

The housekeeper was just folding Chance's clothes so Amy joined her, her thoughts still on the prescription and the note.

"Ruth, has Maggie ever had any heart problems? I mean like years ago?"

"No, never. She's been extremely healthy the entire time I've been here. I can only remember her being real sick once, and that was years ago. Jake brought it home from school. He was so sick. It seemed like the whole valley was. I think his father was the only one in the whole house that didn't get it."

"Has she ever been on medication for her heart?"

"Maggie? No." Ruth shook her head. "She hates to take drugs. I hope it won't be a fight if the doctor puts her on something." Ruth gave a little laugh.

Amy thought over what she'd said, wondering again about the bottle in her pocket. Was Maggie supposed to take them and wouldn't. If so, why were so many missing and why were they in Jake's linen closet? Surely in the last year Ruth would have noticed them. She was too thorough to have missed them.

"Ruth, do you know a Nora?"

The housekeeper stopped and thought about it. "No, not that I can place," she said finally. "Why do you ask?"

"I saw the name and wondered if it was one of Jake's girlfriends. I hadn't noticed him going out." She sounded like she was checking up on him. Amy about groaned at the thought. "It was on a piece of paper in a book and I wondered if it was important, but it's probably nothing." Amy tried to cover the question and not let it disturb her.

"Jake hasn't had that many girlfriends. As a boy, he was always horse crazy. When he wasn't on a horse, he was doing sports. He also took on responsibility real early, kind of like Chance. I don't ever remember him being much of a problem.

"He got serious several times. The first one, he realized, wasn't right for him. With the two others, he found out they were mainly after him because of who he was. Those hurt him pretty badly, and though he's stayed friendly to the opposite sex and is still looking, he's been very cautious. Not a bad thing. It's kept him from letting Clarissa get her hooks in him, and believe me, she has tried, almost from the moment she walked into this house. I shouldn't have said that, but everyone else knows. It's so unbelievable the way she carries on."

Amy heard the garage door and jerked around.

"You okay? You've been a little jumpy this afternoon. What happened this morning must have really gotten to you."

"I'm fine. It has just got me a little nervous. I don't know why."

"You shouldn't worry and that'll probably be Chance and Jake. I think they took Jake's baby," she said soothingly.

"Baby? But they took it to the shop."

"That's his everyday car." Ruth arched an eyebrow at her. "You haven't seen his baby yet? Go out in the garage." When Amy didn't move, Ruth gave her a nudge to the door.

Amy opened the door to the garage just as one of the most beautiful old cars she'd ever seen rolled in. All thoughts of the pill bottle and the name on the paper fled from her mind as the cream and chrome drew her. Jake stopped the car in front of her.

"This was what was under the covering in the corner?" she said in astonishment.

"You like it?" Jake grinned broadly.

She glanced at him and back at the car. "Like it? I love

it. It's beautiful."

"It's a–" he began.

"An Auburn, early nineteen thirties, boat-tail," she said before he could.

His brow went up.

"There was a TV show that had one in it. It was a creamy color, very similar. I fell in love with it. I've seen a couple in car shows, but this one is spectacular."

"Thank you. She's my baby. My father helped me restore her when I was a teenager. We did most of the work ourselves."

"Wow." She was breathless.

"You want to go for a ride?"

"Oh, yes." She didn't even think of holding back.

"Chance, why don't you run in and see if George has a snack for you while I take Amy for a ride?"

Chance got out of the car and held the door for Amy.

Jake gave him a nod of approval when he closed the door after she settled onto the seat.

"Have fun." Chance smiled at her, and she grinned back.

"We won't be gone long. You haven't practiced your piano yet. Why don't you start that after your snack?" Amy suggested.

He made a slight face, wrinkling up his lips. "Okay." He dragged the word out.

"I have a video about five guys playing a piano all at once that's really amazing. I'll play it for you when I get back."

He nodded, backing away.

"You handle him very well." Jake commented as he backed out of the garage.

"He's pretty easy."

"He knows you like him," Jake countered.

"As I said, he makes it easy, those hazel eyes were killers from the first."

ALYSIA S. KNIGHT

"You like hazel eyes?" He stopped the car and leaned a little closer, giving her a good look at his own hazel eyes.

Amy fought to still her lips from twitching but it was no good, and she broke into a laugh. "I hadn't thought of it much before, but the light brownish center, with flecks of gold and the bluish green edge is really striking. Kind of like your opals, you never know what they're going to look like one minute to the next with the way the color shifts."

His hand came up to brush her cheek but instead of commenting on what she'd said, he just said, "We better get going so you can have your ride."

He shifted smoothly and they were off.

Amy looked around her. There was something magical about riding in the car. Even in her plain T-shirt and white shorts, she felt like a princess. "Oh, this is so amazing. How did you ever get it?" she exclaimed after they had gone about a mile.

"Dad and I went to a car show in town. There were a couple there, a bright red, and a cream and black, I liked them. Then one day I went with him to deliver cattle. The guy we took the cattle to had it sitting out in the field. It had been in an old shed he was cleaning out for the space. I wanted it when I saw it. He didn't want it, so my father worked out a deal with him that he was more than happy to take. It became our project."

"Wow," she said again.

"It was actually in better shape than we first thought, all intact, which was amazing. It took us several years because we were busy with the ranch and everything." He reached up and ran his hand over the gleaming wood dash. Fond memories and pride shown in his eyes.

"You did a great job."

"Yeah, she's been in several shows and got a couple trophies before I stopped showing her."

"Her?" Amy questioned, but she knew it was a guy thing to refer to their machines as feminine.

"Yep, she's my pride and joy." He grinned, easing the car around the curve. "Any other old cars you like?"

"Quite a few. Old model T's and A's. The rumble seats are really sweet, but my other top pick would be a 1914 Stutz Bearcat."

He shot her a look of surprise. She laughed. "It was from another TV show. I saw a rerun on it once. It's such a sweet car. The twin barrel seats, spoke wheels and, of course, that one was fitted out with a Gatling gun."

"A Gatling gun?" he said skeptically.

"It was in the TV show. Action and adventure, my type of thing."

"Even now?"

"Yes. I'm not much into chic flicks."

"That's good to know." There was a thoughtful tone in his voice. They fell silent just enjoying the ride back to the house.

Ben was waiting to talk to Jake.

Jake caught her hand as she started to get out. "Before you disappear, I want to talk to you about something. I just didn't want to spoil our fun in the Auburn."

Amy felt a wave of trepidation. "Okay." She moved off to the side, listening as Ben gave the good news that the horse was up and doing better. It was then Amy remembered that Jake had left a sick horse to come after them, and then given up going back to it to take Chance to the hospital.

If she had even a sliver of doubt about Jake and the drugs, they disappeared. Family came first. He would never do anything to harm Chance or any of his family members. Unfortunately, she believed someone else was out there that would, and Jake might be in their sights, too.

☙❧

Jake was aware of Amy standing only a couple feet away. It seemed he was always aware of her. There was no discounting he was attracted to her, but he was coming to accept it was more. When he'd heard they needed a tow, and something about the brakes going out, he'd nearly panicked, even though he knew they were all right. He had to see for himself.

What he found when he got there and talked to the sheriff alarmed him even more. The accidents were already bothering him, and he could no longer reason them away as coincidence, especially with the brakes failing. If Amy wouldn't have known what to do, or had panicked, she and Chance could have easily gone into the ravine and been seriously hurt or killed. He couldn't bear the thought.

Jake forced himself to listen as Ben told him what the vet had said. Delia was going to be alright. Ben would keep an eye on her the next couple days to be sure. When his foreman left, Jake turned to Amy as she walked toward him. He noticed the apprehension in her so didn't wait to start.

"I wanted to talk with you about what you said to Ralph, the sheriff," he clarified in case she didn't remember.

She winced slightly and stiffened.

"I wish you would've come to me first." He tried to sound non-confrontational.

"I'm sorry. I should have, but it all combined with the brakes going out and it kind of burst out. And, I did kind of mention it to Maggie. She told me Clarissa can't inherit."

"But, I can." It burned in him that she might think that. Her head was shaking before he even finished the words.

"I don't believe that." The words rushed out of her.

"You don't?" he pressed.

"No, I never thought that," she said softly then paused slightly before continuing. "Jake, I found something today when I was helping Ruth put away towels while you guys were gone."

He waited while she pulled a pill bottle out of her pocket and handed it over. Her fingers trembled slightly.

He was shocked to see Maggie's name on it. "Do you know what it's for?" he asked.

She nodded. "I looked it up in the book in the library. It's for heart problems."

He frowned. "Maggie's never had heart problems. She wouldn't keep that from me." The thought that she might, hurt him.

"I didn't find it in Maggie's room. I found it in your bathroom, in the linen closet."

"What? Why would …" He broke off looking to see if any doubt shown in her eyes. There was none but there was worry.

"The book said an overdose of this could cause heart failure," she added.

The significance hit him hard. He didn't like it, but right now, it was too much of a coincidence to doubt it. Still, he considered every possibility. When he turned his focus back to her, he knew she expected him to dispute it.

"I wish you would've brought this to me earlier," he said grimly.

Her body eased with released tension. The action drew him forward. When he wrapped his arms around her, she leaned into him. A sigh escaped her.

"You were frightened?"

"I didn't know what to do. I wasn't sure my imagination wasn't running away with me, or that I was looking for mysterious plots," she said against his chest.

"I don't think so. We'll get to the bottom of this." He hugged her tight, running his hand over her hair.

"Jake." She leaned her head back and looked up at him. "There's one other thing. I found a small slip of paper in the medication book. It was stuck on that page, like it had been left. It wasn't marking the page, just there." She pulled it out and handed it to him. "Do you know a Nora?"

"No." He shook his head. "I don't think I've ever met one."

"Not even in your class?"

He thought a minute before shaking his head. "No, I'm positive."

His cell phone rang. Jake hesitated before reaching for it. It was on the fourth ring when he pulled it out. Seeing the sheriff's ID, he quickly accepted the call. "Ralph."

He listened as the sheriff explained one of the bleed air screws had been opened. Jake looked at the spot where the car normally sat. He released Amy and walked over, noticing a few drips on the concrete floor.

"Every time she pressed on the brakes, she lost fluid until it was gone." Ralph was saying in his ear.

Jake knew all about that, and he couldn't see it happening all on its own. He'd had the car too long for it to have come with the problem, and he'd just driven it the day before and hadn't noticed anything wrong with them.

"The mechanic doesn't think there is a way this wasn't done on purpose," Ralph affirmed what was going through his mind. "Jake, I'm going to have to keep your car. It's proof it was no accident or malfunction. I'm going to have to look at this like an attempted murder. If they would've gone off the road—"

"I understand." Jake cut him off, not wanting to hear the possible outcome aloud. "I have one more thing for you. Amy found a prescription bottle for a heart medication. It's in Maggie's name, but she's never taken any."

"Where'd she find it?"

"My bathroom."

There was a pause on the other end of the line. "What was she doing in your bathroom?" Jake understood he was wondering if there was more to their relationship.

"Helping Ruth put towels away. It was in my linen closet."

"And you've never seen it before?"

"No, but it's dated about ten months ago."

"Before Miss Mathews came?"

"Yes."

"And you said it's in Maggie's name," he said as if logging facts.

"Yes."

"I'm either going to swing by and pick it up or have one of the deputies, but how about we do it on the sly? I don't want anyone to know we have it just yet."

"Okay, just give me or Amy a call and we'll come out and meet you." Jake gave him Amy's number which surprised her.

"I suppose both of you handled the bottle?" Ralph asked.

Jake winced. "Afraid so. Amy didn't know what it was when she found it and looked it up. She brought it to me."

"Then, we'll get your prints while we're there. If that's okay?"

Jake looked up at Amy. "Is it all right if the sheriff takes your prints?" He motioned to the little brown bottle and she nodded.

"That's fine."

"Okay, I'll see you in a little while." The sheriff cut the connection.

"The sheriff, or someone, will be by for the bottle and to get our fingerprints. He'll see what he can find out about it. It looks like the brakes on the car might have been tampered with, at least enough that they're going to do some more investigating on it."

She took a deep breath. "I don't know if I'm relieved or not."

He reached out, placing his hands on her arms, rubbing them up and down. "I think I need to thank you again."

She looked confused. "For what?"

"For bringing this to my attention. For keeping Chance safe, but mainly for believing in me. I don't think I would've seen anything besides accidents, and it would have been a very reasonable conclusion to think I was behind it, since everything becomes mine if something happens to Chance."

It was his turn to be surprised when she reached up and touched his cheek. "You love your brother. It's obvious, but even if you didn't, you wouldn't have done anything to harm him. You are the type who takes responsibility, you are a guardian."

Jake felt choked up that she saw him that way. "You make me sound like a hero." He tried to brush the remark aside. "If you ask me, you're the guardian."

"No, I'm the governess." She smiled.

He met her smile with one of his own. "Much more." He then grew serious. "I know it's a lot to ask you to stay, and I wouldn't blame you if you wanted to leave."

This time her fingers touched his lips, stopping him. "I'm not leaving."

"Good, but I want you to be careful." It was his turn to caress her cheek. He then leaned down and placed his lips on hers. There was no hesitation in meeting him, just a sweet welcoming. He accepted the invitation and deepened the kiss. She followed him in it, sliding her arms around him.

"I really like doing this," he said against her lips. "Remind me to thank Maggie for bringing you here. It should make her feel much better."

Amy pulled back and looked slightly alarmed. "You don't think she was trying to play matchmaker?"

"Her? You never know." He brushed his knuckles over her cheek. "She denies it."

"You asked her?"

He grinned. "With Maggie? You bet I did, the first night. She said she brought you here for Chance, and after seeing you with him, I believed that. When I showed an interest in you, I'm sure she found it an amazing bonus."

Amy picked up the grin. "You're interested in me?"

"Believe me. I don't kiss women who don't interest me, no matter how beautiful I think they are." Jake cut off at the small shake of her head. "And, don't doubt you're beautiful, because you are." He stroked back her hair, letting his eyes drift over her face. "I find you very beautiful."

He kissed her again, long and lingering. Finally, he eased back, letting his hand slide down her arm to take her hand. "As much as I would like to continue doing this, I think we better get inside."

He led her to the door then stopped. "Please, keep a close eye on Chance. And be careful."

"I will." Her promise was full of feeling.

Jake placed one more, quick kiss on her cheek and opened the door for her.

C380

"What are we going to do today?" Chance asked as they walked toward the house from the tennis courts.

Amy looked down at him. "I was thinking since George and Ruth are gone, that maybe we'd make a picnic lunch and go for a ride."

"All right! Maybe we can take lunch to Jake." He bounced as he walked.

"I don't see why not, if we can find out where he's at."

"He's checking out the stream in the upper east pasture. He's thinking about shifting some cattle in there." Chance supplied what Jake had said that morning before he left.

"Yes, but do you know how to get there?"

"Of course I do."

Amy laughed at how old and matter-of-fact he sounded.

They walked into the house and it hit her how quiet it was. There was usually music coming from the kitchen as George liked to cook with music. She wasn't surprised that Clarissa wasn't around. She'd made a production out of leaving and going to stay at a hotel until the 'staff' came back.

"Let's go change, then we can start making lunch," Amy suggested.

A few minutes later, Amy walked back into the kitchen wearing jeans, a T-shirt, and hiking boots. She really needed to invest in a pair of cowboy boots since she was going to be doing a lot of riding. She'd gathered bottles of water and juice; apples, trail mix, cookies and was just starting on the sandwiches when Chance came in and slid up on the stool beside her.

"Why don't you call Jake and let him know we're coming, then you can get a sack and start putting the food in it? We'll take it downstairs and find a pack it will fit in." As Amy turned, she caught movement outside the window. "Who?" She didn't get a good look at who it was because he'd gone by so fast. The only thing she knew for certain was that it was a man.

"Amy?"

She turned to Chance. "Sorry sweetie, I just saw someone in the back. It must have been the landscaper or the guy doing the pool.

"They don't come today," Chance said what she'd already been thinking.

Feeling uneasy, she stepped closer to the window to get a better look, but no one was there. "Maybe it was just my imagination." She shrugged. "Did you reach Jake?"

"No, the phone must be dead. It sounded funny."

Another shiver ran over her, but she pushed it away. "We ready?"

"Yep." He picked up one bag while she took the other two.

With one last look at the window, Amy followed Chance down the stairs to the outdoor equipment room. It didn't take long to put the stuff in the saddlebags they'd used on their previous picnic. Amy had just picked up the bag and draped it over her shoulder when she heard the sound of someone walking down the stairs.

Chance looked at her, obviously just as alarmed as she was because he didn't say anything. No one was to be there but them, unless Jake had come back earlier than planned. Still, she held up her hand for silence as she eased forward. They hadn't closed the door when they entered the room. Amy reached over and flipped the switch, turning out the light, then pressed her hand on the frame and peeked out. Amy couldn't explain why she was being so cautious.

There was a shadow at the bottom of the stairs cast by the light coming from above the man, but he didn't take the last step into view. All she saw was the sleeve of a green shirt that she knew Jake hadn't been wearing that morning when he left. She bit her lip to keep from sighing when he turned and went back up the stairs.

Chance pressed against her back. He still didn't make any sound even when Amy pulled back and closed the door behind them.

"Amy," he said in the barest whisper. "I don't think that was Jake."

"I don't either."

"No one else is supposed to be here."

"I know. I left my phone upstairs. It's still in my room. Is there any other phone down here besides in the workout room?"

He shook his head.

"Okay, I want you to stay here while I go make a call."

He was already shaking his head before she finished. "No, don't leave me."

"I'll be right back. You can hide if you want."

The movement of his head became more pronounced. "Please, don't leave," he pleaded and she couldn't.

"Okay, but stay right by me and be as quiet as you can."

He nodded.

Amy cracked open the door and peeked out, then listened before opening it more and slipping out. She reached back her hand, and Chance took it. His small fingers trembled slightly. Amy felt foolish because she knew he was picking up her fear. She just prayed she wasn't terrifying him for nothing. Moving as slowly as they were, it took a full minute to reach the exercise room.

Cautiously, she glanced around the corner. The room was empty. Amy pulled Chance into the room with her. The phone was on the wall just inside. She lifted it and was greeted with a hum.

"Chance," she whispered. "Was this the sound you heard earlier?" She held the phone to him.

He nodded.

"It's off the hook somewhere."

"So we can't call out?"

"No, not unless we go through the house and find out where it is and hang it up."

"What are we going to do?"

It didn't take her long to come up with a plan. "We'll go up the other stairs and get the keys to one of the cars." She placed a hand on his shoulder and gave a light squeeze.

They quickly retraced their way down the hall. At the intersection, they took the stairs up, moving slowly and pressing back against the wall. Amy signaled Chance to stop when she reached the top. Peeking around the corner, the hallway was clear. She was about to step out when a man crossed the opening into the kitchen.

Amy pulled back and held her breath, praying he hadn't seen her. When footsteps didn't sound in the hall, she let out the air and looked once more. Only half the man's body was visible and he was turned away from her. His hair was medium brown. She couldn't tell more than that, and wasn't sure if she knew him. She wished she could get a better look but didn't dare.

Amy glanced from the man toward the place on the wall where the keys were kept. All the hooks were empty. A gasped escaped her before she could stop it. Afraid, she looked back at the man, but he didn't seem to have heard her. He reached for something, and she caught a glimpse of a cookie as he brought it up.

The man was actually eating. She didn't know what to make of it. For a moment, she debated stepping out but something held her back. Feeling Chance's small hand touch hers, she knew she couldn't risk it. She looked back at him and tipped her head downward. He understood and started to move back down the stairs. She followed him. At the bottom, she turned them to the door leading out in front.

"We're going to make our way to the stables. We can call for help there. Do you know the combination to the gun safe?"

Chance shook his head. She knew it was a long shot, but she would have felt better if she was armed. She didn't want to use a gun on anyone, but she wasn't going to let anyone harm Chance either.

"That's okay." She touched his cheek. "Try to keep hidden until we get away from the house. Then we're going to run for the barn. Can you do that?"

"Yes."

"Let's go."

Amy had faith in him, and he didn't let her down. As soon as they made it past the corner of the house, he took off running, not stopping until he reached the barn.

"Ben!" Chance yelled reaching the barn doors. "Ben, Cody, Seth!"

There was no answer.

"Jake!" Amy yelled. She went straight to the office. It was empty, and when she pressed the connect button on the phone, she got nothing but silence. She stepped back out into the barn. Chance was heading down the row of stalls looking in each one.

"No one's here," he said what she already knew.

A quick check outside proved there were no vehicles around.

"The horses," Amy said before Chance could ask. "We'll ride out until we find Jake or Ben." She didn't say that they were the only ones she felt she knew well enough to trust.

Amy draped the bag of food over a railing and went to get the saddles while Chance took care of the bridles. He had no problem with the horses and within a couple minutes, they were ready to go. Amy lashed the saddlebag in place and swung up in the saddle.

"You sure you know where Jake is?" she asked.

"I know," he assured her in a voice too serious for such a little boy.

"All right. You lead the way."

She followed Chance out of the barn, keeping an eye out for anyone coming from the house. She didn't see anyone as she kicked her horse into a gallop.

They rode past the old farmstead and slowed their horses to a walk as they cut up the draw just past it. It put them on top of the hill. Amy stopped them long enough to get a good look of the surrounding area before motioning to continue. They crossed a small dip between two hills, cutting through a herd of cows, and then climbed again.

"Jake should be up here somewhere." Chance broke the silence that settled over them.

Amy wasn't sure if she dared yell for him. "How about we go up to that ridge? Maybe we can see him from there."

The trail grew rockier. Ponderosa Pines dotted the hill, running up to the ridge. When they reached the top, Amy swung down and tied her horse to a branch. She made her way out to a rocky point.

"Do you see Jake?" Chance asked from by the horses.

She shook her head.

"Amy, what's happening? Why was that man in our

house?"

She looked back at him, then used the time of settling down on a rock to think what she wanted to say. Chance came up to her, and she pulled him into her lap.

"I'm not sure, sweetheart. It might've been nothing."

"But, it scared you."

"Yes, it did." She decided she had to be honest with him. "I'm not sure the accidents that have been happening lately, are all accidents."

"Like when the rack fell and the brakes went out?"

She brushed back his bangs. "Yes. Jake's concerned, too. The sheriff is looking into it. Jake wanted me to keep a close eye on you. He would've told me if there was supposed to be someone in the house. Especially, someone I didn't know."

"And the phones weren't working."

"Yes."

"What if Jake's not here, and we can't find him?" There was trust in his eyes that steadied her.

"Well, we have food and water, and there's other stuff in the backpack so we'll be okay to stay out here even if it's for the night."

"We should've brought a sleeping bag," he said sagely, like sleeping out was a done deal.

She ruffled his hair. "Yeah, well, it's not that cold at night so we'll be all right. Jake will be looking for us, but if we do have to spend the night, tomorrow we'll ride to the nearest house and call Jake or the sheriff."

He leaned against her shoulder, and she wrapped her arms around him and laid her cheek on his head. They sat like that for several minutes.

"Do you think the snake in my room … hey." He pulled up, leaning forward. "There's Jake," he exclaimed, pointing out.

A man in a blue chambray shirt riding a bay horse came through the trees. Though she was certain, Amy held her breath until the rider came from behind another tree, and she could see it really was Jake. Relief made her sag. It was okay.

Suddenly, she felt a little foolish at her actions. What if Jake had sent the cowboy to the house to watch over them? She winced, but inside she didn't believe it anymore now than she had at the house.

Amy was about to call out and wave when the sound of a faint snort from a horse just below them caught her attention. She turned in time to see a man on a horse just at the crest of the draw. He looked startled as he pulled his horse to a stop, and then with a jerk, raised a gun pointing it directly at Jake.

"Jake," Chance yelled just before her. The sound of a shot cracked, drowning out their warning.

Jake jerked in the saddle and tumbled off. Even from the distance, Amy heard him hit the ground. Her heart burst with pain. Her first instinct was to run to him. Instead, she wrapped her arms around Chance and pulled him down out of sight of the gunman.

Chapter Seventeen

For a second, shock kept Chance in her arms then he started squirming to break free. "Jake," he tried to call his brother's name just as Amy clamped her hand over his mouth.

"Shh," she hissed in his ear. "Chance," she gave him a light shake to get his attention as he continued to fight. "Chance, you have to be still, so I can go check on him."

He finally quieted.

"Come on." Amy took his hand and pulled him away from the edge. Rocks littered the ground but nothing big enough to hide behind. She shifted their direction to where the trees stretched toward the outcropping, about fifteen feet away. They had to reach them before the man made it up the rise. There was no doubt he'd come to kill them.

Amy tried not to think of Jake but the thought of him hurt, possibly dying, ate at her. She needed to get to him. She prayed he was alive. They'd just reached the trees when Amy heard the sound of hooves on rock. She pushed Chance down behind the closest tree.

"Stay still and hide." She didn't have time to say more. She ran to put distance between her and Chance. Amy made it about twenty feet then ducked down behind another tree to wait and listen. Her gaze landed on a three-foot long branch on the ground about six feet away, but before she could make a dash for it, more sounds from the horse reached her. She could tell it was getting close.

She shifted slightly trying to see Jake. He was on the ground only about a hundred feet away but there might as well have been a chasm between them. His body was completely still. She bit her lip to keep from calling to him. Only the sound of the man kept her in place, but remaining still tore at her heart.

She pressed back against the tree, twisted her head to the side and leaned over an inch at a time until she caught movement. Amy pulled back, drew in a deep breath and repeated the process, this time getting a look at the man as he swung off his horse.

He was turned away from her, looking toward Jake. Out here in the sun his hair was lighter and had a strong reddish tone. She knew it was the same man who had been in the house, and she knew him, well just his name. Todd something. She'd seen him on the ranch a couple times.

Amy was afraid he was about to head toward Jake and wondered what she could do to stop him when he turned. She pulled back but he didn't come her way. He headed toward the out cropping. Amy glanced at Chance. He was hunkered down just like she'd instructed, but if Todd went that direction, he'd surely see him.

Amy risked another glance. Todd stood at the edge looking over. Amy wondered if she could make it to Jake and get to the gun she knew he carried before Todd shot her.

As he turned, she ducked back. This time it was the sound of his boots on the rocks that told her his location. Todd was coming closer, but headed more Chance's direction than hers. Amy looked at the boy. He was crouched down, looking to her. She turned her head a little more to see the man. He'd put the gun away but was only about eight feet from Chance.

Fear filled Chance's eyes.

She raised a finger her lips.

Todd slowed as he reached a tree and peered around it

then moved to the next. He was hunting. He knew they were there. Amy held her breath and glanced at the stick then back. He was only about two feet from Chance. There was no way he'd miss seeing him.

Todd took a step and reacted at seeing Chance. "Got you."

Chance cried out and jumped up, trying to dodge him. Todd caught his shoulder, pulling him back around then wrapped his arm around him, picking him up off the ground as Chance kicked and fought.

As soon as Todd was distracted, Amy leapt for the stick. Her hands locked onto the two and a half inch width like a baseball bat as she ran at the man.

"Todd!" she yelled and was already swinging before he turned. Amy hit him high to clear Chance's head, catching Todd across the shoulder and neck. A loud crack split the air. The stick vibrated in her hands as it snapped in two.

"Run Chance!" Amy plowed into them, taking them all to the ground and came up fighting. Hitting out again, she got in three or four more blows before Todd caught her wrist. She kicked out, almost catching him in the groin.

Todd swung his hand catching her on the side of her head but Amy didn't let up. She changed her focus and clawed at the gun, wrapping her fingers around it as Todd's hand locked over her wrist. Knowing she didn't have the strength over him to win the fight for it, when his hand swung hers to the side, she opened her fingers and let the gun fly, barely keeping track of where it landed.

She kicked out at his knee. He grunted when she connected, but didn't go down. He shook her roughly, swung her away from him then back. Amy saw the blow coming and tried to block it, but his fist powered through catching her on the end of her chin. Tears came to her eyes. Everything blurred.

"Planned to do the boy first." Todd pulled her across

the ground by one arm.

They reached the rocky area before her mind cleared enough to grasp his intentions. He was going to throw her over. Amy started to fight again, clawing at his hand. They were almost at the edge of the cliff when she turned her head enough to bite down on his arm.

He released her arm and brought his hand up to lock around her neck. "They'll find you and the boy's body at the bottom of the cliff, dead. I'll make sure they never find Jake, but they will find the pills that almost killed the old lady."

Amy clawed at his hand and wrist, digging in with her fingers. Around her the world began to swim. A sharp crack ripped through the haze settling in her mind. Above her, Todd jerked. He gasped for a breath. Releasing her, his hand went to his chest, and he staggered back. A red strain spread high on his shoulder. He took another step back and disappeared over the edge.

Amy slumped back drawing in air for several seconds before pulling herself up to look for Chance. He was on the ground next to Jake. Jake leaned on him, a rifle in his hand.

"Jake!" Relief and joy filled her with adrenalin. Amy climbed unsteadily to her feet and stared at the edge. She swallowed and ignored the pain as she stretched out her neck. She didn't want to look over, but she had to know what happened to the man, Todd Wessex, funny how the full name of the man finally came to her.

She looked down at the body and knew immediately he was dead. Amy turned away and almost fell when she tripped over a rock. She steadied herself and looked at the McCarron males. Pain tore at her heart.

"Jake." She broke into a run. "Jake." She dropped down by him.

Blood soaked the left side of Jake's shirt and sleeve.

"How bad?"

"I'm okay." Jake got out as she reached for him. His

dismissal of his injury, combined with her relief that he really was alive and well, shifted her fear to fury.

"Don't give me that, cowboy." Amy gritted her teeth. "There's blood. That means you were shot, and I saw you fall off your horse."

The wince was more mockery than pain. "Don't remind me."

She just glared. "Tough cowboy image. Don't worry it's still safe. Getting knocked off a horse by a bullet doesn't count against you. Let me see."

He grimaced as she started undoing the buttons. "It's not bad," he said softer. "I think it just scraped me."

Amy ignored him. "Chance, are you okay?" She moved to the next button.

"Yes, Amy."

"You did real good, sweetie."

"Is he dead?" Chance asked. His voice trembled.

Amy's hands stilled on the button, and she looked up at Jake's gaze, then reached back to take Chance's hand. Tears came to her eyes, and she blinked them back. "Yes."

Jake raised his uninjured arm and used his thumb to brush the moisture from her cheek.

"Hold still," she ordered, not that it did any good.

His hand lowered to her neck. "You're going to have bruises."

"I'm alive." She took a deep breath and felt the twinges of pain in her throat. "We all are. That's what matters."

His thumb raised to catch another tear as it slipped free. "You're amazing." Lines tightened on his face, and he released a small hiss of pain but it didn't stop him from bending forward to kiss her.

Amy returned it. She wanted to settle in and savor the life in him but pulled back. "Jake." She wiped at her own tears. "I have to keep it together long enough to tend this and get us out of here. I can't curl down into your arms and never leave right now." The words slipped from her.

He cupped her chin, tipping it up so her gaze met his. "Is that what you'd like to do?"

The need in his eyes pulled the answer from her. "More than anything." She didn't try to stop her love from showing. It was too close to the surface to hold back.

"I wouldn't mind holding you the rest of my life."

Amy felt herself lean toward him then saw him stiffen and make another grimace of pain. She stiffened also. "Yeah, well, not until I see to this."

She undid the last button. Opening his shirt, she slid it first from his good shoulder and arm then eased it off the other. The sleeve caught on his arm, stuck to drying blood. She careful worked the material free, conscious of the pain she was causing him. The wound on his arm didn't look too bad. It really was pretty much a scratch like he said, an inch long crease left as the bullet passed by.

Conscious of Chance watching, Amy fought to hold in her reaction when she got a good look at his side. About three inches below his armpit, there was a gash of torn flesh that was easily four inches long across his side to his back. In some spots the blood had already started clotting but blood still flowed down his side to his jeans.

Since his shirt was already ruined, she folded it over and wiped the blood away then tucked it into the edge of his jeans to soak up the rest that had made it that far.

"I need to clean this some and bandage it." She looked up to find him staring down.

"There's a small first aid pouch in my saddle bag," he said.

She nodded. There was one in hers, too. A first aid kit was standard equipment in all packs. "Chance, can you get it?"

Chance was up and moving before she finished asking.

"Do you have a cell phone?" she asked as she bent closer to examine the wound. The width and jagged edges made her worry about how they'd close it.

"Yeah, but we can't get reception up here. You can get it about half way down the draw."

Amy glanced that way. She had a brief thought of sending Chance to call for help while she tended Jake but was unwilling to let him out of her sight even though Todd was dead. "Okay, as soon as I see to this, I'll ride down and call for help. Chance can stay with you until I get back."

"We can go together," Jake said.

"But–"

"I can make it. I've ridden with worse. We stay together."

She nodded.

Chance came back with the kit. His eyes were big with concern as he stared at the blood.

"Hey." Amy drew his attention, smiled and tipped her head toward Jake. "He's going to be all right. This is nothing a tough cowboy can't take. You heard, he's had worse." She opened a swab and started to clean the edges.

"We have our tender side, too." His mock indignation was ruined with another small hiss of pain.

Chance jerked. "Are you going to be all right?"

"Yeah, it really is just a big scratch."

"It looks like it hurts."

"It hurt a lot less before Amy started messing with it."

She glared at him. "That's all I'm going to do." She opened a large sterile pad and placed it over the wound. "Chance, can you hold this while I tape it down?"

He placed his fingers where she showed him, and Amy used a couple pieces of medical tape to tack it down then pulled out a roll of stretchy bandage to wrap around him.

"Now this I may like," Jake winked at his brother. "Do me a favor and make her do it by herself."

Amy rolled her eyes, feeling a smile slip free. "You are definitely going to be all right. In fact, maybe you don't need this."

"Uh huh, you started."

Amy sent him what was meant to be a glare, but failed miserably as she saw the pain in his eyes and knew he was making light for Chance. She shrugged. Placing the end of the wrap over his heart, she held it there. It hit her how close the bullet had come to his heart, just a couple inches. She choked up and tears threatened again. Amy looked up to find Jake watching her.

He dipped his head and kissed her. Not just a light brush but a hard reaffirmation of life that also yelled of claiming. Amy gave herself over to it. When the kiss ended, her fingers were trembling as she started wrapping his side, going carefully over the bandage, but keeping it snug. She leaned in to reach around his back, aware of every inch of his warm, hard muscle and gentle breath on her cheek. She went around three more times before running out of wrap.

"That should do." She pressed down the end, getting it to stick before easing back.

"Thank you," he said, when she looked up at him. "Shall we get out of here?"

"Just a minute." She held up a hand. "Chance, why don't you get two of those blue packs of pills and give them to Jake. He can have all four pills. That is if you're not allergic."

"I'm not."

Chance gave him the pills then got him a drink while Amy wrapped another pad over the scrape on his arm, using tape to fasten it down since she was out of the other bandage.

"Thanks. You know you ought to take a couple of those, too. They'll help the swelling."

Chance followed the lead and opened up a packet for her. Jake handed over his water. Amy drank from it without hesitation or thought until she noticed him looking at her lips and realized they were where his had been an instant earlier, then again, a minute before, they had been on her lips.

Amy ripped her mind away from the thought. She was losing it. Everything that happened had her unsettled. She closed her eyes and took a deep breath to bring herself back under control. When she thought she was steady, Amy opened her eyes only to have everything shift again at the sight of Jake shirtless in front of her with dried blood streaked over his side.

"Maybe I better go try calling for help." She stood moving away several steps.

"I can make it." Jake started to rise.

Amy reached for him and Chance shifted behind him as if to catch him.

"Easy," she ordered.

Jake wrapped his good arm around her, and she helped him straighten. He wobbled slightly and leaned into her.

"Maybe you should–"

"I'm okay, Amy." He gave her a light squeeze then released her and stepped toward his horse. Amy followed, placing herself behind him with Chance in case he fell, but he made it on the horse fine.

"Okay," she acknowledged and looked at Chance. "Let's go."

They retrieved their horses. "What do we do about his?" Chance asked.

"Blue will probably follow us back, but grab his reins and get him started," Jake said.

They made it down the hill. Both Amy and Jake kept their horses in between Chance and the sight of Wessex's body.

"Was that Wessex?" Jake whispered to her.

She nodded.

"What happened?" He finally asked the question she knew was to come.

Amy changed the motion of her head to a shake, not

certain what to say. "He was in the house."

"What?"

"We came back from tennis and were making a lunch to bring to you when I thought I saw him out back. I didn't recognize him. When we went down stairs for a pack, he came in upstairs. The phones weren't working, and the car keys were missing. So we ran for the stables. No one was there, so we rode for you."

"There's a phone in the stables."

"It was dead."

The look he gave her was of utter disbelief but not in doubting her.

"So you just got Chance out of there."

"I didn't know he'd followed us." She caught the bottom of her lip to steady her emotions. "I checked behind us several times."

"It's okay. It's over, Amy."

"When he shot you …" A sob escaped her.

"It's okay."

"I …" she stopped and blew out a breath. "Why?"

"That's a great question. I don't know much about him. He's only worked here a couple of months." Jake fell silent a minute. "We should be able to get reception here." He dropped the reins and pulled out his cell phone. "Not yet." He stared at the phone as they continued down the hill then selected a number and brought the phone to his ear.

"Ralph, Jake McCarron. Sorry to ruin your day, but I have a dead body out here."

Amy shook her head at his phrasing.

"I shot him. He shot me first and was trying to kill Amy and Chance."

Amy reached over and caught Chance's hand, aware of how quiet he was. Then again, she didn't know what to say either.

"I'm okay."

She heard Jake say and sent him a glare. "We're about

a mile and a half past the old homestead up one of the draws. Had to come down to get service. You'll need a four-wheel drive to reach the body. I'll get hold of Ben to take you there. I think Amy's going to insist I go to the hospital." He paused. "Flesh wound on my side." There was another pause. "I can make it down. I don't need an ambulance. I'll have Ben meet me at the homestead with a truck."

There was a longer break. "Todd Wessex. I have no idea why." Jake looked at her. "Okay, see you there."

Jake disconnected. "Ralph and some deputies will meet us at the homestead." He looked to his brother. "You okay, Chance?"

Amy noticed a weariness in his voice that hadn't been there before.

"I'm okay." Chance straightened a little in the saddle.

"Let's get to the homestead then."

Amy was wondering about him calling Ben, but decided to wait until they reached the bottom of the draw to mention it. Jake was flushed when they got there.

"Can I see the phone?" She reached out a hand.

"What?" He blinked at her.

"I'll call Ben."

"Oh, yeah." He brought the number up then handed the phone over.

"What'cha you need?" the foreman answered on the third ring.

"Actually, this is Amy," she said. "Listen, Jake's been injured, not bad, but can you meet us with a truck at the homestead? The sheriff's meeting us there, also. I'll explain then."

"Be right there." The man cut off, not bothering to ask more.

Amy could see the dirt trail thrown up by a vehicle, and another almost directly behind it as they reached the homestead. She led them under the shade of a tree.

She and Chance slid from their horses but Jake remained on his. He was pale, and Amy knew shock was settling in.

"Chance." She handed him the reins and went to Jake, laying a hand on his leg, gaining his attention. He started to swing his leg over the horse, and she stopped him. "Maybe you ought to wait for help."

"I can make it." He continued, but his motions were not his normal smooth form.

Amy caught him as he hit the ground.

He used her and the horse to steady himself and blew out a breath. The trucks skidded to a stop next to each other kicking up more dust. Luckily, air currents carried it the other direction. Ben was the first one out and ran to them.

"What happened?" His gaze took in Jake.

Amy didn't get time to answer as two vehicles from the sheriff's department pulled to a stop and the question was echoed by the sheriff as he got out.

While a paramedic-trained deputy took a look at Jake's side, Amy and Jake took turns telling what happened.

"Okay," the sheriff said when they finished. "Why don't you get to the hospital and have that looked after? I'm going to send a man over to your house to check it out. Is it locked?"

Jake looked at her.

"The front door is. I don't know about the back patio doors. We didn't lock them. I just got Chance out of there."

The sheriff nodded looking over at Chance who was leaning against her. "That was the right thing to do. I'll tell them they can go in through the back. Ben can take us up to the body. We'll get a more complete statement later. I don't want you to talk about it, but go over it in your minds so it stays fresh." He reached over and patted Chance on the head.

As the sheriff pulled out his phone, Amy stood and reached for Jake. He accepted her help, giving her a half smile. Ben stayed by his side all the way to the truck. Chance got in the back seat, and Jake made it into the passenger side just as the sheriff came over.

"I called the hospital to let them know you're coming in. It will make it easier. Gunshot wounds raise all sorts of flags."

"Thanks."

Amy climbed in and started the engine, relieved to be leaving. She glanced over at Jake. He was leaning back against the seat and the door. His eyes were closed. As if sensing her attention, he opened them. "I'd hold your hand but my arm feels better like this." He had it tucked to his side. He'd been keeping it that way.

"How are you doing?" she looked at the dirt road then back at him.

"I think the pain killer is wearing off."

"I don't know if you should take anymore until the doctor looks at it." Concern hit her hard.

"I'm fine."

୧୫

Jake was in the same position when Amy pulled the truck past a deputy sheriff's vehicle and into the garage three hours later. Jake's wound had been tended, and he'd been given an antibiotic and painkiller. With a list of instructions, Amy was allowed to take him home.

Amy got out and opened the back for Chance to hop down. "Do you think we can get your brother in or shall we see if the deputy can help us?"

"I can make it on my own." Jake's groggy voice rumbled out.

Amy exchanged looks with Chance and they both laughed, but managed to get Jake into the house and to his bedroom. Amy waited outside his closet door while he changed out of his blood-soaked jeans. A couple minutes later, she tucked him into bed.

"Where's my kiss?" he said when she started to step

away.

Amy froze.

"You always give Chance a kiss."

"I think the pain meds have addled your brain."

He looked up at her with yearning in his eyes.

"All right." Amy leaned over and placed a kiss on his forehead. "Better?"

"Uh huh." He caught her hand, giving it a light tug, and she lost the fight with her resolve. Leaning in, she brushed his mouth with hers, savoring a moment before pulling back.

"Better," he mumbled the word and fell asleep.

She couldn't bring herself to pull away. She'd fallen in love with him, truly, deeply, in love with him. She didn't know what to do. There was one thing that kept her from panicking, and that was the realization he really did have feelings for her, too. Or was she just being a foolish dreamer? She placed one more kiss on his forehead and stood.

Amy checked on Chance, who'd gone in to shower then went down the hall to the family room. She found the deputy waiting there.

"Miss Mathews, I'm Deputy Morris."

"Amy, please, if it's allowed." She guessed he was in his early to mid-thirties, with a friendly smile that was welcoming at the moment. She was so tired.

"Yes. The sheriff will be here in a few minutes. Until then, I need to ask you some questions."

Since there was nothing else she could do, she nodded and followed him to one of the couches. She went over everything in as much detail as she could remember.

"So you didn't know the man?" he asked one more time.

"I'd seen him before but hadn't talked to him. I didn't recognize him when he was in the house."

"So why did you run?"

"No one was supposed to be in the house. Everyone else is gone. What really frightened me, was that the keys were gone. I'd seen them there earlier."

"Would you mind showing me where that is?"

"Certainly." She stood.

They were just about to the hall when there was a knock on the door. They shifted directions. The deputy opened the door to the sheriff and another deputy.

"Will you wait right here a minute?" Deputy Morris stepped out the door to talk with the other men.

When they came back inside, it was the Sheriff that spoke up. "Do you want to show us the key holder now?"

It seemed odd the way he said it. Amy didn't understand the significance until they were in the hall almost to the garage and she caught sight of the board. There were easily five sets of keys hanging there.

She froze. "They weren't there."

"Are you sure you saw the board?" the sheriff asked.

"Yes, I was on the stairs. I looked right at it." She was confused. Even to her, it seemed odd that Todd would take the time to put the keys back when he was after them.

"Did Chance see them missing?"

"I don't know. He was behind me."

"Where was the man standing?"

Amy turned and pointed into the kitchen. "Just there inside."

The sheriff shifted his stance. "But you couldn't recognize him?"

Amy was sure this time she heard doubt in his voice. "I was looking around from the stairwell. He was backlit with his back toward me. He was eating a cookie." She almost groaned at how it sounded.

The sheriff's eyebrow arched but he didn't comment on it. Instead, he motioned back toward the family room. "Why don't we go sit down? I want to go over it with you one more time while my men check out the house."

Amy knew Deputy Morris had already gone over things but led the way back to the family room. The sheriff went over each detail at least twice then asked her where she'd found the medicine bottle, then about the snake and the wall unit falling.

"It's lucky for the McCarron's you've been there when each thing happened," the sheriff said.

Amy was pretty sure that wasn't what he was thinking. More likely, it was quite a coincidence that she was always right there. His next sentence proved it. "Well, that should do it. I do need to ask you, though, please don't go anywhere. I'm afraid I need to talk to Chance now, if you wouldn't mind getting him. You can wait either in your room or out by the pool."

There was nothing Amy could say to that, so went and got Chance and took the opportunity to take a shower before going out on the patio. They didn't talk nearly as long with him. Chance came out and sat with her on the patio while the sheriff went in to talk with Jake. Amy wanted to argue about waking him but didn't dare.

Nearly thirty minutes passed before the sheriff came out. "I think that should do it for now. Just a reminder, don't go anywhere. We'll be in touch. Jake was wondering if you could bring him some water."

"Certainly." Amy stood. "I'll see you out first."

"That's not necessary." He waved a hand as if waving her away.

"I want to lock the door." Amy led the way. She sighed when she closed the door behind them. She wanted to drop her head into her hands and cry, but if she closed her eyes, she was afraid she'd see Todd going over the cliff or his body at the bottom. She felt sick to her stomach. She knew the sheriff thought she was involved.

A hand took a hold of hers. She looked down at Chance, squatted in front of him and brushed a hand over his cheek. "How are you doing?" It sounded like a silly thing to ask.

He shrugged. "I'm okay. I'm hungry."

Amy almost laughed. Trust a little boy to put things in perspective. "I guess we never did get our picnic. Let me get Jake a drink, then I'll fix us some dinner."

Jake was asleep when she went in, so she left the glass on the nightstand. He was still sleeping when Amy had Chance ready for bed.

"Can I sleep in Jake's bed tonight? Jake lets me sleep in his bed if I need to. We never told the other governesses."

Amy wasn't sure how to answer. It was a big bed, and she really couldn't blame Chance. "You'll have to stay on your side, so you don't bump him."

"I will." He made a cross over his heart.

As she tucked him in and dropped a kiss on his forehead, Amy decided it was a good thing having Chance there, because then she could keep an eye on both of them. With Chance asleep, she went through the house checking all the doors and windows even though she'd done it after the sheriff and deputies left. She then grabbed a fluffy throw from the linen closet and settled down on the couch in Jake's room.

ᘓᘔ

She couldn't find Chance. He was gone. He was her responsibility and she loved him. Jake loved him. She ran, searching everywhere. The man came out of the shadows where he'd been lurking all along. His hands wrapped around her throat squeezing. She couldn't breathe. Her throat burned. She wanted to scream, to warn Jake but nothing would come out.

Chapter Eighteen

Something hit the ground. Amy jerked awake, sitting up, looking around at unfamiliar surroundings. Her throat felt like it was on fire. She raised her hand to her neck. The gentle touch brought more pain.

Across the room a groan from the bed pulled her the rest of the way out of the nightmare and she remembered what happened. Jake was sitting up on the edge of his bed. His shoulders hunched, pulling in deep breaths.

Amy threw off the blanket and ran to him. "Jake," she whispered his name.

He reached for the drink he'd obviously been trying for when he knocked his clock off. She helped him drink and picked up the clock, turning it to see the numbers.

"It's time for your pain pills."

When he didn't complain, she knew how much pain he must've been in.

She laid her hand on his face, checking for fever. He caught her fingers bringing them to his lips.

"You should get some sleep." He drew out the words.

"I was sleeping." Her voice sounded scratchy and hoarse.

He looked over at the couch. "That can't be comfortable."

"Actually, it is." She found whispering the words easier to get them out.

He handed her his glass of water, and she gratefully

took a drink.

"The bruises …" He stopped what he was saying to run his finger over her collar bone just below the area.

"It's okay, just a little sore."

"Like I hurt just a little. We're quite a pair right now."

Amy looked down at his bare chest. There was a bruise on his shoulder where he'd landed on it when he went off the horse, but it didn't detract from the beauty of him. He had an incredible, well-defined chest and stomach.

"You're probably starving." She pulled her thoughts from her inspection of him, feeling herself flush.

"I could eat."

"I made some dinner, but you were sleeping, and I didn't want to wake you. Yours is on a plate in the fridge. I'll just go heat it up." She stood, catching sight of the body in bed next to him. "Chance wanted to sleep with you. I let him so I could be close if you needed anything."

"I could use more water." He looked down at the empty glass in her hand.

She went to the bathroom to refill it and stopped long enough to take some pain relievers of her own.

Jake was watching Chance when she came out. "He hasn't slept there for a long time. After our father died, he needed to be close. That's one of the reasons I moved his room over here. It used to be down the other hall, though he stayed in the room he's in now while our father was away on his vacation." He took a drink.

"I'll be right back with your dinner." Amy hurried to the kitchen though her thoughts stayed in Jake's room. He was so much more than a brother to Chance. He'd be a wonderful father. The thought of having his baby came to her mind. She tried to push it away, but it held. Luckily, the microwave beeped, and she was able to get herself under control on the walk back to his room.

Jake stood by the window when she came back in.

Her first reaction was to say he should be in bed, instead she said, "Does it feel good to be up?"

"Yes."

"Do you want to get back in bed or eat this at the table?"

"The table." His movements were metered as he made his way over. Amy placed the food in front of him then went to get his glass.

"Thanks."

"You're welcome. That's what I'm here for."

"Being my nurse isn't part of your job description." Weariness toned his words.

"I'm not doing it because of my job."

"I know." He looked up at her and motioned to the chair across from him.

She settled in it.

"I don't think any part of what you do is because it's your job. It's because you care."

Amy shrugged it off. "I'm not that altruistic. I needed the job."

"That may be, but it's not why you treat Chance the way you do. Loving him is not part of the job. I'm glad you're here."

It warmed her heart until her eyes dropped to the bandage wrapped around him. "I don't think the sheriff is." She glanced away not able to look at him. "He believes I'm behind what's happened."

"What makes you say that?" His head leaned toward her.

"Just a few things he said." When Jake didn't make a comment, she continued. "He pointed out I'm always around when anything happens, like saving the day to get noticed."

"I'd say it worked, but I was interested the moment you ran into me in the hall."

She laughed. "Right. I was in a robe and a towel, just

out of the shower. Very attractive."

"I thought so."

His seriousness caught her breath, and she had to look away. "Besides, I think you ran into me."

"An excellent move, I may have to do that more often."

She shook her head, uncertain how serious he was. When he reached over and caught her hand, she knew. The warmth in his eyes carried over her in the gentle brush of his work roughened thumb over the back of her hand.

"I shouldn't …" She stopped, afraid to say the words, but he got it loud and clear.

"I think we've had this discussion before. Shouldn't doesn't play because you already do, and since I do too, it just doesn't matter."

"Jake." Amy wasn't sure what she was asking for and Jake didn't get time to answer as a whimper from the bed drew their attention.

Amy reached the bed before Jake even made it to his feet. She slid across it, instead of going around. Chance stirred restlessly, small cries escaped in his sleep.

"Shh." Amy stroked his cheek. "It's all right Chance. We're here. Shh," she repeated over and over again.

Jake sat on the bed next to her. His voice joined hers in calming sounds.

There was fear in Chance's eyes when they opened, but as soon as he saw her and Jake it faded. "He was trying to kill us." The words trembled from him.

"It was just a nightmare." She pulled him into her arms. "It's all over now." Amy placed a kiss on the top of his head.

Jake settled close so he could reach Chance with his uninjured arm. "We're all right here together."

"He was going to kill you, me and Amy," he restated what he'd said probably a half dozen times that day.

"And I don't know why." Jake took up trying to

answer him. "We'll have to wait for the police to figure that out."

"Will they?" Fear poured from Chance.

"Yes. Now what do you say we all lay down and get some sleep." Jake met Amy's look when she turned to him. "Amy and I will be right here."

Chance looked from one to the other then nodded. Lying back down, he closed his eyes, already drifting back to sleep.

"Jake," Amy whispered.

"You're not sleeping on that couch. You'll be much more comfortable here. Besides, Chance will feel better if you're here." He paused slightly before adding, "And so will I."

Amy knew she should object but looking at him, she couldn't.

He stretched out beside her, sighing once he was down.

Giving up, Amy reached down and pulled the covers up over him. She wrapped an arm around Chance, but was aware of the man beside her, especially when he reached up and ran his fingers through her hair.

She turned to him. "You should be still so you don't pull your side."

"I wanted your attention."

He was clearly visible in the light from the other side of the room. His eyes were heavy as sleep snuck upon him. Whiskers shadowed his chin. She didn't realize she'd raised her hand until she felt the roughness as she ran her finger over it. He turned his head slightly and kissed her fingers.

"I shouldn't be here," she whispered.

"I was serious earlier today when I said I wanted to hold you the rest of my life."

"Your side—"

"Is the only thing keeping me behaving myself." The corner of his lips tilted up, giving him a wickedly playful grin. "Sleep well, Amy." He closed his eyes and to her surprise, he went right to sleep.

Amy lay awake staring at him. He settled deeper into her heart. As sleep drifted over her, she wondered if she was already dreaming.

ೞ

"So this is how it is. How cozy."

Amy jerked awake at the caustic tone. She was shocked to see Clarissa standing at the end of the bed. On both sides of her, Amy felt a shifting in the bed. Chance opened his eyes but just cuddled into her side, while on the other side of her, Jake groaned.

"What are you doing here, Clarissa?" Jake ground out.

"I came to join the pajama party." The scathing tone deepened in her words. "It's time for fun and games."

A growl rumbled in Jake's throat. "Go away." He shifted, covering his eyes with the back of his hand, and groaned again.

Amy started to climb out of the bed to get him a pain pill but Clarissa's comment stopped her as did the sight of the man standing just behind her. Knowlton held a gun in his hand pointed directly at them.

"Oh, I plan on it." Clarissa drew out the words. "I just need to get a few things first."

"What are you talking about?" Jake was still not paying much attention to her.

"Jake." Amy got out through the tightness in her throat.

Jake lowered his hand and eased up in the bed. "What is this?"

"Our plans have gone a little awry. Thanks to her." Clarissa glared at Amy. "The police are looking into what's been happening around here, as I'm sure you know. They contacted me about you getting shot." She looked at the bandage on his chest, showing no remorse. "I need you to get up now."

219

Jake glanced at the man behind her.

"Get up." Clarissa snapped.

Chance flinched and clung to Amy tighter, now fully alert.

Jake eased up and swung his feet to the floor. He sucked in a breath as he straightened.

Clarissa looked him over. "Tsk, tsk, does it hurt? It's too bad Todd was such a lousy shot. This wouldn't have been necessary if I could have fired the governess." She spat the last word out as if it had become distasteful to her, "and controlled the boy's inheritance. Should have done that in the first place, but there was you and the old lady."

Jake straightened to face her, his face hardened. "Now what?"

"Everyone up!" Clarissa said curtly, there was no more of the honey-sweet tone in her voice.

Amy urged Chance up as she stood, but kept him tucked just behind her.

Clarissa gave her a sour expression. "Still going to protect him? I really am surprised. A sensible person would have cut and run by now. Then again, I guess you were holding out for the big prize, though I can't see what he sees in you."

"Clarissa what do you want?" Jake drew the attention back to him while his was still focused on Knowlton.

"A few things that were denied me. If you behave, I will leave you alive, if not…." Clarissa shrugged. "This way." She turned and moved to the door.

Knowlton stepped back and made a motion with his gun for them to follow her. Jake went first. Amy led Chance in behind him. She was aware of Knowlton and the gun but was unprepared when the man reached out and caught Chance's arm, ripping him away from her side.

Amy reacted without thought, reaching back for Chance. "N–"

Knowlton whipped out his hand catching her on the side of her head with his gun. Amy slammed into the doorway. She would have gone down except Jake caught her. It took a second for her mind to clear and steady herself.

Chance struggled against the man's hold despite the gun pointed at his head.

"Precaution," Knowlton said smoothly, giving Chance a shake. "Don't try anything or the boy dies."

"Chance, be still." Jake caught hold of Amy's arm.

"This way," Clarissa sneered.

Jake helped Amy steady herself, wrapping his arm around her keeping her tight to his side. Worry was in his eyes when she looked at him. "I'm all right," she assured him.

"You're bleeding."

She fought not to raise her hand and touch the area. She could feel the stickiness making its way down the side of her cheek just in front of her ear. She looked back at Chance and felt a wave of panic, but let Jake lead her down the hallway behind Clarissa.

"Where are we going?" Jake asked as they crossed the family room.

"Downstairs. My brother found your vault but couldn't get into it. Which is surprising, he's quite good."

"Brother?" Jake glanced back over his shoulder.

"Yes." Clarissa headed down the stairs.

Knowlton held Chance back. When Clarissa reached the bottom, she turned and now also held a gun on them. "Come."

Amy found Clarissa's calmness more eerie than having Knowlton at her back.

Clarissa ran her eyes over Jake as he came down the stairs. "You know, I would have enjoyed having you. Your father was a fine-looking man, but he wouldn't touch me."

Jake took the opening she gave him. "Then how did

you get him to marry you?"

"Oh, at first he was flattered and interested, but he was too cautious. So I helped him by spiking his drink."

"You drugged him."

Amy felt anger seethe from Jake.

"So how'd you get him through the ceremony?" His words were clipped.

Clarissa gave a little laugh. She looked at the two brothers. "I paid the man to make up the marriage certificate and got your father to sign it."

Jake's hand tightened on Amy's. She stroked her other hand over his. He loosened the grip, but his stance remained tight.

"Unfortunately, I didn't know he had all his holdings incorporated and couldn't get hold of them. He'd done it as a precaution before his trip. Does your little hick know that?" Clarissa looked directly at Amy. "Or do you even understand what that means? You can't get your hands on any of the money, just what he keeps in his own personal account. If it's like his father, it isn't much." This time the fury burned in Clarissa's eyes. "Open the vault." She motioned to the door to the vault room.

Jake remained still.

"Open the vault or your new play thing finds out what it feels like to get shot." Clarissa growled out the words, raising her arm to point the gun directly at Amy's chest.

"Amy!" Chance cried out, fighting against the man holding him.

Jake stepped away from her to the door, put in the combination and opened it.

"Inside," Knowlton ordered. "And remember, your brother gets my first shot."

Amy's heart pounded as she stepped into the room. Tension poured from Jake. He knew as well as she did they would never be left alive. Odds were they wouldn't walk out of that room.

"The vault." Heat flared in Clarissa's eyes as she looked at the vault door.

"I don't keep much money in there." Jake tried to reason.

"But, you have the jewelry that was denied me." Fury crackled in her words.

Amy knew the woman resented that. It was probably made worse when she was allowed to wear their mother's necklace.

"Once we get upstairs," Knowlton spoke up from the doorway, where he held Chance. "You'll transfer the money to an off shore account."

So they weren't going to die down here, Amy thought. The money was the real objective. That made more sense. Knowlton was just placating his sister by letting her have the jewelry.

"Now open it." The man tightened his hold until Chance let out a squeak.

The look Jake sent back was pure challenge, but he stepped to the keyboard and put in the combination. Jake kept his body blocking Clarissa and her brother, but when she caught a glimpse of him hitting the o twice, Amy knew the combination. Earth, moon and stars. Jake looked back at her as he finished, and she also knew it wasn't by accident that he let her see. He was telling her, he loved her.

Jake stepped back, pulling the heavy door with him. Light came on in the inner room illuminating shelves stacked to the ceiling holding trays of jewelry and gem stones. Amy felt her own breath catch at the sight of them.

Clarissa's reaction was a mixture of glee and euphoria. "I told you. It's better than I thought."

"We need a duffle bag for that," Knowlton said. "There is one in the other room. You." He motioned to Amy. "Go get one."

She didn't move until she saw Jake nod.

Knowlton pulled Chance out into the hallway to let Amy leave and kept an eye on her. "Be quick," he said as she passed. "You wouldn't want the boy to develop a hole."

Amy ran down the hall. She wished she could dart into the room with the gun safe but didn't know the combination. As she entered the storage room, backpacks and duffle bags were on one rack. She paused to look around the room for anything that could help.

She hoped to see a hatchet or knife in the camping gear, but they must be in the gun room because she didn't see any. She grabbed a metal tent peg and slid it into her waistband. Unfortunately, the cast-iron fry pan was too big to hide. She grabbed up a duffle and was about to go when an incendiary road flare next to luminescent sticks caught her attention.

Amy grabbed it, pulled off the cap to reveal the striker. Palming the striker in one hand, she hid the flare behind the bag in the other and stepped out into the hall just as Knowlton yelled.

"You better hurry!"

Amy rushed back toward them.

Knowlton eyed her as she approached, the muscles around his eyes tightening. "Get in there," he ordered.

Amy felt weak with relief that he detected nothing. Jake stood in the center of the room when she entered. Clarissa was in the vault holding the Earth, Moon and Stars in her hands.

"Let her in there to get the stuff." Knowlton followed Amy inside the room this time. Knowlton still had Chance's arm, but Chance was to his side and the man's attention and gun was focused on Amy and his sister.

As Amy stepped by Jake, she caught his gaze and looked down at her hands, tilting the bag away from her a fraction so he could see the flare. His eyes jerked back up to meet hers and he gave a slight tip of his head.

"Don't forget the money," Knowlton snapped.

Amy turned as if to answer him. She brought her hand over striking the flare. It burst to life at the same time she dropped the bag. Amy shoved the flare up toward Knowlton's face. Instinctively, the man raised his arm to shield his eyes, releasing Chance.

Clarissa shrieked but couldn't get her gun pointed at them before Jake slammed the door closed, engaging the lock.

Amy rushed at Knowlton with the flare still in her hand. Knowlton jerked back, but swung the gun her direction, firing. The shot pinged off the vault before plowing into the concrete wall.

Jake dove passed her, colliding into Knowlton, knocking him back against the wall. Amy directed the flare away from Jake as he locked his hand around Knowlton's hand holding the gun, forcing it up away from Amy. Jake shoved his other arm up under Knowlton's chin, forcing the man's head up, while he slammed Knowlton's gun hand repeatedly against the wall over his head.

Another shot went off hitting the ceiling, sending down a small shower of debris into Jake's face. Jake jerked and Knowlton took the seconds of distraction to drive his free hand into Jake's injured side. Jake gasped and staggered back but didn't release the man. Knowlton hit him again. This time Jake was able to get his arm in between them to take the blow, but he groaned and staggered.

Amy dropped the flare, pulled the tent peg from her pants and drove it into the man's shoulder as he swung at Jake again.

Knowlton hollered and fell back. He dropped the gun. It clattered to the cement floor.

Jake stepped in and rammed his fist into the man's stomach, then sent his other fist into Knowlton's jaw. Knowlton slumped to the floor.

Amy reached for the gun to get it out of the man's

reach, but there was no need to worry, Knowlton was unconscious. She straightened to look at Jake. He leaned against the wall. Blood stained the bandage over his side, but he opened his arms to her.

Amy stepped into his embrace, taking some of his weight on her. He wrapped his arms around her, pulling her tight to him. She felt his lips on her forehead. He sighed heavily against her.

"Chance," Jake called his brother and reached down to wrap an arm around him drawing him into their huddle. Amy felt tears trickle down her cheeks but didn't care. They were safe now.

They stood like that for some time before Jake released his hold. "Why don't you give me that?" He took the gun from her hand. "And, go upstairs to wait for the sheriff's department."

"Wait?"

"I activated a silent alarm. They should be on their way."

She looked at the man on the floor.

Jake followed her gaze. "I'll be all right."

She hesitated. "They won't shoot me will they?"

Jake actually laughed. "No, but why don't you take Chance, just in case."

Amy glanced back down at Knowlton one more time.

"I'll be all right," Jake repeated. "Go."

Chance clung to her hand as they ran up the stairs. They opened the door and walked out into the curved drive and saw cars heading toward them. They pulled back and waited while four vehicles screeched to a stop.

"Ms. Mathews." The sheriff looked her over as he got out of the SUV. "We had an alarm."

Amy nodded and immediately regretted the action. Without the adrenaline and fear running through her body, the blow to her head was making her dizzy and kind of nauseous. "Jake has Knowlton, the chauffer who is also

Clarissa's brother, in the basement. Clarissa is locked in the vault."

"Are you all right?" the man asked reaching her.

"I've had better mornings. If you follow me, I'll show you."

The group of five men and one woman followed her inside and down the stairs. Jake was leaning against the wall when they entered. Seeing him in just pajama pants and bare feet, Amy realized how they all must look. Chance too was in pajamas, and she just wore a pair of stretch athletic shorts and a T-shirt, with no bra under it.

She went to stand by Jake moving Chance in front of her.

"Ralph." Jake handed the gun to the sheriff.

"I'd say you have quite a tale for me," the man said accepting it.

Jake nodded. "This is Timothy Knowlton, or at least that's what I was told. It seems he's Clarissa's brother. She's locked in there, but you'll want to be real careful when you open it. She has a gun."

The sheriff cocked an eyebrow. "Maybe I better hear the whole story. First, is there any chance of her suffocating?"

Jake shook his head. "No, there's a ventilation system."

"Okay. Someone get rid of that." He motioned to the flare that still burned on the floor.

One of the men came over and picked it up, leaving the room. Jake started to tell what happened. Knowlton stirred as two officers handcuffed him.

After hearing the preliminary story, the sheriff had Jake put in the combination, then cleared the room but for three officers in full protective gear, who eased open the vault door while giving instructions to Clarissa. The precaution ended up being unnecessary as she came out quietly, though she glared in hatred as she was led past them.

Jake took Amy's hand, and they walked upstairs to wait for the sheriff. "You know as much as I hate to admit it, but I could use a pain pill." Jake sank into the couch.

Amy smiled and went to his room to get one.

When she came back, Chance was sitting on one side of him. Amy handed Jake the pill and a glass of water and sat on the edge of the coffee table in front of him. After taking the pill and a drink, Jake placed the glass beside her and reached for her hand, running his fingers over her knuckles.

"Who would have thought being a governess would be so hazardous," Jake said.

She gave a little laugh. "I should've asked for combat pay."

"At the minimum, but maybe I can make it up to you. You know, we have a real good university here. You could start taking classes when Chance starts back to school. I'd cover your tuition," he added quickly.

Amy got the feeling he was trying to say more. She waited as he looked down at her hand in his.

"Maybe you ..." He didn't get to finish because the Sheriff came into the room. Jake straightened but didn't release her hand.

"Well, Clarissa's not talking. Knowlton is awake and isn't saying anything yet either, but we'll be taking a close look into them." The sheriff looked at Amy. "By the way, Todd's fingerprints were on the cookie jar. It's just a guess, but I bet he was working with Clarissa. At least, we'll be looking into that, too. Now, I probably ought to give you a ride to the hospital. You should have that checked." He nodded to Jake's side. "And, you," he looked to Amy, "may need a couple of stitches."

"Thanks," Jake said. "Neither of us is probably up to driving. I can get someone to come pick us up."

Chapter Nineteen

"It's so good to have you home," Amy said the next day as she helped Maggie get settled in her bed.

"That's about a dozen times you've said that." The older woman laughed.

"Well, it is." Amy settled on the edge of the bed.

"And it is thanks to you I'm here. I owe you my life." Maggie patted her hand.

"I'm just glad I was there. It was one of those things I learned but never thought that I would ever use."

"Hopefully, you'll never have to again. The doctor's positive the heart attack was brought on by those pills you found. So, I owe you for that also."

"We're even. You gave me a great opportunity bringing me here."

"You can say that after all that's happened?" Maggie brushed the lock of Amy's hair next to where the doctor had glued the cut on her head.

"At least it's not stitches." It was Amy's turn to laugh.

"I still can't believe I missed all the excitement. To imagine John was not even married to her. His marriage never made sense to me." Maggie shook her head.

"The police are still working on that. I know Ralph called Jake this morning and gave him some details. Clarissa is not even her real name. It's Nora, but she and her brother have at least a dozen aliases."

"Yes, I was told. They've made a living by taking

turns marrying and inheriting." Maggie looked sad.

"I'm sorry." Amy clasped her hand.

Maggie forced a smile. "Things seem to be going well for you and Jake." Maggie changed the subject, giving her a knowing look.

Amy glanced away and blushed. "It's not ... I mean ... it's too soon." Amy stumbled over the words.

"I'm glad it's working out. I knew you'd be perfect for him. There was just something about you that fit so well."

Amy looked up, shocked. "You mean you really did bring me here for Jake? I thought it was for Chance. Even Jake thought..." She broke off unable to go on.

"I did bring you here for Chance. You were good for him. I wouldn't have hired you otherwise, but it didn't take me long to see you were what my other grandson needed also. Maybe even more than Chance. They both need someone to truly love and care for them. And that, my dear, is you."

Amy opened and closed her mouth not knowing what to say. "He hasn't even ..."

"He will. Are you sleeping with him?"

"No!" Amy felt her cheeks heat.

"Good. I'd have been kind of disappointed if you were. I'm still old fashioned about that."

"Maggie, I've never." She didn't go on, but the older woman was already beaming.

"That's just fine. A wedding night's a good time to figure it all out."

"I think you're jumping the gun."

"We'll see. We'll see." She glanced at the French doors. "I think I'd like to get some rest now. Will you open the doors a bit more on your way out?"

"Sure. Rest well. I'm glad you're back," Amy said again, giving her hand a light squeeze.

Amy crossed the room pausing to take one last glance back at the older woman, who had become as important to her as her grandsons, before stepping out.

An arm snaked around her waist pulling her back against a hard male body. Amy was startled, but no fear came as she instinctively knew who the man was. Jake drew her off the patio, behind the trees and gave her a swift but thorough kiss that stole her breath.

When he pulled back, his eyes sparkled mischievously. "So you've never?" He arched his brows.

"You were listening?" She fought to still her heart.

"Yes," he said totally unrepentant.

"Maggie was just–" She tried to explain, but he cut her off.

"So our wedding night will be your first?"

"What? Jake!" Embarrassment flooded over her.

"You know if we hurry, we'd have time to go somewhere for a honeymoon before the summer is over and you start back to school."

Amy shook her head, thinking he had to be teasing her.

"Amy, you're fired."

It came so fast, she was unprepared. "What?" Amy thought he might be serious. "Jake?"

"I thought I'd better get it out of the way first. It would be improper for me as your employer." He dropped to one knee and reached into his pocket. "This isn't the Earth, Moon and Stars," he said, opening the small box he'd removed. "But, it means the same thing. You are my world." He held up a ring with a large diamond solitaire set in white gold.

"Jake," she repeated his name once again with no less shock.

"Do you love me?"

She couldn't hold back the answer. "Yes."

"Will you marry me?"

The answer came just as easily. "Yes."

He rose catching her in his arms, kissing her. One kiss turned into another. When they broke they both were breathless, but as Jake set her on her feet, he grinned. "Are you mad that I fired you?"

"Well." She dragged the word out. "I've never been fired before."

"You could think of it as just a different job description."

"Oh, and what's the pay scale for it? I was making pretty good money as a governess."

"Well, if you take this for a down payment," he slipped the ring onto her finger, "I'll have to think about it. The benefits are good. At least, I'm really looking forward to them." He kissed her to show her, as if she didn't know.

"Okay," she gasped for air. "I accept the terms."

"Maybe we'd better seal the agreement."

She put her hand on his chest to hold him back. "I don't know if I can handle it," she said as she led the way into the kiss.

This time Jake blew out a breath when they separated. "Hiring you was the best thing Maggie ever did and firing you was definitely the best thing I ever did."

Amy laughed. "We better go tell Chance he doesn't have a governess anymore."

He nodded but stared intently at her lips for several seconds as if he wanted to devour them.

They found Chance sitting on the couch playing a video game. They watched a couple minutes until the level ended. Amy released Jake's hand and settled by Chance.

"We wanted to talk to you about something," Amy started.

"Is it about Clarissa?" He looked up. He'd been on the quiet side since the day before.

Amy wondered if this was a bad time to tell him their news but felt Jake's hand on her shoulder as he took over.

"No, that's all over. Nothing more for you to worry about. This is something we hope you'll think is good. How would you feel about Amy and me getting married?"

Joy flashed in Chance's eyes then he got a very serious look. "What about my governess?" he ventured.

"You won't need one," Amy said. "I will be here to take care of you, all the time."

Chance nodded to that but still didn't seem totally reassured. His next sentence let them know why. "When you get married, you'll have a baby. Is it okay if I'm here?"

"Oh, Chance." Amy understood immediately what was bothering him and hugged him to her.

Jake knelt down and wrapped his arms around both of them. "This is how we are," Jake said firmly. "One family."

Amy took over. "When Jake and I get married, I'll be your sister-in-law. We'll be family. You will always be part of that family, even when it grows and expands." She looked at Jake and smiled before looking back at Chance.

"And, when we have a baby, you will be its uncle. You will have to help me watch over it. You'll be more like a big brother than an uncle. Do you understand? We will be one family." She cupped his face in her hands, lifting his chin to meet his gaze. "The only thing I worry about is that when you get older, and I set rules you don't like that you won't be happy with me anymore."

"I'll always love you." He hugged her.

Amy wrapped her arms around him and kissed him on the top of his head. "And I'll always love you, even when you think I'm mean and ornery and tell you to eat your vegetables and go to bed."

He smiled, joy again bursting in his eyes.

Jake touched his head and Chance looked up. "Is it all right if I marry her then?"

Chance beamed and nodded enthusiastically. "I want Amy with us forever."

"Me, too." Jake's gaze shifted to hers. "No more governess, just the earth, moon and stars."

About the Author

    I grew up in a small town in Wyoming loving the outdoors, sports, art, and reading Hardy Boys books. After reading them all at least a half dozen times, I started writing my own stories.

    Thirty years ago I married a wonderful, honorable man. I'm mother of five children and grandmother of six boys. I love traveling. Through my husband's work and vacations, I have visited much of the United States, all over Eastern Europe, Canada, Mexico, China, Thailand, Cambodia and Australia, giving me many intriguing locations and experiences for my stories.

    I am a storyteller. I write the classic hero story because I think there's a need for more heroes, love, and adventure in our lives. I'm not out to change the world with my writing; I'm just hoping to make your day a little better.

Hope you enjoy.
Alysia S. Knight

Please feel free to visit me through my website:
www.alysiasknight.com